THE Valentines

HAPPY GIRL Lucky

HOLLY SMALE

HarperCollins *Children's Books*

First published in Great Britain by
HarperCollins *Children's Books* in 2019
HarperCollins *Children's Books* is a division of HarperCollins*Publishers* Ltd,
HarperCollins Publishers
1 London Bridge Street
London SE1 9GF

The HarperCollins website address is
www.harpercollins.co.uk

1

ISBN 978–0–00–825414–8

Holly Smale asserts the moral right to
be identified as the author of the work.

Typeset in Plantin Std by
Palimpsest Book Production Ltd, Falkirk, Stirlingshire
Printed and bound in Great Britain by
CPI Group (UK) Ltd, Croydon CR0 4YY

MIX
Paper from
responsible sources
FSC™ C007454

HOLLY SMALE wanted to write from the age of five when she discovered that books didn't grow on trees like apples. Her passion for stories led her on a number of adventures, including modelling, teaching children in Japan, PR and backpacking across dozens of countries around the world. She has a degree in English literature and an MA in Shakespeare from Bristol University.

The Valentines series is the much anticipated follow-up to the number-one, internationally bestselling Geek Girl series, which sold over three million copies in thirty languages and won the Teen and Young Adult category of the Waterstones Children's Book Prize.

Happy Girl Lucky is the first in a brand-new series that follows the famous Valentine sisters.

This is Hope's story.

Follow Holly on Twitter and Instagram @holsmale.
Follow Geek Girl on Facebook/GeekGirlSeries.

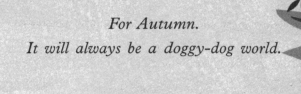

For Autumn.
It will always be a doggy-dog world.

FADE IN: REGENT'S PARK, LONDON, A SPRING MORNING

HOPE, fifteen, stands with her back to the sunshine, blue silk dress fluttering in the breeze. Her hair glistens, her posture is excellent and you can tell right away that she is the star of this film. In front of her is A HANDSOME BOY.

BOY

(*entranced*)

We've never met before,
but somehow it feels like we know
each other already.

HOPE

You feel instantly familiar to
me too.

BOY

(*even more entranced*)
Do you believe in fate,
beautiful stranger?

HOPE

(*shyly*)
Of course I do. Everything
happens for a reason.

BOY

Then . . . perhaps *you* are my
reason?

BOY holds out his hand. 'Teddy Bears'
Picnic' music starts playing.

HOPE

This is all happening so *BEEP*
fast . . .

BOY

And yet we've waited our whole
lives. Now *BEEP* take my hand
and together we will – *BEEP*
BEEP BEEP-BEEP—

BEEEEEEPPPPP

Blinking, I stare at the hand reaching towards me.

'You want toppings on this?' the BOY continues, yawning through his nostrils. 'We got chocolate sauce and chocolate sprinkles. Strawberry sauce and nuts, but that's extra. Or butterscotch sauce or toffee sauce. Chocolate flakes are extra too, so are toffee pieces and –'

I sigh. He's getting this script *all* wrong.

A few seconds ago, I was the romantic heroine poised to run away with my true soulmate – now I appear to be in a meeting with Willy Wonka's accountant. As usual, I *infinitely* prefer my version.

'Yes, please –' I smile sweetly as the car behind me starts beeping its horn again. 'Actually . . . never mind. Plain is just fine.'

'That's one pound thirty, then.'

Smiling harder so my dimples show, I hand the money across while gazing over the counter as intensely as possible, using all my advanced actressing skills to communicate complex, award-winning emotions.

The BOY stares back. 'You're ten pence short.'

'Whoops!' My eyelashes must have been fluttering too fast to see properly. 'Here you go.'

Our fingertips touch lightly and I stare at them, waiting for a flash of light, a few sparkles, maybe a bit of casual levitation. Up close, his fingernails have a thin line of black under each one, there are bright red spots marking his cheeks and his apron has melted chocolate smeared on it. Although I'm actually in black jeans and a neon cropped jumper – and it looks like it's about to start raining – so reality isn't exactly doing either of us a favour.

But there's *definitely* Potential. I just need to harness this new cinematic direction – fast.

'So,' I say as the car horn starts blaring again, 'what's your star si—'

'HOPE! WHAT ARE YOU DOING? YOU WERE SUPPOSED TO BE LOOKING FOR A

4

TOILET! DO YOU HAVE CONSTIPATION OR WHAT? GET IN THE CAR RIGHT NOW OR WE'RE GOING WITHOUT YOU!'

OK, the word *toilet* is absolutely not going in my big opening scene; I am also editing out *constipation* immediately.

The BOY's eyes slide over my shoulder, then widen as he spots the huge luxury car parked behind me.

'Whoa,' he says, abruptly waking up. 'Is that—'

'Yep.' I take a step backwards. 'Thank you so much for this ice cream, kind stranger. I shall treasure it forever and ever, until it melts or gets eaten.'

Quickly – while he's still watching – I take my hair out of its tangled knot and give my black curls a quick, charming shake.

Then I glance adorably back over my shoulder.

```
              HOPE
   I'm afraid I must leave you
   here, but this moment will be
   engraved upon my heart for the
              rest of time.
```

'Bye, then!' I call brightly, waving.

BOY
Goodbye, my dream girl. I will
never serve ice cream in the
same way again.

Ice Cream Boy stares at me for a few seconds with a deep furrow between his eyebrows. 'Bye?'

I feel an abrupt *whoosh* of pleasure.

Next time I visit, he's going to recognise me and ask my name and declare his eternal love for me and *everything*.

This One is almost definitely The One.

'HOPE, YOU TOTAL MUPPET!' my sister screams helpfully. 'GET OVER HERE RIGHT NOW!'

'Coming!' I call back.

Then – delighted with how the morning is going – I skip towards the car with the blue dress I'm not wearing fluttering behind me.

FADE OUT.

♋ Cancer: June 21–July 22

Your natural gift is in connecting with others, Cancer.
Today Mercury and Venus are in your fourth house,
which emphasises home, family, roots and parents.
Use your talents to bring those bonds even closer.

I'm Hope, your new leading lady.

Nearly sixteen years ago, my parents took one look at my beaming, newborn face and thought: *There's a girl who'll embody rainbows, sunrises and the kiss at the end of a film. There's a girl who'll skip when everybody else is walking, and try to see the best in all things; who'll never need to look for a silver lining because for her there'll be no clouds.*

And you know what? It totally worked.

Hope is somehow buried inside me, planted deep

in the middle of who I am, like the pip of a cherry or the stone of an avocado. My eldest sister, on the other hand, shoved her name into the ground and then tried to get as far away from it, as fast as physically possible.

A bit like a . . . potato.

'What is *wrong* with you?' Mercy snaps as I climb carefully into the back of the limo, precious ice cream held reverently in front of me. (His ice cream! The Ice Cream Created By Him!) 'Seriously. It's not a rhetorical question, Poodle. I'm looking for a clinical diagnosis.'

Twisting, I stare longingly out of the window at the ice-cream van retreating slowly behind us, my fingertips pressed up against the glass. Saying goodbye is so hard sometimes.

                    HOPE
            Until next time, my
        chocolate-covered paramour.

Music swells.

                                END SCENE.

'Don't call me Poodle,' I object, turning to face my sister and licking my ice cream. 'You know I don't like it.'

'How about Poo, then?' Mer sighs, propping her high-heeled boots on the seat next to me. 'Smelly, inappropriate in public and constantly disrupting plans.'

'I am not.'

'Are.'

'Am *not*.'

I stick my tongue out and she pretends not to notice. Mercy's seventeen and permanently glamorous; today her hair is in a tight black bun, her lipstick's red, her silk T-shirt is black, her hooded coat is black and her trousers are black leather.

The car seats are black leather too, so every time she moves there's a loud squeaking sound. Maybe it's the souls of the poor cows greeting each other in another format.

Without warning, I start giggling.

'Do you have brain freeze?' Mer snaps, picking at a perfect red nail. 'Or are random hysterics yet another side effect of having literally nothing in your head?'

'*Mercy*,' Effie says, looking up from her fitness tracker. 'Would you please leave Hope alone? Does it matter if we get there a little late?'

Because, if I grew with my name inside me, and Mercy grew without any of hers, then sixteen-year-old Faith holds hers up like a flower: always gentle, always adored, always sweet.

She's also always beautiful.

And yes, I know that's not a character trait, but if my middle sister was being cast in a movie that's exactly what would be written on the script. Effie's perfect face is always the first thing the rest of the world notices, yet somehow the last thing she does.

Which makes no sense because, when my visage eventually decides to blossom into hers some time over the next year, I'm *totally* going to make the most of it.

Broken hearts *everywhere*.

'Yes,' Mercy snaps, glaring at me pointedly. 'Because I've got better things to do on a Sunday than watch my irritating kid sister making cow eyes yet again at the zitty ice-cream boy.'

'First off,' I explain patiently, 'they were *not* cow

eyes. They were mysterious eyes designed to woo and captivate. And second off his acne is clearly healing because he has a lot of scabs, so *ha*.'

I fold my arms in triumph.

'We're coming up to the gates,' Effie says as Mercy smacks a palm against her forehead. 'Please stop squabbling for, like, forty-five seconds? Be nice. And game faces at the r—'

The car screeches to a stop.

'Yo, yo, *yo*,' Max shouts, swinging a door open and poking his close-shaved head into the back of the car with a grin. 'I see the three witches eschewed their broomsticks for the day. How's tricks, my hubble bubblers?'

All I need to say about my nineteen-year-old brother is that he takes his name *very* literally.

'For the love of—'

'*Language*, Mermaid,' Max laughs, shoving our sister over and clambering to the other side of the car, brown knees poking out of his ripped jeans. 'Aren't you happy to see me, sister-face? You are. I can tell you are. Look how *incandescent* my mere presence makes you.'

He leans forward and uses his fingers to stretch

Mercy's mouth into a scary, red-lipped, horror-film smile.

She immediately punches him. '*How* are you so annoying?'

'Dunno.' Max slumps in the seat and stretches his hands lazily over his head while he thinks about it. 'I'd like to say it was a gift from the gods, but I won't lie – I've been taking a few night classes. Really honing those skills.'

Then he yawns widely, showing all his back teeth, his tonsils and a single string of saliva, yet still managing to look handsome.

'What does *eschewed* mean?' I ask, leaning forward.

'It's a sneeze in the past tense, baby bear,' my brother grins, fluffing my curls with his hand. 'And I should warn you there are paps and journos *everywhere*. But don't fret, sibs, I got here early and gave them a few choice nuggets. How we're all being strong for each other, pulling together in our time of need and so on and so forth . . .'

He grins wickedly and Faith glances at Mercy.

That explains the mirrored sunglasses Max is wearing, even though it's now fully raining. (My hair wasn't really glistening in the sunshine earlier, either: that was done in my brain's fully staffed Special-effects Department.)

'God, Max,' Mercy hisses, clearly livid she didn't think of this first. 'Attention-seeker much?'

'God, Mer,' he laughs brightly. 'Jealous much?'

The car turns a final bend.

Excitement starts bubbling in my stomach. It's very important to make the best out of every single situation.

With a practised hand, I quickly tidy my hair and reapply my lipstick. If only somebody had told me the paparazzi would be here today, I'd have contoured much more carefully – really made sure my bone structure can be seen through a tinted window.

The car glides to a stop. My siblings and I stare at each other, united briefly by what's waiting for us outside.

'Ready?' Faith says, biting her lip.

'Steady,' I agree, trying not to look too exhilarated. '*Rock* steady. Or whatever's steadier than a rock. Stone. Cement?'

Mercy rolls her eyes, pulls up the hood of her black coat and nods in silence.

Max pops his sunglasses down. 'AND . . . GO!'

Simultaneously, we swing open the back doors of the massive black limousine.

There's a flurry of lights and clicks.

'Valentines! VALENTINES!'

Click. Flash.

'This way! Faith! Max! Mercy! Look over here!'

Flash click flash click flash.

'Talk to us! Can you tell us what happened? What's the news? How's Juliet?'

'What can you tell us, kids? This way, turn this way!'

Flash.

'Talk to us! Faith! Faith! Look sad for the cameras, ladies!'

Flash flash flash flash flash

Because there's a couple of *tiny* things I forgot to mention.

Mum's in rehab.

And we're one of the most famous families on the planet. A dynasty of movie stars stretching back four generations.

So, when I was introducing us a minute ago, it was probably our *surname* I should have started with. Aka the one name the entire world knows us by.

We are the Valentines.

3

You didn't recognise me, right?

It's OK, you're not supposed to. I'm not quite sixteen, which means I'm not allowed any of the fame or money or acting jobs or awards or parties or swanky restaurants or designer clothes and shoes, etc. for another four months: it's a Family Rule.

And that means I have time to *practise*.

When I'm finally unleashed on my adoring, impatient public, I'll be so talented and glamorous that my world-renowned siblings will collapse with jealousy. They'll beg me to explain my wondrous movie-star ways so they can copy me exactly.

I'll be the heroine you've all been waiting for – the kind that gets the lead in every romance without even auditioning – and every boy who co-stars will fall madly in love with me before the end of the first read-through.

In the meantime, I've just had a jumper put over my head.

'Can I come out now, please?' I think I'm being led by the hand through the giant electronic metal gate – I can hear the beeps. 'My nose tickles.'

'*Stop* snotting on my Burberry cashmere.' Mercy pokes my waist. 'Have you ever considered gluing a layer of fluff straight on to your face, Poodle? Then we wouldn't have to do this every single time.'

Effie gently takes my covering off and the world reappears: a cute little cottage with a muted grey-green front door, pretty flowers, neat hedges, tiny trees and an enormous six-metre-high steel fence shutting everyone else out.

'You won't have to do it much longer,' I remind them as we crunch up the soggy gravel path. 'In just over a third of a year, I'll be so famous you'll be able to sell my snot on eBay for millions and then some creepy boy, who's totally obsessed, will buy it and grow a mini snot version of me in a test tube to keep forever.'

Mercy checks her jumper in horror before stuffing it into her Fendi handbag and Faith laughs.

'I'd get one of those,' she smiles, kissing my forehead. 'To put in my pocket for when you're not around, Po.'

'Exactly how much is this ridiculous Privilodge of Mum's anyway?' Max asks as Effie punches yet another complicated passcode into a metal box embedded in the stone wall. 'Twenty grand a month? Thirty? It's *insane*.'

The cottage door swings silently open.

'We shouldn't use that word here,' Effie objects as we're beckoned down a shiny corridor.

'Mum's *not*,' I say quickly. 'She's just really tired.'

'Sure. Because it must be *so* hard doing nothing all day for twelve weeks solid. I'm sure our mother is absolutely exhausted, sitting in a steam room, getting facials and drinking green tea. She must be *worn out*, poor thing.'

I'm glad Mercy understands. Obviously, Mum wouldn't be here if she didn't need to be; she'd be at home with us, or on a film set, or maybe on an extended holiday in the Maldives like last summer.

'Selfie!' Max demands loudly as we cluster outside a familiar door, holding his phone in the air. 'I'll post *GONE TO SEE THE MAD WOMAN IN THE ATTIC LOLZ* hashtag sadface.'

Effie shakes her head at him, then clears her throat.

'Mum?' she says softly, knocking on the door. 'Can you handle some visitors?'

There's a very long silence.

A few rumbling sounds of furniture moving and bags unzipping; the snap of a mirror compact shutting. Then a weak voice says: 'Oh yes, I think so. Please do come in, my darlings.'

We push into an enormous suite.

Everything is shiny monotone, as if we're in an old black-and-white movie. Even the huge vases of flowers on every available surface are white and silver.

Mum's lying on a chaise longue positioned artfully in a flattering ray of sunshine. She's wearing loose white silk pyjamas and is fully made-up. Her platinum-blonde hair is perfectly smooth, her eyes are closed and one hand is held delicately against her forehead. I'm deeply impressed. My mother really knows how to command a scene.

'Oh, you have got to be *kidding* me,' Mercy sighs flatly.

'My darlings.' Mum opens her silvery eyes with a flicker and stares at the ceiling. 'It's *so* good of you to come. I've missed you all so very much. Right in my bones, in the very essence of – *oof.*'

I've lobbed myself on top of the chaise longue too.

'Oh, *Mum,*' I say, trying to wrap my arms round her. 'We miss you too! How are you? Have you been for a walk in a field yet? You should, because you're a Taurus so it would be an *excellent* health remedy for your pacific constitution.'

'Would it?' Mum says, patting me vaguely with three fingertips as I scooch over to give her more space. She struggles to her feet. 'Goodness.'

Calmly, she smooths out the crumples I've made in her silk pyjamas. Then she looks down at me.

'Hope, darling,' she says with a tiny frown, 'you must sit up straighter. You're going to get a curved spine and that is *so* difficult to correct at your age.'

I immediately snap to attention. 'Sorry.'

'Faith.' Mum glides over and takes Effie's beautiful face between her hands. 'My love, are you using that cream I gave you? Your pores are looking quite large. Don't forget that those high-definition cameras will magnify each flaw.'

'Every night, I promise, Mum.'

'Good girl.'

Now it's Max's turn. 'And how is the Barbican, my dear? I know the ghost doesn't have any lines, but it's a solid part. I did try to call in a few favours, but a lot of it is down to your own acting skills, I'm afraid.'

My brother's left eye twitches. 'It's good. I mean, I'm dead before the curtain goes up. That's the dream, right?'

Mum ignores him and turns to Mercy.

'Those leather trousers are glorious on you, darling. But have you considered a size fourteen? They look *uncomfortable* in a twelve.'

A muscle in Mer's jaw goes *ping*. 'They fit perfectly, thanks.'

'Of course they do.' Mum smiles wanly. 'I'm only thinking of *you*, darling.'

'Are you? That makes a nice change.'

There's a silence.

'Mum,' Faith says, stepping abruptly forward. 'You might want to move away from the window. Max brought the paps and they've got long lenses.'

Mum's back straightens immediately.

'Ah,' she nods, gliding nearer to the window and opening the curtains wide. 'Such *vultures*. Is there no privacy any more? No respect for our personal space? Do these coyotes do nothing but take, take, take while we give, give, give?'

Mercy, Faith and Max glance at each other with lifted eyebrows.

'Yeah,' Mercy snaps. 'Weird, that.'

Mum angles her beautiful high cheekbones towards the light, then stares bleakly into the far distance, silvery eyes shimmering. 'Did you, perchance, happen to see anyone from the *LA Times* out there?'

'Nope,' Max grins. 'But I *did* see the *Telegraph*. Wait, Grandma reads that, doesn't she?'

Mum abruptly closes the curtains and steps away. 'How . . . is she?'

'She wants to know why you're living here instead of at home with your children,' Mer says, looking at her blood-red nails. 'It's a question we're all quite eager to have answered, when you get a *spare moment*.'

'Oh, my darlings,' Mum says with a soft smile. 'You are *so* sweet to worry about me. I *will* triumph,

I promise you that.' She perches neatly on the chaise longue, legs crossed elegantly at the ankle. 'Although I'm afraid I'm feeling terribly tired. I have a two o'clock appointment with a very well-respected herbologist, so . . .'

There's a silence while Mercy looks pointedly at her watch. It's not quite ten in the morning yet.

'Sure,' Effie says, chewing on her bottom lip. 'You must be wiped, Mum. We'll see you next Sunday, yeah?'

Impulsively, I fling myself at Mum again.

'Neptune is in retrograde,' I whisper into her neck as she steadies herself on the plumped cushions behind her. 'Which explains *everything*. So get lots of fresh air, stay away from the colour red and put this inside your pillowcase.'

Before my mother can respond, I sneak a little pouch of lavender into her hand, kiss her cheek and flit out of the room.

Exiting the scene beautifully.

LOCATION SETTING: REHAB RECEPTION

'Well,' Max says as my siblings and I stare at each other blankly. 'That was quite a lot worse than I thought it would be.'

Faith nods. 'What are we going to do?'

'Does she have no shame at all?' Mercy screws up her nose. 'It's pathetic. Tragic. *Sad.*'

We're reading from exactly the same page of the same script at the same time, like a seamless run-through of a Tony Award-winning sitcom.

'So tragic,' I agree emphatically, trying to grab all six of their hands at once in comfort. '*So* sad. Mum's last big romantic film was so intense and so *all-consuming* that, to wall intensive purposes, it has totally worn her out. I think it's time for Dad to hurry up and come back from LA as soon as possible.'

Max abruptly glances at me.

'Hope,' he says, studying my face carefully. 'It's *for all intents and purposes*. Mum's not in rehab for bricks. And you do understand what's going on, don't you? You don't *actually* believe—'

'Effie,' I burst out cheerfully. 'That's a *good question*. What *are* we going to do? We should compile our brainpower and find a way to stay positive. We need to keep Mum happy until Dad arrives home, because happiness is the most important thing there is. Apart from love, obviously. Any ideas?'

Max, Mercy and Faith stare at me.

'I don't have any,' I say quickly, because they look very expectant. 'You're going to have to think too. I can't do it all on my own.'

'*Blime-y*,' Max exhales. 'How were you even *made*, Po? Were you put together in a doll factory, wrapped in pink tissue paper and left randomly on our doorstep?'

'Are you trying to tell me I'm adopted?' I reply in amazement. 'Because, if so, your sense of dramatic timing is truly terrible.'

There's a light cough and I jump. An incredibly

hot blond boy with deep brown eyes is hovering behind us.

You see? This is what happens when you take your eye off the ball: The One can sneak up while you're not even pushing your chest out properly. Quickly, I flick my hair, open my eyes wide and bite the inside of my cheeks so my cheekbones look sharper.

Too hard. *Ow.*

Max laughs loudly. 'I don't think they put in enough bubblewrap, Fluff-pot.'

You know what? In my next life, I'm coming back as the oldest sibling and giving Max stupid nicknames in front of *his* soulmates too.

'May I assist with transport?' my new The One asks politely with a subtle dip of his head. 'There are a range of options we could organise: a Bentley, motorbikes, a . . .'

Wow, he's so powerful and efficient. I bet he'd know how to call me a rescue helicopter if I fainted subtly in his arms and everything.

Mer snarls. 'Do you think we *swam* here?'

'We have a car waiting,' Effie says quickly, giving him a devastatingly gorgeous smile. 'But thank you.'

My One goes red and blinks at my middle sister as if she's suddenly spotlit – even though she's wearing no make-up, a shapeless orange hoodie and neon-yellow leggings – and I immediately send him to my reject pile.

He failed the audition.

Next.

'VALENTINES!' the crowd shouts as the metal gates swing open again. 'What happened? How's Juliet? When's she coming out? Can you tell us anything? Anything at all?'

There's a nanosecond for me to give them my most enigmatic movie-star smile before Mercy's jumper goes over my head again.

'Is it exhaustion?' I hear a journalist yell through the fluff. 'Depression? Insanity? Total mental collapse?'

'Have divorce papers been issued? What about reports that your dad's engaged to another actress already?'

'Will Juliet be at her film premiere next weekend?'

'Where are those boots from?'

That last question must be aimed at Mer because Max, Effie and I are all wearing trainers covered in

Nike ticks. Mercy has stiffened, so – curious – I rummage around inside her jumper until I can peer out of an armhole.

Slowly, eyes blazing, my big sister turns to face the crowd.

'This,' Mer says coldly into a sudden silence, 'is an intensely private matter. While the three of us may live our lives in the spotlight, it is not a spotlight of our choosing. We owe you nothing and you do not own us. Please try to remember that . . .' She pauses for a fraction. 'We are just teenagers, trying to . . . hold on to our mum.'

There's a tender crack in her voice and Mer's chin quivers as her eyes fill with tears. The journalists are completely still, Dictaphones frozen in the air.

I stare at my sister in amazement.

'Please,' Mercy continues, her voice hoarse. 'Let us deal with our heartbreak in peace. Let us be, for a moment, the normal family we *are*.'

She blinks quickly, then turns, but not before we all see a tear trailing down her left cheek. 'Gucci,' she adds quietly. 'My boots are Gucci, although I don't see why on earth it matters.'

And she disappears into the limousine.

Stunned, the rest of us climb in after her.

The second the doors lock, I rip the jumper off my head and wrap myself round my sister's neck.

'Oh, *Mercy*,' I whisper, patting her left ear awkwardly in an outpouring of compassion. 'Don't you worry – Mum's going to be *fine*. She'll be home any day now. They're just horrible rumours. But we're here for each other. I love you so much and—'

There's a shout of laughter.

'You *total* cow,' Max chuckles, taking his sunglasses off and rubbing his eyes. 'You almost had me there for a second, Mermaid. God, you're *good.*'

I pull away, feeling slightly sick.

Mercy wipes the single tear off her face with a red nail and flicks it away. 'Runs in the family,' she shrugs, smiling tightly. 'We're *very* skilled at pretending to be something we're not.'

She stares out of the darkened window.

'Well, what are we waiting for? Drive the hell on.'

♋ Cancer: June 21–July 22

Mars and Saturn send thunderbolts today, leaving you feeling slightly restless. But a pleasurable surprise is on its way, so harness that energy and put your best foot forward!

The next morning, it's all over the papers:

HEARTBREAK FOR THE VALENTINES

There's a large photo of Faith's face – luminous in its orange hood – much smaller photos of Mercy and Max, and a blurry insert of Mum staring wistfully out of the window.

And – *ooh!* – there's my left arm peeking out in the corner!

Elbow looking good, if I do say so myself.

'Seems like you had *quite* the day yesterday.'

Our housekeeper, Maggie, dropped off the papers first thing, then made us all a large breakfast. Now she's drinking a coffee and leaning against the Aga, calmly watching us stuff our faces.

'Right? Listen to this.' Max piles egg into his mouth and waves a full-page article in the air. 'Wait –'

He stands on a chair and flings his arms out.

'After *months of silence,* following a *brutal dumping* by prominent African-American film director husband, Michael Rivers, the *full mental breakdown* of now *single and lonely Juliet Valentine,* one of Britain's *most beloved stars of stage and screen,* has been confirmed—'

I roll my eyes and Maggie frowns at him. 'Max . . .'

'Wait, Mags, it gets better. *Mercy Valentine, Up-and-Coming It Girl and Professional Big Nose,* whose eyes filled with *eloquent* tears yesterday—'

'It's not my fault you're not quoted,' Mer shrugs,

savagely pulling apart a croissant. 'If you didn't want to be outshone, you probably shouldn't have invited the media in the first place.'

'You *invited* the media?' Maggie frowns and puts more eggs on the table. 'Why on earth would you do that?'

'They were writing about Mum anyway,' Max declares defensively. 'I figured they might as well hear it from us.'

'From *you*, you mean,' Mercy corrects.

'It's such nonsense,' I pipe up through a mouthful of toast, shaking my head humorously. 'Where do they get this crazy gossip from? And they call themselves professionalists!'

'No, they don't, because that's not a word, Po.' Max looks back at the article. 'What else have we got? *Natural beauty, Faith Valentine, girlfriend of pop sensation Noah Anthony, said everything without saying anything.*'

'Please stop,' Effie says, sipping orange juice. 'They're toxic.'

'And yet they still like you the best,' Max laughs. 'Looks like you're going to need that nose job if you want the main shot, Mermaid.' He nudges

Mercy with his foot and then hops to another chair so her punch doesn't reach him. 'Let's see how *online* feels about the Valentines today, shall we?'

He picks up his iPad and clears his throat.

'Grandmother, no comment . . . diva posho Mum's finally lost it . . . Dad's upgraded . . . the kids are talentless nonentities . . .'

'Max.'

'A century of privilege . . . entitled brats, living off their parents' money . . .'

'*Max.*'

'Who do these people even think they—'

'THAT IS *ENOUGH*, MAX!' barks Maggie.

Max sits down abruptly. 'Apologies, Mags. At least Dad told them to – direct quote – *kiss my American butt,* so you can take some comfort in that.'

'Of course he did,' I say cheerfully, licking blackcurrant jam off my fingers. 'I mean, I've never heard such trash in my entire life. Always jumping to ridiculous conclusions! Hahaha – journa*lists* or *journo-nots*, am I right?'

I look triumphantly at everyone, but they're busy eating.

'*Anyway*,' Maggie says smoothly, cleaning the top

of the Aga, 'I'm afraid I'm not around this evening. Ben's back for a holiday so I'm taking the rest of the week off.'

Max, Mercy and I swivel immediately towards Faith.

Ben is Maggie's son and has been madly in love with Effie since they were both six years old: he used to follow her around the grounds, giving her caterpillars to eat as a sign of his eternal devotion. I thought it was very romantic, but she never ate them.

'He is?' Faith flushes and avoids our eyes. 'How's he finding school up north? You must miss him so much.'

'I do.' Maggie nods and wipes her hands on a tea towel. 'But he loves living with his father in Edinburgh so I try not to show it. And I know I'm biased, but he's turning into a bit of a heartbreaker. Every girl in sixth-form chess club seems absolutely besotted.'

Max and Mercy start sniggering.

'How proud you must be,' Faith says, flashing them warning eyes.

'*How* proud,' Mercy agrees, snorting. 'Is he still

obsessed with Scrabble too? Do you remember when he used to meaningfully play words like *beguile* and *ardour* all the time, Eff?'

I should probably mention here that Ben is short and skinny with crispy mouse-coloured hair in a side parting. The last time I saw him he had a spidery moustache that he stroked every now and then as if for luck.

'Umm,' Faith says, fiddling with her spoon. 'I don't really remember. It was such a long time ago.'

Mercy and Max are twiddling air-moustaches and pretending to play the bagpipes until Maggie quirks her eyebrows at them. 'You want to make your own dinner tonight, Downton Abbey?'

That shuts them up: none of us know how to cook.

'I can't wait until I'm famous,' I sigh with starry eyes, gazing at the newspapers. 'I wonder what nonsense they'll make up about *me*. Right now, I could get attacked by zombies and there'd only be a picture of my elbow, slightly nibbled on.'

'Oh, please.' Mer's nose twitches slightly. 'If zombies ever invaded England, you'd just fall in love with the most rotten one, Poodle.'

'Oh, Handsome Zombie!' Max cries, pretending

to reach into his chest and throw the invisible contents across the table. 'You have my heart, now and forever! Do with it as you will!'

Pretend slobbering, Mer catches my heart and eats it.

'There's no harm in a bit of romance,' Maggie says sternly as my siblings start sniggering again. 'Now, you lot, behave, please. I don't want the media circling while I'm trying to cook my top-secret shepherd's pie.'

Then she puts her cardigan back on and leaves us to it.

'No harm in romance . . .' Max erupts as soon as she's gone. 'Unless it's with the *flesh-eating undead.*'

'I'm sure the zombie will love you to pieces, baby,' Faith says, leaning over and kissing my cheek. 'Like we all do.'

'Yeah, *literally bits and pieces.*'

'You know what?' I say as my siblings laugh and get up from the breakfast table. 'If I *did* fall for a zombie, I can promise you that our great love would ultimately triumph against the odds. It'd be a blockbuster romance that my adoring public would pay millions to see, so *there.*'

'Don't worry, little sis,' Mer grins, finishing her croissant in one bite. 'You'll find a boy with a huge chunk of his brain missing one day, I have no doubt.'

Now they're draining their drinks and checking their phones. So I jump up and do that too.

'What are we doing now? *Oooh*, why don't we watch a film together? How about *The Heart of Us*? We haven't seen that in *ages*.'

It also happens to be the very film Mum and Dad met on: an epic, sweeping romance set in London in the Second World War. And, yes, *I* watched it last night, but it doesn't count if it's on your own.

'Sorry, Poodle,' Max says, shoving toast in his mouth and heading towards the stairs. 'Three whole lines to learn. Just in case Messenger Two literally breaks a leg.'

I look hopefully at Effie.

'Not this morning.' She winces as her phone starts buzzing. 'Noah's been touring Europe for weeks, which means he has to tell me about every single meal he's eaten in exquisite detail.'

So I turn to Mercy, much less optimistically.

'Not in a billion, trajillion years,' she yawns. 'It's

a dumb film, you're annoying and I'm going back to bed. Go play fetch with Rabbit or something.'

I used to have an imaginary puppy when I was little, and my siblings still think it's hilarious to mention him, even though I haven't played with him for *years*. Obviously.

'His name was *Rocket*,' I say indignantly. 'And if you just wait a minute maybe we could—'

Nope. They've already gone.

6

RICHMOND, A SUNNY MONDAY MORNING

The camera scans over an enormous, stately red-brick mansion with fifteen bedrooms and a swimming pool set in the middle of large grounds. It's surrounded by trees and an enormous wall, a long gravel drive runs up to the front door and a babbling brook winds through the bottom of the garden.

HOPE, fifteen, stands gazing out of a large front window, wearing a T-shirt that says I LOVE YOU A LATTE and pale blue jea—

PAUSE.

Quickly – before I lose the flattering lighting – I run to the laundry room and rummage through Mercy's reject pile from last week until I find a gorgeous black Chloé jumpsuit, way too big, with a stain on the front, but *much* more appropriate.

Delighted, I tug it on, tie it up with a coat belt and snatch some towering pink suede Prada heels from the hallway. Then – inspired – I find a stray red Chanel lipstick in Mercy's coat pocket, slick it on and totter back up the stairs again.

OK, universe, as you so rightly advised me, my best foot is now forward.

And – *PLAY.*

HOPE gazes out of a large front window, wearing a Chloé jumpsuit and red lipstick. She looks glamorous yet casual and laid-back, as if she can sit down easily at any given moment. Her expression is thoughtful, her posture excellent.

A HANDSOME BOY strides up the long driveway.

BOY

(*looking up*)

How have I walked this path so many times and never seen that girl before?

HOPE

(*amazed*)

How have I stood at this window so many times and never seen that boy before?

BOY

Beautiful girl, will you open the window and talk to me?

HOPE

What?

BOY

(*makes gesture with hands*)

OPEN. THE. WINDOW.

HOPE

Oh!

She opens the window.

                    HOPE (CONTINUED)
          Sorry, I couldn't hear you.
        I was just lost in my poetic
           thoughts that were focused
        over there in the far distance.
                    Hang on.

Violins start to play. She runs down
the stairs, opens the door. They gaze
at each other for a few seconds.

                    BOY
        It's like we already know each
                other somehow.

                    HOPE
And yet you are also totally new.

He leans forward. **They k—**

  'HOPE!' Mercy yells down the stairs. 'TAKE MY
CHLOÉ OFF RIGHT NOW AND STOP

LURKING AT THE WINDOW. YOU ARE NOT IN SOME BASIC HORROR FILM.'

Her door slams.

Sighing – *I'm in a* romance, *thanks very much* – I return to my room to get changed. Any day now, a handsome newspaper boy or somebody gorgeous who works for Harrods food delivery is going to show up unexpectedly, but I won't be at the window to bewitch him. I will blame my eldest sister for this tragic misdirection *entirely*.

Back in my jeans again, I click on my phone for more details of today's horoscope. There's a *ping* and a garish pop-up – *IS LOVE ACTUALLY DEAD? EVERYONE'S FAVOURITE COUPLE IS OVER AND WE'RE CRYING* – next to photos of my beautiful parents in their heyday. I immediately close the shameless journo-not clickbait.

Then I swap around my film posters so the giant one of a couple kissing is directly in front of my bed. The universe works in its own mysterious ways, but it might be open to direct hints, right?

Carefully, I rearrange my favourite bits of memorabilia: a clapperboard from Great-Grandma's 1920s silent classic *It Didn't Happen Here!*,

Grandma's silk gloves from *Evening Rain*, the long, jewelled sword Mum carried in *The Hurtful Ones* and the director's chair from Dad's Golden-Globe-winning *Waves of Time*. (Although – if I'm being honest – I'm not entirely sure why it won: it's about the navy and there isn't any love story at all.)

Smiling, I straighten a little old photo of my grammy and grampy on Dad's side – beaming outside the adorable frilly house they had in New Orleans – so they don't feel left out.

I turn on *The Heart of Us* so it's running very loudly in the background. Then I grab my phone and hit speed dial.

'Hey there,' a deep American voice booms. 'This is Michael Rivers. If your call is work-related, try my agent at First Films. If not, go right ahead and leave your message after the beep.'

Beep.

'Hello, Dad!' I chirp, turning the film up two more notches and holding my phone out so he can hear the amorous *ack-ack-ack* of the opening gunfight. 'How's the filming going? You must be nearly finished, yeah?'

I prod his old director's chair with my toe.

'Anyway, I think it's time for you to wrap it up and come home, OK? By Friday ideally. Also, can you bring me an expensive and irreplaceable memento from set? Like the leading lady's shoes? Size six, although I can totally scrunch my toes into a five if I have to.'

Trailing my finger along the peacocks in the wallpaper, I wander vaguely back into the corridor.

'So I'll see you at the end of the week. Have a safe j—'

Out of the window I can see an enormous silver Mercedes crunching slowly up the driveway, followed by five much smaller cars in blue, red and black that I definitely don't recognise. Holy horoscopes, the surprise sent by Saturn! The pleasurable one! Thank *goodness* my best foot is permanently forward.

'Gotta go,' I say, hanging up.

Then – with studied grace – I get right up against the glass, gaze into the distance and make my face as wistful as possible.

Hold it for five, four, three, two —

Then, hanging on tightly to the bannister, I swish down the stairs, still wearing the gigantic pink heels (I was told to take her jumpsuit off, but Mer said *nada* about footwear).

Next, I use my remaining few moments to prepare with dramatic breathing exercises the way Effie taught me: pulling air deep into my stomach and then letting it out with a loud *SSSHHHH SSSHHHHH* and an *AAAAAAAHHHHHH* and a *HA! HA! HA! HA! H—*

'Stop that,' a sharp voice says from the other side of the front door. 'What are you doing? This is not a zoo.'

Heaving the huge door open, I beam and hold my arms out. 'Grandma! What a *pleasurable surprise* this is! I didn't know you were coming!'

An emerald green velvet coat is dropped over my arms.

'Yes,' my grandmother says coldly, surveying the hallway. 'Although I think you probably should have guessed.'

7

You obviously know Dame Sylvia Valentine already.

But – to aid my very busy casting team – she's exactly the same now as she is in her fifty-six films: small, rigid, with grey eyes, platinum-blonde hair in a bun and a withering gaze. (Except in real life she gets to invent her own lines and facial expressions so they tend to be even less friendly.)

'How are you?' I ask, expertly air-kissing – *mwah mwah* – so I don't stamp her with borrowed red lipstick. 'It's not Wednesday yet, is it? Don't you normally come on Wednesdays? And hello, Genevieve! You're here too! What a wonderful addition!'

My grandmother's assistant nods silently from behind her.

'Darling, you're far too enthusiastic,' Grandma snaps, leaning on her walking stick. 'Try to attain a higher level of *ennui*, especially so early in the

46

morning. This Americanised zeal for living is utterly exhausting.'

'I'm half American,' I point out cheerfully.

'An unfortunate fact I remain painfully aware of.' Grandma picks non-existent fluff off her brocade skirt and stares round our vast dark hallway with her nose wrinkled delicately.

I have to say it: her posture is *excellent*.

'Are your wayward siblings here? Or can I assume that they're currently running amok, as befits a colony of teenagers with no parental guidance?'

I glance up the stairs. Mercy pokes her tousled head over the bannister, widens her eyes and pulls it back again.

'Umm,' I say loyally, looking subtly in the opposite direction. 'I'm . . . afraid . . . they're . . . not . . . here . . . right now . . . so . . .'

'Come down, please!' Grandma calls without raising her eyes. 'Mercy, I presume.'

There's a short pause, then Mer thumps down the stairs.

'FAITH!' she yells over her shoulder. 'MAX! NANNA VEE IS HERE.'

My grandmother flinches with one eyelid. *Nanna*

Vee is not on her approved list of terms of endearment.

Seconds later, Faith appears. And I swear I'm not editing this, but a ray of sunshine appears at exactly the same moment, settling on her skin and hair as if it's literally coming from *inside* her. Unfortunately, it's also settling on her electric-blue leggings, orange sports bra strap and huge lime-green T-shirt, and those really didn't need emphasis. She already looks like a bag of highlighters.

'Oh!' Eff says sweetly, skipping down the stairs. 'Hello, Grandma! Have we moved our lesson to today? I was *just* about to go for a long run, but it's not a problem! Shall I go and get my books instead?'

Mercy rolls her eyes.

Every Wednesday since she turned sixteen, Faith has been getting secretive lessons in *How To Live Forever As An Immortal and Internationally Beloved Movie-star Goddess* (we assume).

All we know for sure is that Mercy definitely didn't get them.

I'm excited to find out if I will.

'Not today, Faith,' Grandma says curtly, using her walking stick to punctuate her words on the stone floor. 'We have more preoccupying matters to discuss, such as how this family ended up splashed across the front pages of the tabloids this morning like marauding *soap* stars.'

She says *soap* as if she's just eaten it, and Effie and I glance guiltily at each other.

Mer sticks her nose in the air. 'It was Max,' she states defiantly. 'He told them we were going to be there. I was just—'

'Yes,' Grandma says, holding up a pale, ring-spangled hand. 'I believe we know what you were doing, Mercy. Where is your brother?'

Now we all shrug: ranks closed.

'Let me make something very clear.' Our grandmother tightens her lips. 'We are *not* reality-television celebrities or popular musicians. We are *not* Beauty Loggers or what they call *Tubers*. We do *not* air our dirty laundry in public for the entertainment of the masses.'

Now is probably not the time to tell her that Max started his own channel nine months ago: 600k+ followers watch him give loud opinions weekly, often with no top on. Also, *Beauty Logger* makes it sound like they're using lipsticks to cut down trees.

'We are *actors*,' my grandmother clarifies in her small-theatre voice. '*Artists*. And, while I appear to be unable to prevent your mother from throwing her emotional toys out of the perambulator, I will *not* allow the Valentine name to be cheapened further.'

Eyes closed, Genevieve is nodding as if in prayer.

'*My mother did not build this dynasty a hundrrrrred years ago,*' Grandma projects beautifully, now in her big-theatre voice, '*for her prrrrrogeny to destrrrroy it with unscrrrrripted doorrrrstep drrrrama. Am I making myself abunnndddaaaaannntly clear?*

'VALENTINES. ALWAYS. ACT. WITH. CLASS.'

And there's the family motto, somehow spoken in a different font.

We are suitably chastened.

'Sorry, Grandma,' we chime together. 'We won't do it again, Grandma.'

I don't know why I'm apologising – I had literally nothing to do with it – but it's *lovely* pretending for a minute that I did.

'So,' my grandmother concludes, 'I have taken the necessary steps.' She gives the tiniest nod.

Outside, the other car doors start opening and

dozens of people emerge: glamorous, expensively dressed men and women laden with huge bags, boxes, lights, cameras, hangers full of clothes. It's like a signal only big brothers can hear.

'Grandmother!' Max calls, bounding down the stairs three at a time. 'What a joy! I was *just* examining my lines for my big stage role – inspired by you, dear matriarch! – and thinking, *What would Grandma do?* And here you are!'

Mercy sticks a finger down her throat.

'Yes.' Grandma nods, unruffled by either of them. 'I suspected you would appear around now, Maxwell.'

Together, my siblings and I spin towards what is clearly a *crew*. They look very official – a million miles away from the yelling and shoving and lying on the floor of the paparazzi camped outside the rehab centre yesterday.

'But,' I say blankly, 'who *are* they?'

'*Variety* magazine.' Grandma looks at us sharply. 'Otherwise known as Damage Control.'

8

Now *this* is more like it.

'You may shoot the cover in the drawing room,' Grandma announces as everyone troops in, filling the hallway with designer handbags and glossy shoes. 'I grew up in this house, and it has the best light at this time of day.'

'We thought maybe the garden, Dame Sylvia?' a small lady in a beige trench coat murmurs nervously. 'There's such a pretty patch by the tr—'

'Yes, the drawing room.' Grandma nods as if in agreement. 'By the purple silk chinoiserie wallpaper. That will work perfectly. And make sure you ask about their mixed heritage, please. This interview should focus on the diversity of the modern Valentines, should it not?'

Within seconds, our Least Used Room is rammed.

A rack of designer clothes is set up in the corner,

antique dressers are piled high with make-up bags, the marble mantelpiece is crammed full of hair products and a circle of powerful lights is being propped up by our enormous leaded windows.

People are suddenly everywhere, holding up outfits against Faith, flattening Mercy's already straightened hair with hairspray and complaining that it's hard to find the right foundation shade for Max's skin tone.

'It's a good thing I'm so comfortable with my masculinity,' he tells them cheerfully. 'Or I'd be outraged by the implication that I'm not already perfect.'

This is by far the most exciting, important thing that has ever happened to me, and just a small *slice* of the epic gloriosity of my wonderful life to come.

Maggie pops her head round the door and I wave cheerfully from where I'm sitting patiently in the corner, waiting for my turn.

'We're going to be cover stars!' I explain in delight. 'With an eight-page spread officially launching the new generation of Valentines! Grandma arranged it all! What a *pleasurable surprise*, wouldn't you say? Isn't that just the best-ever *gift*?'

'I'd prefer a new casserole dish myself,' Maggie

says, wiping the top of a chair. 'Oh, for pity's sake, I never dust in here.'

Mesmerised, I watch the chaos unfold. It's extremely important for me to absorb each tiny detail because, in the near future, I'll probably have to do a photo shoot every single morning and an interview every single lunchtime and—

Oooh, the photographer's assistant is cute*!*

He's fair and short, and is bending over a little black box with his blue underpants poking above the top of his trousers. Of *course* this is how I meet The One! In my very own house! In my very own drawing room! It's a *pleasurable surprise* cosmic double whammy!

I'd better go and speak to him before my big glamorisation happens. I need to know he wants me for *me*.

                        BOY
                    (stunned)
    I don't know who you are, beautiful
       girl, but I have just looked up
          from whatever this box is and
            I am now deeply in love.

54

Shoulders back, I sidle up behind him.

Then I lean casually against the wall, toss my head back, straighten my I LOVE YOU A LATTE T-shirt and clear my throat. 'Hello there, so . . . what's your star si—'

'H-hi,' he stammers, sticking his hand out at Effie. 'I-it's meet to nice you. N-nice to mate you. Nice t-to— *Dammit.*'

My One goes bright red and leaves the room.

Yet another failed audition for my Romantic Leading Man. Honestly, you just can't find the *cast* these days. Undaunted, I wander over to inspect the clothes rack for items I can borrow.

'I read yesterday the mother is having the whole lot done,' someone whispers from behind it. 'Nose, boobs, eyes, cheeks, knees. That's why nobody's seen her: they're replacing parts bit by bit like an old car.'

'*Knees?*' someone else breathes back. 'Is that a thing?'

'Totally a thing. Apparently, the hotty hubby wants younger, less saggy knees, if you know what I mean.'

'*So* sad when natural beauty falls apart. Like watching an apple slowly rotting in a fruit bowl.

The daughter we've put in gold certainly got the best of both worlds, didn't she? What a *face*. Dull as a cabbage, though. Always the way.'

My cheeks have abruptly got very hot; my darling Effie is not a *cabbage*! She's a rare, exquisite bloom of sweetness and beauty. Also Mum's knees are super perky. I've seen both of them.

'Actually,' the other continues, apparently steaming a pair of trousers, 'it's the eldest girl I feel really sorry for. That *nose*. That nineties eye make-up. Used to be quite cute, back in the day. Remember that show?'

'Oh my God, right? But you can't blame her. Didn't she—'

'Hello there!' I part the clothing abruptly and peer through with a confident smile. 'If you're not too busy, would you like to get me ready now? You may have my autograph, if you like.' Stepping over, I hand them both a pre-signed photo.

Mainly because I am a professionalist and a Valentine, and I'm pretty sure *Acting Classy* does not include punching your adoring potential public right in the face because they're spreading nasty rumours about your family again. Also, Mercy is my big sister and therefore exclusively mine to be mean about.

'I'm sorry,' the tallest one says, staring at me. 'Who . . . are you?'

'Hope.' I give a little twirl so they can take my measurements in a single glance. 'The youngest Valentine, and very soon to be the most famous. I'm right on the end of your list, but don't worry. I'm already highly trained in the subtle art of beatification so I can totally assist you.'

They glance at each other in alarm, then I guess they think that I can't have heard anything and visibly relax.

'Isn't beatification what happens when the Pope turns someone into a saint?'

'Yup,' the other nods. 'But sure. Can't see the harm in it.'

'I won't harm anything,' I reassure them, beaming. 'Indeed, you will find me an absolute *parasite* of professionalism.'

Thrilled, I select a gorgeous purple Vera Wang gown.

After a bit of frustrated tugging – my hair has looser waves on one side, tighter ringlets at the back and short bits of fluff at the front – they give up and secure my hair in a ponytail again. Then they spend six minutes searching for the right foundation before compensating with a heavy layer of bronzer. I also get shimmery purple eyeshadow, lipstick and gold highlighter that *pops*.

In the meantime, I've been practising my range in the mirror: biting my lip and smiling, looking enigmatic and adorably confused, etc. That photographer's assistant is going to be kicking himself when he realises I exist, which is going to be literally any second. I am a freaking *vision*.

Glittering, I race over to my siblings.

They're grouped tightly together, shimmering in front of the lights: Faith in gold, Mercy in silver and Max in bronze.

'I'm here!' I say breathlessly, shoving between them. 'Sorry I'm late! Don't worry – we can start now!' Then I suck in my cheeks, push my chest out and turn at an angle so I look two-dimensional. 'And . . . *shoot*!'

There's a long silence while my siblings stare at me.

Then at each other, then at Grandma.

Then at each other, then at the photographer.

Then at me again.

'Umm,' says Max.

'Po,' says Faith.

'Idiot,' says Mercy.

'Hope.' Grandma frowns at me from her position directly behind the photographer. 'I assumed you understood the situation. You won't be in this shoot or the interview.'

I stare at her. 'But—'

'You know the rules. You're not sixteen yet.'

It feels like my character's been killed off seconds before the opening credits roll.

'But I'm sixteen *any minute*,' I blurt desperately, wiggling further into the group and sticking my elbows out so they can't dislodge me. 'Like, so *very* nearly. My birthday's less than four months away. By the time the magazine comes out, I'll be basically sixteen already!'

'I'm afraid this is non-negotiable.' Grandma looks round. 'Margaret, please remove my youngest grandchild from the room before things get . . . emotional.'

'No!' I use Max as a shield. 'Please, please, please, *please.*'

My big brother smiles sympathetically, but then peels me away and nudges me out of the group. I'm then dragged across the room by Mags, dropping my pre-signed photos on the floor as I go.

Emotional? I'll give them *emotional.*

Pulling air into my diaphragm, I clench my fists, lift my chin high and prepare my vocal cords for maximum dramatic output: lights, camera—

'THIS ISN'T F—'

The door is closed in my face.

LOCATION SETTING: THE CLASSROOM

It's two hours later, and my friends and I are sitting together at the back of class, furiously passing indignant notes and discussing this absolute injustice. Olivia can't believe it and Sophia is sympathetic; Madison's calling for mutiny, but she always overreacts so we ignore her.

Finally, we simmer down and our conversation turns to normal topics: parties, clothes, teachers, the new boy who's just started at school. He's clearly very bad news (he has piercing green eyes), but he keeps staring at me across the classroom. We all suspect that, deep down, he has an interesting backstory and a secretly good heart.

And Olivia is all, 'Oh, Hope, when are you going to *realise*?'

'Hope.'

Sophia is all, 'You two are *meant* for each other.'

'Hope.'

Except I can't see it, because—

'HOPE.'

Jumping, I blink at Mr Gilbert. 'Mmm?'

'Are you listening, or shall I take this absorbing lesson outside and teach a squirrel to pass their fast-approaching exams instead?'

Umm, good luck getting *them* to hold a pen.

'I'm listening,' I ad-lib quickly: we world-class actresses have to be able to think on our feet. 'And . . . in . . . ah . . . 1052 William of Normandy claimed that he was the rightful heir to the throne, and thus began the Norman Conquest!'

'In 1052?' Mr Gilbert frowns.

'1053? 54? 55?'

His ancient bushy grey eyebrows are going up a fraction at a time.

'56 . . . 57 . . . 58 . . . 59 . . . 60?'

They're still going up.

'61 . . . 62 . . . 63 . . . 64 . . . 65 . . . 66 . . .'

They stop moving.

'In 1066!'

'Excellent. I'm glad we finally got there, Hope. What a shame we're studying chemistry this morning, not history.'

I stare at the red book in front of me.

If only Sophia or Olivia or Madison or New Boy had pointed this small technicality out to me earlier, but they didn't. Mainly because I've never been to school. I study alone in our library with a tutor and none of my friends actually exist in real life . . . which makes it hard for them to warn me about stuff.

'Ah,' I nod.

What does Mum say when she's not listening?

'I'm just *multitasking*, darling.'

'Let's see if we can single-task first,' Mr Gilbert says, closing his eyes briefly. 'Then we'll consider branching out to more than one. And please don't call me darling.'

He looks tired, which is strange because up until two years ago he had to teach *all* the Valentine kids and now it's just me. You'd think it would be a lot less hard work.

'Shall we push on?' Mr Gilbert coughs. 'We write the molecular formula of the *repeating unit* in brackets, putting an n where—'

My eyes start wandering around the room.

I can't believe I'm in here, surrounded by thousands of books in brown, beige and snot-green, when I could be out there, telling *Variety* my entire life story. What does a nearly movie star need with this information anyway? They're not exactly going to quiz me on repeating units for a feature in *Vogue Japan*, right?

Bored, my eyes flick across the chintzy wallpaper, windows, wallpaper, books . . .

Finally, they reach a small, oily and deep grey/ brown painting I haven't paid attention to before because it was made before they invented proper colour paints.

'Is she dead?' I ask abruptly. 'Or sleeping?'

Mr Gilbert pauses from polywhatsits and rubs his face. 'Who?'

'That woman. The one lying in the boat.'

I peer more closely. She's got long blonde hair, her eyes are shut, she's covered in flowers, people are crying . . . and I *may* have just answered my own question.

'That's Elaine,' my tutor says in an exhausted voice. 'She was in love with the knight Lancelot,

64

but he loved Queen Guinevere who was married to King Arthur.'

He says this in a flat tone, as if it's not the *most* interesting thing he's ever told me.

I lean forward. 'And *then* what happened?'

'She was trapped in a tower, cursed to only watch the world through a mirror.'

'And *then*?'

'Lancelot rode past and Elaine spun round to see him.'

Mr Gilbert has *no* ability to tell even a basic story properly. 'And *then*?'

'The mirror breaks and she dies.'

My heart is swelling; my eyes are losing focus. 'That is . . . the most . . . beautiful . . . and . . . romantic . . . film . . . I have ever . . .'

'It's not a film, Hope. It's *The Lady of Shalott* by Alfred, Lord Tennyson – we studied this poem last month. Have you been listening at *all*?'

Umm, no.

Honestly, I heard a lot of dull stuff about barley and rye, and figured it was a vegetable-based poem about baby onions. This is exactly why titles and visuals are so very important.

I'd have called it *Lancelot's Lover is Dead* and it would have been *huge*.

'OK,' my tutor sighs, shaking his head. 'So where were we? *Hydrogen atoms*, Hope. How many electrons do they have?'

Kill me. 'Five?'

Mr Gilbert and I are in tune: he clearly wants to kill me too.

'One. And, because they only need one more to complete the first shell, they seek out other easily available atoms to combine with, which means they're weaker and less stable . . .'

'But . . . what if they're *not*.' I lean forward and jab the page with my finger. 'What if they're *meant* to be with other atoms, Mr Gilbert? What if they *want* to be? What if it's their *atomic destiny*?'

'It kind of is, Hope,' my tutor nods, unexpectedly delighted. 'Chemically speaking. Well done.'

I glow at him, even though I was obviously talking about myself.

'So,' he continues, '*hydrogen perox—*'

There's a soft knock at the door.

'*OH NO!*' I shout, jumping up. 'It must be someone from *Variety*, come to disrupt my pivotal lessons! They've realised I am an *integral* part of the interview and they can't go on without me! What an unexpected twist! What will I do?'

Effie's head appears. 'Sorry for butting in, Mr Gilbert.' Then she grimaces at me. 'Bad luck, Po. I tried my best to talk Grandma round, but . . . you know what she's like. If it helps, I can't answer without Mercy or Max interrupting me.'

I sit back down again with a sigh. 'At least you're not an ostrich.'

Faith blinks. 'An . . . ostrich?'

'Yes.' I nod sadly. 'I have been ostrichsized by my own family.'

'Do you mean *ostracised*?'

'That is what I said.'

Opening the door fully, Faith laughs and swishes towards me – shimmering and gold – and kisses the top of my head. 'You're my favourite,' she whispers into my hair.

'Is it over now?' I ask hopefully, tidying my ponytail again. 'Can I come out? Is the . . . photographer's assistant still there? I just . . . thought he might need . . . help. With his little black box or . . . other photography-based props.'

I am prepared, on very careful reflection, to give him a second audition.

Not *everyone* nails it first time round.

'We're not done yet,' Faith says with a small twist of her mouth. 'It's just they . . . uh.' She hands me a bag full of my crumpled jeans and T-shirt. 'They need the dress back, sweetheart.'

Devastated, I look down at my beautiful purple Vera Wang gown.

Can't I even study chemistry flawlessly?

Sighing, I walk behind a jammed bookshelf and clamber back into my jeans and T-shirt. *Four months, only four months, although frankly, if my family don't stop using up all the attention, we're going to run out.*

Then I hand the beautiful dress to my sister.

'Do you want to hang out tonight?' I ask as Faith heads towards the door. 'Maybe watch *Waves of Time* together? Then we can quiz Dad on all the behind-the-scenes information and ask him why there isn't a single kiss in it.'

'I . . . *would*.' Effie smiles slightly. 'But Noah's cooking dinner so I need to get there before the papers rifle through his bins to work out if we've split up yet.'

I nod resignedly because Max will be at the theatre and Mercy will be Out.

'Cool,' I say as the door closes. 'That's cool.'

It's at times like this that I really miss Rocket.

'Right,' Mr Gilbert says, tapping the book. 'Where were we? Hydrogen peroxide.'

♋ Cancer: June 21-July 22

Jupiter is in transit, which should bring luck and growth. But, as a water sign with Pisces rising, you might be feeling extra sensitive this week so try to avoid unnecessary confrontation and find harmony.

I wouldn't call the rest of this week a classic. Honestly, if Monday to Thursday was a film, I'd have given it one star – *Where's the narrative arc? What direction is this going in?* – and switched it off by now.

I've stayed upbeat by focusing on Friday night – the premiere for Mum's new film (the third most expensive movie ever made).

On Tuesday morning, Mars and Saturn kick in and I get my *pleasurable surprise*:

Sorry, snowed under! Will catch up at the weekend! Love you. Dad xx

Finally.

Nearly two days late, yes, but I'm not going to be churlish about it. The universe has a *lot* to get through on any given day, what with all the moving about it clearly has to do.

Either way, my father will be arriving on a First-class flight from America late on Friday afternoon, just in time to collect Mum from rehab, take her shopping for a new dress and grab a bite of dinner at The Ivy before they arrive at the launch together. At which point there's going to be a huge family reunion, photocall and announcement to kill off the rumours and set the paparazzi straight.

So obviously I have to be there too.

Mum was thirteen years old when she attended her very first premiere. There's a photo on her bedside table of her next to Grandma, skinny, slightly shiny and beaming on the red carpet – two *full years* younger than I am now – and if that's not proof that just one enormous celebrity party won't damage me for life then I don't know what is.

'No,' Max says when I finally track him down on Friday evening. He's been out of the house pretty much all week, doing I don't know what because his role lasts literally twenty-six seconds. 'Nope.'

I open my mouth.

'Not happening.'

'But—'

'Nu-uh.'

'If he could just—'

'No way.'

'All I want is to—'

'*Noooooooooo.*'

My brother is laughing while eating peanut butter out of a jar. He's using the spoon to conduct me as if I'm an orchestra.

'*YOU DON'T EVEN KNOW WHAT I'M GOING TO SAY.*'

'I do, Poodle, because you've been dropping the world's least subtle hints all week. Now you're just going to straight up demand that you attend tonight's party for *just a second* because you're *so nearly* sixteen and Mum was only thirteen and we're all going without you and it's not fair I tell you it's not fair it's not *fair it's not fair.*'

'*Pffft,*' I say, walking out of the kitchen with dignity. 'I was only going to say *it's not fair* twice. Idiot.'

Then I climb the stairs and stand outside Mer's bedroom.

For a split second, I can see a much smaller girl grinning goofily, her hair in a crazy, curly cloud and missing a sock. I blink, then rap hard on the door.

'WHAT? I'M BUSY.'

Apparently, my big sister has become nocturnal: sleeping all day, disappearing every night and having her activities logged by tabloid newspapers every morning. She's having the *Valentime of Her Life*, according to Thursday's headlines.

Quickly, I gather my best acting skills in one bundle.

As Mum said when she was preparing to play Anne Boleyn at the Old Vic, you can't *pretend* to be the Doomed Queen: you have to fully *embody* her, find a way to step into her skin and walk around. It's an acting technique Faith calls *Being the Orange*. My sister says if you can convince yourself you're an orange then you can basically convince anyone you're anything.

'Oh,' I project through the keyhole. 'Are you getting ready for the launch tonight, Mer? Me too. Premieres are *so* difficult to dress for, aren't they? *So* important to strike the right *note.*'

A pause, then her door opens. 'You're not going.'

'I *am*, as it happens.' *Be the Orange, Hope.* 'I actually got permission from Mum this morning, so—'

'Stop leaning on door frames.' Mercy scowls at me. 'It doesn't make you look casual. And you didn't get permission because Friday is silent day at the clinic, you lying little toad. There's no way I'm letting you snot under my jumper tonight, Desperado. Try asking somebody who gives one.'

The door slams so I knock again.

'GO. AWAY. MORON.'

Undaunted – that went exactly as expected – I wander down the corridor and knock on Faith's door. Mercy was my dress rehearsal, but *this* is my opening night.

FADE IN: HOPE, FIFTEEN —

'So,' I say as it opens, leaning casually on the door frame. '*How* are we *both* preparing for this big glamorous party tonight that we *both* happen to be atten— Wait, aren't you ready yet?'

Effie looks down at her shapeless lime-green T-shirt dress. 'What's wrong with what I'm wearing?'

'You look like a popped *frog* is what's wrong with it.' Shaking my head, I walk into her room with my hands on my hips. 'Oh, Faith. Faith, Faith, Faith. *Sooooo* much raw potential, *sooooo* much natural beauty, but you never make the best of yourself. What on *earrrrth* will people think of us?'

Effie blinks a few times, then bursts out laughing. 'That was a superb impression, you little mousebear. Brilliant.'

I have no idea who I was impressing, but I nod anyway.

'Thanks,' I say proudly, looking at my watch. It's 7pm and the party starts at 8. 'But we don't have time for random pleasantries, Eff, so what are the other options? Let me be your fashion *goo-roo*.'

My sister points guiltily at her bed. It's strewn with glittering Valentino, Armani, Dior, Givenchy and Chanel in blues and pinks and purples – thousands of pounds' worth, lent for free – but, as per usual, my beautiful sister has selected what looks like an old nightie.

'Take that thing off,' I command. 'You're not Shrek. And instead . . .' I pick out a beautiful, bright yellow, low-cut, halter-neck Elie Saab maxi dress. 'Wear *this*. Tidy your hair. And don't give me any of your sassy backchat, Faith Valentine.'

Effie nods, nostrils flaring. 'I wouldn't dream of it, Granny.'

Once she's changed, I drag in my massive Rejects Makeover Kit (everything Mercy gets tired of and leaves scattered around the house). Then I prime and buff, powder and highlight, contour and blush, shade and enhance and gloss. I give Eff beautiful smoky eyeshadow and orange cut-ins and pink lips and huge fake eyelashes and eyebrows that are *much* more suitable for her face shape than the ones nature provided.

On an artistic roll, I smooth down my sister's tight curls with serum and add a diamond headpiece, six rings, eight bracelets, an anklet, a necklace, dangly earrings and a little gold belt. A pair of sparkly electric-blue heels and a bit of glitter spray, plus three crystals on each cheek, complete the look.

Then I lead her proudly out of the room, down the stairs and into the hallway like my most prized pony.

'Jeez-us,' Mercy says, appearing from the kitchen in a black tux and burgundy lipstick. 'Look at the state of *you*.'

'Yes,' Effie says firmly, raising her beautiful, brand-new eyebrows. 'Look at the state of me, which our little sister has gifted so carefully, with much generosity and patience.'

Mercy looks at me, hesitates, then nods. 'Good job, Poodle.'

Honestly, I'm so proud I could burst.

My sisters look like *angels*, although admittedly one of light and joy, the other of darkness and pain (there's possibly a can of pepper spray hidden in Mercy's spiky-heeled black boot).

'Rightio,' Max says, whizzing out of his room and down the stairs in black trousers and a white shirt, trying to do up a bow tie. 'See you in the—' He double-takes. '*Blimey*, what happened to *youuuu*—' Faith widens her eyes '—*uuurrr* handbag? She's going to need a *handbag* with that lovely get-up, Poodle.'

Quickly – oh, he's so right! What a fool I am! – I run into Mum's room and grab a gold Gucci one with a silver clasp and speed back downstairs.

'Aren't you supposed to be working tonight, Max?' I point out, handing it over. 'In the Shakespeare play? You know, your job?'

'Oh.' He coughs loudly and puts a hand on his forehead. 'Yeah. I'm very sick for the next six and a half hours. Possibly dying. Possibly even dead already. Fingers crossed, tomorrow I'll be able to play the ghost for *real*.'

'No wonder they don't give you any lines, Max,' I say sympathetically. 'You're a *terrible* actor. I can help you with that if you like. Give you some professionalist tips.'

Max laughs and pinches my cheek. 'Cheers.'

'Thank you for your help, little one,' Effie smiles, clipping a subtle fitness tracker to the waistband of her dress, transferring a handful of items from her sports rucksack to the handbag and giving me a bright pink kiss. 'You're the most helpful mousebear ever.'

Then my glamorous siblings head out of the front door – chattering and glittering and smelling like Christmas.

And I've only just realised that in all the excitement of getting Faith ready I totally forgot about *me*.

'Guys!' I shout at their retreating backs. 'If you just wait a mi—'

But they've gone again.

11

OK, unexpected scene edit.

It takes only a few seconds to recalibrate: being able to respond *positively* to direction is one of my strongest life skills. In *this* version of events, I can focus on getting ready without any distractions. I can make my own way to the party at my own speed and thus ensure I turn up just late enough to make a dramatic entrance.

Those idiots are going to get there on time in a limo, like total keen-beans.

Ha! *Amateurs.*

'Has Mercy double-locked her bedroom door, though?' I wonder out loud as I lay place mats on the dining-room table. 'Because if she has I'm going to need to climb on top of the conservatory and slip through her window that doesn't latch properly.'

I polish two champagne glasses by breathing on them and rubbing them on my jumper.

'If not, a hairslide should do the trick.'

Five white candles are placed in the middle of the table.

'I'm thinking the long black Prada, or maybe the short Calvin Klein, and *definitely* her favourite McQueen heels.'

Two glasses of fresh orange juice are poured and I put two croissants on plates next to them.

'Or maybe she's left something in the laundry again, although honestly I'm really looking for something without deodorant stains all over the—'

'Hope? Who are you talking to?'

I blink at Maggie in the doorway.

'Oh.' I glance round the empty room. 'Umm. Monologuing skills should be practised wherever possible, Mags. It's important to *nuance* your cinematic voice, and also prepare for award acceptances, interviews, charity announcements – that kind of thing.'

Also, *my imaginary friends* just sounds weird.

Maggie lifts her eyebrows into her hairline as she looks at the awesome breakfast setting I've laid. It's my big surprise for Mum and Dad, giving their first morning home together a nice romantic start.

With a flourish, I make a big heart out of pink petals in the middle of the tablecloth, then – with Maggie still watching – quickly grab the newspapers from the week and head up to my room with scissors. There's *so* much news to catch up on and I need to do it fast.

On Monday the moon entered Gemini, which resulted in an energetic shift inwards (I was particularly thoughtful that day), then *on Tuesday Jupiter started traversing and my sixth house of health was highlighted* (I sneezed, like, three times). *Wednesday, Saturn and Mercury were in conjunction* – that's probably why I failed that maths test – and yesterday's *transit* inspired a lot of chocolate eating.

I mean, it's not that I completely believe in horoscopes. As Max said, it does seem highly unlikely that there are only twelve personalities on the planet, allocated by the time our parents procreated, but . . .

That's also *exactly* what a Leo would say.

Checking my watch – I've still got another hour and a half before I have to leave in time to be perfectly late – I quickly scan Max's fate for the last few days, then Mercy's (Aquarius) and Faith's (Pisces). They're having quite nice weeks, which is reassuring. Then I cut out my own horoscopes for this week and stick them round the glowing bulbs of my Mirror of Destiny so I can keep track of what's going on.

It goes without saying that I'm a Cancer, aka the Crab: imaginative, loyal, emotional, sympathetic, intuitive, easily attached and sentimental. There are some other qualities – less attractive ones about scuttling away and hiding – but they don't seem to match me so they're not important. I also have Pisces rising – another water sign – which is probably why I officially don't have a favourite sibling but I do and it's Effie.

'Hope?' There's a knock on my door. 'I made you a cup of tea.'

'Come in!'

I'm flicking through this morning's paper: I totally forgot to check today's forecast. Sometimes I get them online, sometimes from the paper – it really depends which prediction I like the best. 'Thanks!'

Maggie walks into the room and puts my

FUTURE OSCAR-WINNING ACTRESS mug down on my dressing table. Then she automatically goes over to smack my long red velvet curtains. Apparently, they collect a lot of dust, but that seemed like a small price to pay for year-round Hollywood glamour.

'*Casablanca*'s wonky again,' Mags sighs, straightening the framed kissing couple on my wall. 'These two are so unnecessarily passionate that they must keep pushing each other over.'

I cough and nod: that, or I sometimes stick a photo of my face on top of Ingrid Bergman's to see how I look in an intense make-out session.

Pretty romantic, it has to be said.

Smiling, I keep flicking through the paper, pausing briefly on page six – taken up mostly by Mercy falling out of a taxi – then whizzing past a blurry, long-lens shot of Dad jogging next to a brunette under the headline *Rivers Runs Through It*.

'You know,' Maggie says, gazing at my Marilyn poster, 'it must be hard when you're stuck at home on your own like this.'

'Not really,' I say cheerfully, scanning through the zodiac: *Aries, Libra, Scorpio, Sagittarius* . . . 'I'm very happy. There's lots to keep me busy. And there's only four months left before I'll be out *all* the time so this way I get to build my strength up in preparation.'

Capricorn, Leo, Gemini, Aquarius—

'Still,' Mags continues, 'it must get lonely.'

'Oh no.' *Taurus, Virgo, Pisces*. 'I mean, there's always a film to watch or a horoscope to—'

Cancer!

> As Venus moves, so your love destiny moves with
> it. Someone very special is on their way, Cancerian,
> so keep your eyes open or you'll miss them.
> Romance is calling!

My heart just stopped.

Quickly, I scan the horoscope again: *someone very special someone very special.*

Someone. Very. Special.

Every hair on my arms is standing on end. Deep down, I knew it was coming. I could feel it – the change in the air, the planets aligning, the stars shifting in their course, a build-up of dramatic tension – and I was RIGHT.

This is it.

Because, honestly, who cares about Saturn and Pluto? It's *Venus* – the Goddess of *Love* – I've been patiently searching for every morning.

And now she's finally *here.*

'. . . difficult couple of years . . . You've all been through so much . . . it's not surprising that you feel so . . .'

Clutching the paper, I jump up and run to the window.

Where is he? *Who* is he? Maybe a floral order is on its way and he's driving the van? A newspaper or milk delivery? Maybe he saw my elbow in the papers, fell in love instantly and spent the entire week tracking me down. Oooh, I wonder what he's going to look like, what he'll be wearing, what he's going to say, what I'll say back . . .

'. . . things will get better . . . your time will come . . . You're still so very . . .'

Except . . . Of. Course. He's at the premiere tonight, isn't he?

Keep your eyes open or you'll miss them.

Alarmed, I glance at my watch – it's already nine thirty. All the other Cancers have been out there all day, meeting their Special People and falling in love for hours and hours. What if I'm so cool and late that one of them takes mine?

What if – oh no! – they've *already taken him*?

A wave of panic surges through me. I can't believe I might miss my soulmate because I was trying to make a dramatic entrance.

'. . . so I've texted Ben and he said he'd like to pop over in a bit – keep you company. Maybe you can watch a film together . . .'

Blinking, I stare into my Mirror of Destiny.

We only get one opportunity for true love. What if my soulmate turns up to meet me and I'm not there yet?

What if Venus gets bored and doesn't come back again until I'm, like, thirty-six and it's too late?

What if, for the sake of a couple of hours, I get a second-rate boyfriend or – worse – end up *single forever*?

If you thwart The Stars, they might get really offended and give up permanently. There is *no* more time to waste.

Quick as a flash, I run into my walk-in wardrobe and slip on the dress Mum wore in the end scene of *The Heart of Us*, just before she got (spoiler) blown up by a hand grenade. It's a pretty, vintage, knee-length dress in silvery grey. I tie the satin belt and quickly stick some cotton-wool puffs down my bra.

Then I slick on some lipgloss and head towards the door. I'll have to do this barefaced. It's a shame, but my Special Someone is going to think I'm beautiful anyway because that's how it works.

'. . . over in half an hour, after he's been to the . . . Hope? Where are you going?'

I spin back to Maggie.

'Mum's premiere,' I say, tugging on some of Effie's sporty pumps. I'm going to need to *run* to meet my fate – this is no time for heels. 'There's someone I'm supposed to meet.'

Because it's official: *romance is calling.*

And I'm going to answer.

HOPE sprints along the banks of the River Thames. The night is warm, the air is fragrant, the stars are shining. A HOT BOY—

OK, I think I might be running the wrong way. And *reshoot*.

HOPE sprints along the banks of the River Thames in the opposite direction. A HOT BOY, busy examining the stars because he has a poetic soul, slams into her.

                    BOY
          (*blinking in amazement*)
     I thought all the beauty of the

universe was above me, yet nothing could compare to the wonder standing in front of—

No, he has to play a *bit* hard to get.

BOY
(*angry*)
HEY! Watch where you're—

Just rude.

BOY
(*embarrassed*)
I'm terribly sorry! Can I make amends by taking you for a long, meaningful walk in the moonlight?

Ooh, I *like* that one.

Obviously, this scenario is ridiculous. I'm going to meet Him at the party, not running as fast as I can from Waterloo Station. But it's a good idea to prepare my shocked-but-humble-yet-illuminated expression.

Once I meet Him, I might need a brief sit-down and maybe an energy drink.

Plus, it's such a *great* setting.

Twinkling lights are reflected in the river, a busker is playing the violin and kissing couples are scattered like rose petals every few metres. My epic romance is on the verge of starting, I can feel it. By tomorrow, half of one of those couples is going to be *me*.

Tingling, I arrive at the Tate Modern.

It's impressive – immense and squat with thin windows and a long chimney sticking out of the middle like a nose. And it's 10pm so the party's in full swing. The floodlights are blue, the trees in the grounds are blue-lit, there are blue lasers shooting into the air and there's an ice-blue carpet running up to the front doors. It's surrounded eight-deep by my future adoring public, patiently screaming and cheering and clapping.

Somewhere inside this very building are Mum, Dad, Mercy, Max, Faith . . .

And *Him*.

Huffing and slightly sweaty, I shove with effort through the crowd, shrug off Mercy's coat and hand it to a bouncer.

'Will you look after this, please?'

I pull my shoulders back. Posture: excellent.

'Please don't crumple it! It's Prada and not mine. Thank you so much.'

The bouncer's mouth drops open.

Then I dip under the blue rope, put a hand on my hip and sashay rapidly down the carpet, waving and nodding, pausing once or twice so people can take my photograph. I'm in deep trouble once Mum and Dad catch me here, but I might as well enjoy this moment of glory while I can.

'*WHO EVEN ARE YOU?*' somebody yells.

'It's top-secret!' I call, blowing them a kiss. 'But check the papers in about four months' time and my identity will be revealed!'

With a dazzling smile, I slip through the glass entrance.

The windows are dark, and there's yet another bouncer. This one's got a clipboard and a list of names – time to *Be the Orange* again, Hope. Quickly, I inflate my already heaving diaphragm, lift my chin and make sure I truly *embody* my role of very-much-invited-party-attendee.

Casually, I lean against the door frame with one hand.

'Oh, hello there,' I puff as a glamorous couple nod at the bouncer and are immediately waved through. 'I'm afraid I can't give you my real name right now –' another sparkling couple glide past me, followed by an old man I know from action films – 'but let me assure you –' a girl a few years older than me pushes past – 'that I am in *no way* banned from this party. Relax in the knowledge that you can totally let me—'

A shout of laughter. 'You flaming little *mousebear*.'

I freeze.

'Why are you breathing so hard?' Max steps out from a dark corner and puts his phone back in his pocket. 'Did you *run* after us, Poodle? Ears flapping, tongue trailing in the wind?'

A really gorgeous boy with a Mohican walks past and winks at me. Then he disappears through the door.

I automatically stretch after him – a wink! He's The One! – and get pulled back by the shoulders. Max is wearing a new black felt hat. His new hat is dumb. The hat is dumb and my brother is dumb and I hate them both.

'*Actually*,' I tell the bouncer desperately, shoving

my hand in Max's face. 'I'm afraid this is just a maniac fan of mine who wants to ruin my life. I've got a restraining order so if you could escort him out of the area and into the river that would be very helpful.'

'Is this one being a nuisance, Mr Valentine?'

'Usually,' Max grins at the bouncer, dragging me by the arm towards the exit. 'Almost always, actually.'

Another beautiful A-list couple swish past us, disappearing into the Magical Kingdom of Party filled with All the Hot Boys. A pulse of alarm ripples through me.

My Love Destiny is happening in the other direction.

'Oh, *please*.' Bending my knees, I shove my heels into the floor, tense my leg muscles and grip on to a snowflake-covered cloth hanging from the wall. '*Please*, Max, you don't understand. Tonight is *so* important. I'm already late! It's in my *stars*, Max – it's my *fate*. The *universe needs me to be here – it told me, Max. VENUS IS MOVING.*'

To our left, there's loud music and chatter.

Glasses are being clinked and flashes of light glint through the edges of the door. Every time the door opens, I see slices of life: beautiful clothes, beautiful food, beautiful people, beautiful conversations. Mum's in there being beautiful with Dad, Faith and Mercy and Grandma, and photographers, and olives on sticks, and loads of boys I have the potential to fall in love with.

I stretch towards it again.

'The universe needs you to be here?' Max frowns at me. 'Hope, you have *got* to stop doing whatever those horoscopes tell you. They're not *instructions* – they're random lines made up by a loser sitting in a cupboard somewhere.'

'*You're* made up by a loser in a cupboard somewhere.'

'That doesn't even make sense. Do you know how much trouble I'd be in if I let you in, Poodle? I'm already playing a dead person every night as it is.'

To our left is the clink of champagne glasses.

'*Please*, Max.' My voice is wobbling, which is weird because I'm telling it to be confident and assertive. '*Please*. Life is happening in there, but I'm always out here. I don't think I can wait any longer. I'm so tired of always, always, always being *on my own*.'

My brother blinks. 'You are, aren't you?'

'The point is— Max?' He's staring blankly at my forehead. 'Max.' I pull hard on his tux sleeve. 'Hello? *Listen to me! I am talking to you, Max.*'

'Pipe down, Poodle. I'm thinking.'

Before I know it, there's a hat on my head.

'What are you *doing*?' I snap in irritation, taking it off again. 'If you want to look like a fashion-tasteless idiot, that's up to you, but don't destroy *my* Look.'

'You'll have to look like an idiot too if you want to go to this party.'

I stare at him. What the hell is that supposed to—? 'Oh my GOSH, REALLY? If I wear the hat, you'll take me in? Do you really mean it? Really, *truly*? Inbu— Inbudi—'

'Indubitably? Yes.' Max smiles. 'You need a night out. Possibly a mindfulness app. Definitely a dictionary.'

With a happy squeak, I spin in a circle.

I *love* my brother! He's the best big brother that ever lived and I retract *everything* I just thought about him.

'Do me a favour, though,' Max says, grabbing my shoulders. 'Keep a low profile and *stop with the twirling*. Bring anyone you meet to see me first. *Anyone*. Avoid Granny, Mer and Faith, keep your head down, stay quiet and stick to the edges of the room. You're a phantom this evening, understand?'

'Absolutely.' I nod passionately, holding my hand in the air. 'Nobody will see me. I'll be invisible. A ghost. I will make an absolute *spectacle* of myself. I won't even say hi to Mum and Dad when I see them, I promise.'

'It's *spectre*, mousebear.' Max frowns slightly and puts his arm round me. 'Remember, Po, you make your own destiny, OK?'

I roll my eyes. What does he think I'm trying to *do*?

'This one's with me.' Max grins at the bouncer, plopping the wide-rimmed hat back on my head. 'Who doesn't like a bit of trouble, eh?'

With an unnecessarily grand gesture, my big brother bows and flings the doors of the party open with an attention-seeking bang.

'It's time to party.'

13

And the hunt is *on*.

'Hi there!' I beam at the cute skinny boy offering me a welcome drink, pushing Max's hat back so it frames my face properly. 'So tell me, what's your star s—'

'At least get through the *door* first,' Max laughs, handing me a shimmering glass of blue crushed ice and pushing me firmly into the room. 'For crying out loud, sis. *Try* to be cool.'

My brother is so wise. I don't want to accidentally pick a terrible soulmate just because he's holding a tray of – I take a sip – admittedly delicious beverages.

Grinning, I gaze around to get my bearings.

The lower floor of the Tate Modern is vast, with ceilings a hundred metres high hung with enormous white icicles. Real-looking snow crystals sparkle on the floor, there are overstuffed white leather sofas to lounge on and blue lasers criss-cross the air above us. At this end is a circular bar – lit blue and covered in frost-covered glasses – and at the other a DJ is bopping up and down with one hand on his outsized headphones.

Around us, IMAX-sized photographs of mountain peaks have been projected on to the walls, and Mum's flickering in tiny filmed fragments between them: a graceful arm, a swish of blonde hair, a flash of grey eyes.

I glance quickly across the crowd, but there doesn't appear to be any sign of my parents yet, though it's pretty late.

Told you they'd be cool; they are total *professionalists*.

'Max!' A man swings in front of us and a camera starts flashing. 'Max Valentine! Can I ask you a few questions? Max, over here!'

'*Go*,' my brother whispers to me, pulling the brim of my hat down low and pushing me away. 'Run like the wind in what actually used to be the Turbine Hall, little Poodle. You're *freeeeeee.*'

Buzzing all over, I clutch my frosty drink and deliberately head into the deepest, most crowded and therefore most interesting part of the party.

Beautiful people I recognise but have never met are twinkling, laughing, drinking, chatting: radiant and lit vaguely blue.

There are so many hot boys I'm light-headed.

'Some *ridiculously* basic theming going on here,' a woman says loudly in a South African accent, lifting a heel up and staring at it in disgust. 'Tacky as you like. This fake snow is *ruining* my shoes.'

Her friend laughs. 'You wanted subtle from *Juliet Valentine*?'

'True. Guess that's what happens when you're too old to be a romantic lead. You have to produce schmaltzy mountain movies yourself. I haven't seen it yet but I bet *Pinnacle* is a flop.'

I swallow hard. My mum is the *ultimate* romantic lead and *Pinnacle* is going to be the ultimate romance film. But Valentines Always Act With Class so, as a future icon, I'm going to rise above it.

Be the Orange, Hope.

'Hey there,' I say as a really good-looking waiter with big brown eyes and brown hair in little tufty peaks offers me a goat's cheese vollyvont. 'So . . . what's your star sign?'

He stares at me. '. . . Aries.'

'Ah,' I nod knowingly. 'The Ram. I should have guessed from the hair and the snacks.'

Honestly, it's not a *great* love combination – Arians can be aggressive, competitive and prone to smashing things with their heads – but I'm sure we can work through his flaws together. 'And . . . do you come here often?'

'. . . Every Friday night. It's my job.'

'How *lovely.*' I shove a vollyvont into my mouth. Although this *does* mean we won't be able to go out on Fridays, which is traditionally a Date Night. 'And tell me, do you work on Saturday nights, Valentine's Day, Christmas Eve, New Year's Eve or July the second, which happens to be my birthd—'

Faith and Grandma are moving in my direction.

Weirdly, Effie seems to now be wearing a simple white dress and has a completely bare face again; maybe she fell in mud on the way and had to remove all my styling or something, poor thing.

Quickly – before they see me – I pull Max's hat low over my face and hand the waiter one of my pre-signed photos. 'I'd very much like to continue this fascinating conversation later. Check the zodiac calendar for an auspicious time!'

Then I swing away behind a column.

Straight into yet another handsome boy standing directly behind it. It's like a free-range hot-boy farm in here. This one has shiny black hair, green eyes and smells like a coconut. I recognise him from a TV show about . . . wolves. Vampires. Angels. Doesn't really matter: they're all basically the same.

'Crikey,' he says, looking up from his phone and smiling widely. 'Where did *you* come from?'

'Richmond,' I beam back at him. 'Where did *you* come from?'

He laughs. 'Stevenage. And where are you going?'

'*Such* a good question,' I say in delight, flipping my hat to the side in a thoroughly charming manner. 'Hollywood eventually, but that's more of a *long-term* plan. My mum says it's important to build a prestigious stage career in England first so that everyone knows you're a *serious* actor – maybe a key role in the West End first, then an award-winning British indie film, at which point I'll move to Los Angeles where I'll—'

My arm is grabbed and I'm pulled away.

'Nope.'

'Hey, Max,' the wolf-vampire-angel boy laughs. 'How's it hanging?'

'Round your neck if you try that again, dude. That's my baby sister, she's fifteen and I've read the papers, so hop it.' Max spins me round, pats the top of my hat so it falls over my eyes and pushes me back into the crowd. 'Try again, Poodle. Try *better.*'

Disorientated and partially blind, I wade further into the crowd.

There's still no sign of my parents – their coolness is really quite mesmerising – but there's another tasty-looking Potential Hero standing over by the—

'WOOOOOOO! WHO'S HERE TO PEE AY AR TEE WHY IN A MODERATE, BORING AND UPTIGHT FASHION!'

Person by person, the whole party stops talking and turns to stare at the far end of the room. My entire body has gone cold. Slowly, I turn too.

'Oh, LOOSEN UP, GUYS!' my big sister screams into the DJ's microphone. 'We're rich and famous and lucky, remember? We're the *happiest* people on earth! *Happy, happy, happy! HAPPY. So WHY AREN'T WE ENJOYING IT?*'

Wobbling dangerously, Mercy climbs on top of the DJ's decks.

'Get *off*,' she adds, kicking the poor guy with the toe of her high-heeled leather boot. 'Anyone would think you're not being paid ten times what you get in McDonald's.' Then she whacks the top of the microphone with her rings. 'Time to *dance*!'

Silence.

'I SAID TIME – TO – DANCE!'

Bending down, Mer hits a button and music starts thumping.

'Wooooo!' a few of what I assume are her friends shout awkwardly, waving their arms. 'Yeah! Bring it!'

'Those poor Valentine kids,' somebody mutters, shaking their head. 'What a mess that family is.'

Pulling Max's hat firmly over my face, I slink round the edge of the hall towards the DJ booth. Mer's arms are in the air and she's wiggling her bottom violently, straightened hair flying in all directions.

No wonder Grandma never invites her anywhere.

'What are you *doing*?' Effie has suddenly appeared at Mercy's feet and is tugging urgently on the hem of her trousers. 'Mercy, get *down*.'

'I am getting down,' my big sister crows wildly. 'Look at me, I'm *getting down* like nobody's business.'

'You're not doing this tonight.' Faith's face is rigid. 'Down. *Now.*'

Mercy tries to kick her away too, but Effie nimbly dodges Mer's foot and takes off the heels I put her in. She clambers with bare feet on to the DJ table, grabs Mercy round the waist and hauls her back to the ground again. My beautiful sister is surprisingly strong.

'Sorry, everyone,' Faith murmurs into the microphone, holding Mercy in an effortless headlock. 'Page six is alarmingly short of content for tomorrow and my sister is nothing if not altruistic.'

A few people titter uncomfortably.

Then – as the DJ clears his throat, puts his headphones back on and starts playing music again – Effie drags a still struggling Mercy into a private side room.

And I slip after them.

14

Sometimes it's easy to forget that, while your big scene plays out in one room, other people's lives are unfolding in the room next door.

Because all we really see of people are when their stories cross ours.

Especially when they're not supposed to.

Silently, I flatten myself against the door.

'What the hell?' Mercy spits furiously from the other side. 'What gives you the right, you *stupid, smug* little—'

'Enough.' Faith's voice is almost unrecognisable. 'That is enough, Mercy. You do this every single time, and I'm done.'

Mercy gives a nasty bark of a laugh. 'Oh no, have I embarrassed you, Eff? Am I ruining your perfect future and flawless reputation? Please, *allow* me to lie down quietly and disappear into the carpet so I don't get in your illustrious way any longer.'

'You're getting in your own way, Mercy. You're a selfish, self-destructive mess. You're ruining your life and frankly I'm no longer sure I give a fish.'

Except Faith doesn't say fish. My eyes widen.

'Oh, as if you ever have, Effie. You pretend to be so sweet and gentle and kind – oh, I'm *Faith*, look at this beautiful *face*. I'm so perfect and skinny I have to wear big jumpers and crummy old leggings just to hide how pretty I am. Don't pay attention to little old *me*. But you know what you are? You're a fake. A liar. *I see the real you and you can't handle it.*'

'As opposed to being what? An angry, bitter witch with an attention-deficit disorder? If people don't look at you constantly, you *crumble*, Mercy. Oh, see me, listen to me, notice me. Me, me, me, me, *ME*.'

Except Faith didn't actually say witch, either.

My heart is starting to thump and my hands are sweating. Where on earth is all this hatred coming from? How long has it been there? How have I never noticed it before? We're *sisters*. We *love* each other. We're part of the same team, aren't we?

'Oh, *please*,' Mer snarls. 'At least there's something to listen to, Faith. You're so boring I want to cry every time you open your mouth. *Yes, Grandma, no, Grandma, three bags full, Grandma . . .* All you have is a pretty face you got through luck and, once that fades, you are *over.*'

'Well, at least I'm not an entitled, wannabe It Girl with a *giant nose!*'

'COW!' Mercy screams. 'YOU CAN'T ACT!'

'AND YOU'RE A SELF-ABSORBED, SELF-OBSESSED NIGHTMARE!'

I'm taking tiny steps away.

This is a smoking pit of rage I had no idea was there. I'm scared of getting too close in case they suck me in too. Why can't they just be *happy*? I think I'm just going to go back to the waiter with the vollyvonts and the floppy hair and the—

'We *all* are,' Mercy snaps into the silence. 'I mean, look at Hope.'

I stop edging. *Hello?*

'Leave Hope out of this.' Faith's voice crackles. 'This has nothing to do with her. She's just a baby – we need to—'

'Hope isn't a *baby*,' Mercy snorts dismissively.

'She's a *bimbo* – too dumb to have a single original thought in her whole fluffy, empty head. She's a walking cliché. Face it, our little sister doesn't even pass the Bechdel test *as a human being*. Plus, she's not even smart enough to remember—'

'Which is a good thing,' Faith interrupts quietly. 'And you know why Hope is the way she is. For heaven's sake, Mercy! Isn't there enough to deal with, without having a go at each other too? This family has imploded, the divorce is about to get as messy as hell—'

'No thanks to some blonde, twenty-year-old wannabe with a perky nose and tiny feet and a too-small bikini and an eye on a lead role she can't handle.'

'We don't know that for sure, Mer. And, yes, maybe we're all biding our time until we can take our trust funds and go our separate ways. But this party wasn't about you. Why can't you see that?'

'You're right,' Mercy says in a low, tired voice. 'This party wasn't about me, Faith. Or you or Max or Hope. It's never about *any* of us.'

There's a long silence and I want to run away, but I'm frozen, heart hammering. *I need to leave, I need to get out, but I can't move I can't move I can't move I can't—*

'I didn't mean what I said about your nose,' Faith says softly. 'I'm sorry, Mer. I love your nose, I do. It's unique and beautiful and dignified and it suits you perfectly.'

'I know it does. You still can't act, I'm afraid.'

'Whatever.'

There's another silence.

I can't see them, but I know my sisters are both slumped, exhausted, against the wall.

Then there's an *ow don't pinch me oh you're so annoying get off—*

They start giggling.

'I suppose we'd better get back out there,' Faith sighs after a few moments. 'Carry on this ridiculous charade for however long it takes. Although, after that little performance, Grandma's going to kill us.'

'She's going to kill *me*,' Mercy corrects. 'You'll be the saviour of the Valentines, as per usual. But it's fine. Grandma will just tell everyone I'm the tragic loose cannon nobody can reach.'

Effie laughs. 'Good old Nanna Vee. Oh, Mer, your make-up is *everywhere*. You can't go out like that.

Wait a second, I think I've got a wet-wipe in my bag.'

'You're such an old lady, Eff— *Ow*, don't rub so hard. Have you got mints in there too? Balled-up tissues? A tabby cat?'

'No, just a spare catheter. There. That's better.'

They stand up and the door opens a fraction. I finally manage to blink and unfreeze.

Go go go.

Stiffly, I push through the crowds, past the DJ booth and the waiter and the TV actor and the other waiter and the Welcome Drinks boy, through the lights, under the mountains, past flickering images of Mum, out towards the entrance.

'Po?' Max says as I race past him. 'Are you OK? What's happened? Where are you going?'

I reach up, grab his stupid black hat and fling it at him.

'Anywhere but here.'

15

HOPE runs through the—

HOPE waits at the—

HOPE sits on the—

'The train to Hounslow is now leaving from platform seven.'

Fluffy empty dumb bimbo bimbo—

'This train is calling at Vauxhall, Queenstown Road, Clapham Junction, Wandsworth Town, Putney, Barnes—'

You know why Hope is the way she is you know—

'Barnes Bridge, Chiswick, Kew Bridge, Brentford, Syon Lane, Isleworth—'

She doesn't even remember—

'Terminating at Hounslow.'

HOPE is on the wrong train.

Blinking, I stand up.

HOPE jumps off the—

HOPE drops her—

HOPE picks up the—

'The train to Windsor and Eton Riverside is now leaving from platform eighteen.'

HOPE breaks into a run.

Platform eight, platform nine, platform ten . . . *Fluffy*— Platform eleven, platform twelve, platform thirteen, platform fourteen . . . *doesn't even pass the Bechamel test*— Platform fifteen, platform sixteen, platform seventeen—

HOPE can't find her ticket—

'The train now leaving platform eighteen calls at

Vauxhall, Clapham Junction, Putney, Barnes, Richmond—'

Shut up shut up shut up—

I slam Mercy's debit card down and push through the barrier. All the lights in my head have smashed, there's glass everywhere, the cameras have broken, the set is falling apart—

HOPE jumps on the—

The script is ripped—

Stop it stop it stop it I'm not listening I'm not listening I'm not—

BEEP BEEP BEEP BEEP

The train doors shut on HOPE.

OW!

I don't have to hear it I don't have to—

BEEP BEEP BEEP BEEP

The train doors shut on HOPE again.

OW!

Block it block it block it block it—

BEEP BEEP BEEP BEEP

Happy happy happy happy happy happy happy happy—
Hands get slammed on the doors.

'Whoa,' a warm voice says as I'm pulled gently forward on to the train. 'You OK?'

Shaking my head, I focus until everything's silent again. Until the words ringing in my ears stop smashing my world up. Then I stare through wet eyes at the most beautiful boy I've ever seen.

16

'Is it midnight yet?'

'Eleven forty-three.'

'Just in time.'

Blinking, I gaze at the boy standing over me, glowing in the train carriage lights.

'Not you,' I clarify quickly. 'I meant me. This is the last train home.'

The boy laughs; there's a tiny gap between his front teeth.

'Close, though. You definitely OK? That looked pretty painful.'

He's very tall, with golden skin and bronze freckles scattered across his nose and cheeks. His hair is platinum white – flicked across his forehead – and his face is heart-shaped, with a little dip in his upper lip and a slightly pointed chin and ears, a bit like a pixie. His eyes are electric blue: the colour of a winter sky, bright and cloudless.

Obviously, I knew the stars were sending me Someone, but even in my wildest fantasies I didn't know it would be Someone as Special as *this*. Every other Potential is disappearing like bubbles: Waiter, *pop*. Photographer's Assistant, *pop*. Receptionist, TV Wolf Actor, Welcome Drinks Boy: *pop pop pop*.

Did I *really* fancy Ice Cream Boy?

'N-no,' I manage, still staring at him. 'I didn't feel it. Not at all, really. I was . . . thinking about . . . something . . . else.'

'Here. You must be in shock.' I'm led gently to a seat. The train is rocking from side to side, beetling out of Waterloo. 'Sit down. And just let me—'

Before I can breathe, the boy sits next to me and puts a golden hand gently under my chin, thumb and finger lifting my face towards him. Then he uses the right sleeve of his jumper to gently rub at my cheeks, studying my face carefully as he does so.

'Oil,' he explains, smiling. 'From the doors.'

I can feel warm breath on my nose, and we're so close I can see intricate splashes of turquoise and sky blue in his eyes, ringed by cobalt like round the edge of a swimming pool.

'There,' he says, pulling away but still looking at me. 'Much better.'

It's suddenly as if the camera has flipped and I can see *me* through his eyes: dark brown eyes, brown skin, button nose, full bottom lip, the little heart birthmark on my cheek and the tiny curls collecting on my forehead.

Then the camera pulls back and I can see both of us.

I can hear the *click click click* of the smashed spotlights in my head trying to switch back on.

'You're American, right?'

He laughs brightly. 'I am indeed. Although I'm native Californian, which is basically a different nationality in and of itself.'

'My dad's American too!' I beam, even though I totally thought California was in the States. 'From New Orleans originally, but he got together with my mum in London many years ago so I'm half British too. He's in Los Angeles at the moment for . . .' *some blonde with a perky nose and tiny feet* – 'work. He's in the film industry,' I add proudly.

'Yeah?' The beautiful boy grins. 'Cool. I'm not really into movies, if I'm being honest. I'd rather be outside, in the fresh air and sunshine. A typical Cali boy, I guess.'

I stare at him, trying to understand.

What does he mean, *outside*? Doing what, exactly? Surely you mostly go outside to collect the stories you can then go back inside and make films about?

'*So* much other stuff going on,' I agree, nodding. '*Soooooo* much stuff. Like, ah . . .' *What other stuff?* 'Well, there's breakfast for starters. Lunch. Dinner. The bit in between dinner and lunch.' *Umm.* 'And parties where everybody is happy and lovely and everything goes perfectly.'

'Sure,' he laughs. 'You're cute. Hey, are you cold? Why don't you have this for a second? I don't need it right now.'

I hadn't realised I was trembling, but thank you once again, universe. Obviously, I was *supposed* to forget to collect Mercy's coat from the bouncer because now this beautiful boy is taking his jacket off and wrapping it round my shoulders.

I glow at him. This is *exactly* like a film. I couldn't

have written it better myself, and I know because I've tried to repeatedly.

The stars must have *foreseen* that I would read my horoscope late this evening, must have known Max would lend me his hat and let me into the party, then accurately predicted that I'd get caught in those train doors. Destiny had my back right from the start, just like I *knew* it would.

So auditions are over, my romantic lead is found, everyone else can go home – the most important part has been won.

Thank you, Venus, and in your face, *Max*.

'I'm Hope,' I smile, holding a hand out. A puff of cotton wool has started poking curiously out of my bra so I subtly prod it back in with my finger. 'Great to meet you.'

'Jamie,' he smiles and shakes my hand. 'Jamie Day.'

'Hi, Jamie,' I say, feeling shyer than I've ever been before. The entire right side of my body has gone tingly and warm and kind of numb. 'And thank you. For . . . you know . . . saving my life and stuff.'

I honestly don't think that's an exaggeration. I mean, who knows how many times I was going to get shut in the train doors before I snapped back to consciousness? It could have been *hours*.

'You're welcome,' Jamie grins. 'I guess you could say I'm an accidental hero.'

We both laugh and the train crunches to a slow stop. 'Train now approaching Vauxhall,' the tannoy says loudly.

Jamie Day stands up. 'Well, it's been a pleasure running into you, half-American Hope. And an absolute honour to pry you out of the evil demonic train doors of South London.'

I stare at him.

Why is he standing up?

'This is my stop,' he explains as the doors beep and swing open. 'Catch you later, Hope. Who knows? Maybe we'll run into each other again one day in the future.'

Then The One grins, waves, steps off the train and disappears into the darkness.

I stare numbly at my reflection in the window.

Umm, that's not how this scene goes. I have seen a *lot* of romantic movies, and at no stage do the male leads go around saving girls from almost certain death, touching their faces, breathing on them, cleaning them up with jumper sleeves and calling them cute if they're just going to get off at the next station.

I mean, if that was supposed to happen, my horoscope would have said *Romance Is Calling But Don't Get Too Excited Because It's A Wrong Number LOL!*

Vauxhall is less than three minutes from Waterloo. This isn't an epic romance; it's barely even a *trailer*.

Maybe Jamie Day doesn't realise he's *my* The One?

Maybe he saw the cotton-wool puff poking out of my bra and it sent fate spiralling in a different direction.

Maybe he didn't read his horoscope this morning, or he met *another* Cancerian while I was in class, or we were actually *supposed* to meet on the way *to* Waterloo and then we'd have had more time together to really bond and—

'Hope?'

I spin round in my seat.

'So I was thinking, you know that day? The one in the future I was talking about? Maybe we could make it a particular day?'

I blink. 'What?'

'We could run into each other again.' Jamie grins and scratches his head. 'Like, on purpose, at a designated time, in a specified place. Maybe tomorrow? Same place?'

What . . . ? Is he—

'Wait.' I stare at Jamie, then at the open train doors behind him. There must be some kind of delay because they're not closing yet. 'Did you just leave the train, walk to the next carriage and come back in through the doors behind me to ask me on a *date*?'

Jamie laughs. 'Sure. I realised there's a chance I wouldn't stop thinking about you if I didn't. But, if I need to wait till the next stop for an answer, then I totally will.'

My eyes open wide.

Heart hammering, I reach speechlessly into my handbag and pull out one of my pre-signed photos with my number on it.

'Sweet.' Jamie smiles easily as he takes it, putting it in his jeans pocket. 'And can I have my jacket too?' I blink at the coat, then nod silently and hand that over too.

'I'll text you, 'kay?'

Beep beep beep beep –

'There go those demon doors again.'

He bounces down the train and leaps through them.

I suddenly snap back to life.

'Wait!' I shout in a panic, jumping up and running after him. 'I forgot to ask! What's your star sign?'

'Gemini,' Jamie grins as the doors slam between us and the train starts pulling away.

And, just like that, I hear it.

A tiny click.

As the train rocks away from the platform and into the darkness – tracks beneath me thudding like drums – there's a faint tinkle of piano music. Slowly, it swells until there's flutes, violins, trumpets. Cameras whir, hot white lights blink on. A spotlight, glowing and warm, is aimed straight at me.

And we are *Back. In. Action.*

With a rush, the camera pans over all of London – how big it is! How unlikely the odds! How mysteriously the universe works and yet how accurately predicted! – before slowly focusing in on the train hurtling through the night.

Then it zooms in for a tight shot of my glowing, happy face.

And in that moment HOPE knew that nothing would be the same again.

Finally, the BOY had a name.

END SCENE.

COMPATIBILITY

Cancer and Gemini are directly next to each other on the zodiac wheel, which can result in a curious but intimate bond. Outgoing and intellectual social butterfly Gemini quickly becomes Cancer's knight in shining armour, while thoughtful, romantic and sensitive Cancer makes Gemini feel cherished.

Ruled by Mercury, mutable and airy Geminis are the zodiac's communicators – enjoying wordplay and discussions – while Moon-led water sign Cancer is the universe's emotional cornerstone, struggling to say how they feel and tending to bottle things up. These two are therefore opposites, but can make a great team if they manage to find compromise, combining key skills and bringing out the best in each other.

Overall, a solid potential love match.

17

HOPE sits in a Richmond field by the river, under a pink blossoming tree. Her red dress is spread around her. Holding her hand is JAMIE JAMIE JAMIE. They are laughing, a breakfast picnic laid out on a blanket.

                    HOPE
        I've never truly noticed how
        beautiful it is here before.

                    JAMIE
            (gazing pointedly at her)
                It really is.

HOPE
(pretending he means the scenery)
I just wish we could stay here
forever.

JAMIE
Me too, because I don't have
anywhere more interesting or
important to be.

JAMIE leans towards—

'Hope.'
  I frown.

JAMIE leans towards—

'Hope.'
  Oh, for goodness' sake, give me a *second*.

JAMIE leans towards HOPE and—

'Oy, earth to poop-head!'
  And my perfect moment is destroyed forever. I'm

going to have to think of a whole new scene now: nobody wants faeces associated with their first-ever kiss.

'Mmm?' I smile, shifting my beatific gaze from the sunlit fields outside the window – so lush! So green! So pretty! – to Mercy, with alarmingly smudged eyes, who is waving a hand in front of my face. 'Sorry, what did you say?'

It's so weird. I thought I was living life in colour before, but now I can see that everything was muted, the details were blurry, the colours somehow dimmed, as if I was watching everything through a foggy lens.

Or . . . maybe the foggy lens was *me*?

Maybe *we're* the glass the world shines through, and every morning life is tinted by the way we feel and who we are and how we—

'She's gone again.' A hand is slapped on my forehead five times. 'What. Is. Wrong. With. You?'

'We were just asking if you had a nice time last night.' Effie smiles as I refocus my eyes on the kitchen again. 'What with the party and everything.'

My smile fades and I look in alarm at Max.

'The big film launch of our mother's that you

didn't go to because you were safely tucked away at home as per the Valentine rules,' my brother prompts me from the seat opposite, with a lightning-fast wink. 'Remember?'

'Oh.' My dazed smile returns. 'I . . . ummm . . . had a bath, watched a couple of films, read my horoscopes, went to bed. Ordinary Friday night. No adventure or excitement or epic romantic meet-cutes with hot boys here.'

Beautifully done, Hope. Very convincing.

Then I gaze back at the garden.

Look at the beautiful butterflies, the fluffy squirrel, the velvety flowers, the yellow sunshine, that green hedge, two trees, a bird . . . Life is so precious, so fragile, we are all so momentary, just flickers of beauty in a river of time that—

A blue bag gets slammed on the table in front of me.

'Goody bag,' Mercy says briskly. 'And here's another one. And another one. Four.' They're getting piled up in front of my face. 'Five. Six. Seven.' She starts aggressively pulling out contents: perfume, silver pens, more perfume, chocolates. 'We thought it might . . .' A cough. 'Make up for you missing last night.'

It's weird watching guilt at work when you know exactly where it's coming from. But if my mean-girl sisters think a few bags of expensive merchandise are going to make up for—

Ooooh, a Fendi wallet!

'So how did it go?' I ask as airily as possible, cramming all seven bags safely under my chair. 'Was it lots of fun?'

Mercy and Faith glance at each other.

Oh, *come on*. I'd have noticed that even if I wasn't already fully aware of the situation. I might be easily distracted sometimes, but I'm not literally blind.

'It was a bit boring, to be honest,' Faith says sweetly, sipping her orange juice. 'And the DJ was *terrible*.'

Mercy lifts one eyebrow. 'Just didn't know when to shut up.'

'Never does.'

They snigger and I'm starting to wonder just how much of an ordinary conversation between my siblings I normally miss, given how many in-jokes, lies and codes there are that would normally go straight over my head. Have my siblings *always* been speaking another language?

And, if so, do I even want to understand it?

'That's nice.' I smile vaguely as the left side of my chest suddenly vibrates twice: *dzz-dzz*. For a second, I assume I'm having a mini heart attack, but then I remember I put my phone in my MAKE LAVA NOT WAR T-shirt pocket.

Quickly, I reach a hand under my jumper and grab it.

Thought about you all the way home last
night. Can't wait to see you again. Jamie x

My entire body just melted.

This is what movies are written about: exactly the way I'm feeling right now. An entire multibillion-pound industry has been built on this moment. The warmth, the giddiness, the soaring happiness, the way I'm smiling all over my body until I'm beaming with my toes.

Furtively, under the table, I write back:

You too. What are you thinking? x

Three waving dots:

I'm thinking as soon as possible, please. x

I give a little squeak and bounce in my chair.

'Who's that?' Mercy frowns at me suspiciously. 'Who are you texting, Poodle? Everyone you know is sitting at this table.'

'I'm not *texting*,' I lie with award-winning conviction. *Be the Orange, Hope Valentine.* 'I'm playing an online game, and I just won—' What do people win online? 'Three goats. I am so very happy with my goat! Goats are great! Yay, goats!'

Mercy rolls her eyes. 'Loser.'

Then I look back at my phone, still grinning. I'm not quite ready for anyone else to know about Jamie yet. I don't want their starred reviews or judgemental critiques on my personal romance.

Right now, this movie is *mine*.

Lunch? Or is that too soon? x

Immediately!

Never too soon – see you at midday,
Waterloo, by the clock. x

I bounce up, shining like a lamp.

Oh, *so* much to do: hair to style, 'natural' First Date make-up to apply – that takes much longer than full glam – a casual-but-flattering outfit to borrow, identity-defining perfume to steal . . . *Ooh*, and today's horoscope to read. At least I've already checked our compatibility – I did that on the train home, with huge success.

Now I've just got to find today's newspap—

My phone starts vibrating in my hand, and I look down.

DAD.

I hesitate for a few seconds – I really do want to find out what delayed his return last night – but I'm guessing it was some kind of directoring emergency. I really have to prioritise: there's only just time for one face mask as it is.

Quickly, I send Dad's call to voicemail. I'll ring him when I'm back from my *First-ever Date*.

Oh my goodness, that is *so* fun to say.

'Poodle?' Max says as I grab the newspaper and head out of the door. It's particularly full of my family today: Mercy's DJ pics are on page six, and there's a tiny photo of Eff and Noah eating dinner with blank faces and *IS THIS YEAR'S HOTTEST ROMANCE ON THE ROCKS?* written underneath. 'Wait a minute.'

My brother pulls the kitchen door shut behind him.

'Is everything OK?' His voice is low. 'I got cornered by my agent and by the time I escaped you'd disappeared. Did something happen? I swear if anyone hurt you I'll—'

Pain flickers but I push it away.

'Not even a little bit,' I say brightly, kissing my brother's cheek. 'Everything happened just like it was supposed to. I just had to go right then, that's all. But thank you for letting me in, Max.'

'As long as you're OK.' Max studies my face. 'I was thinking, Po, I'm free this morning. Do you want to . . . go shopping or whatever? Hang out together – Little Sis and Big Bro time? I could treat you. Get you out of the house for a change?'

My phone buzzes again.

PS I literally cannot wait J xxx

'Hmm?' I smile distractedly, bouncing on my toes again. 'Oh, I'm actually busy today. Sorry, Max.'

Then I send:

Me neither. x

And it suddenly feels like I'm a movie star, lit by my very own spotlight.

Warm and bright and seen.

♋ Cancer: June 21–July 22

Cancer, Venus has now moved into your eighth house of regeneration and transformation, leading to a very passionate encounter. It's also the turning point of the first lunar cycle, so as a key moon sign it's time for a new beginning.

And *HERE. WE. GO.*

Skipping through the barriers of Waterloo station, I see Jamie immediately; he's standing in the middle of the crowd, under the ornate clock, with his hands thrust in his jeans pockets, turquoise eyes scanning the exit.

Then he sees me and his whole face lights up.

All the extras – security guards, commuters, families on a Saturday day trip, couples – are abruptly thrown into darkness. The rest of the world is just background.

'Hope,' Jamie beams as the blurred crowd parts and I surge forward, stomach fluttering. 'Great timing. I got here early so I could work out the best way to stand with my hands casually in my pockets, as if I'm not overexcited about seeing you. How'd I do?'

I laugh. 'Amazing. It's like you don't care in the slightest.'

Impossibly, he's even *more* beautiful than he was twelve hours ago.

'Then I'm amazed at myself too,' Jamie laughs. 'Because I usually can't stand casual people. Why pretend you don't care if you do? It's like living your whole life with the volume turned down. Which leads me to—'

Smiling, he reaches under his jacket and hands me a branded paper bag. 'There's a shop over there and I couldn't help myself.'

Inside is a small book with the title BRITISH TRAINS. There's a picture of an old black steam train on the front and in biro Jamie has added (messily):

AND HOW TO NEGOTIATE THEIR EVIL DEMON
DOORS.

I burst into delighted laughter.

'This is so thoughtful.' I glow at him as we push through the station doors into the spring sunshine. 'Thank you, Jamie. I . . . didn't bring you anything. I was in such a rush, and there are no shops near my house, and—'

'You did bring something, Hope.' Jamie crooks his arm so I can hold it. 'You brought you, and that's plenty.'

My heart just tripped and fell over.

'So,' he adds as we start wandering towards the river, 'all my plans are going to seem super touristy to you. But whatever – do you want to explore this magical capital with me?'

He could have just asked me to eat spiders with him and I'd have said, *Yes, please, one leg at a time to make it last longer.*

'Of course.' I grin happily. 'Super cheesy touristy sounds fun to me.'

'I mean, I'm talking Camembert cheesy, Hope. Swiss cheese cheesy.'

'Parmesan cheesy?'

'Monterey Jack cheesy.'

We laugh together. My hand is resting on his arm and my shoulder is just touching his chest. My stomach is dancing so hard it feels like it's about to trip over too.

'But don't google Romantic Things To Do in London,' Jamie adds with a wry grin. 'Because then you'll see my plans for all our *other* dates too.'

A giddy little wave of surprise.

Nine minutes in, and he's already making future plans to see me? I'm *so* good at this dating thing. Not that I'm surprised – I've been practising in my head for a very long time.

'What I *can* promise,' Jamie continues, 'is that we're *not* challenging another couple to a pedalo race in Hyde Park or visiting London Zoo for a selfie with lions.'

'*Awwww*,' I laugh. 'We're not boating down the Thames and feeding the swans?'

'No, and we're not seeing an opera or a ballet or a horse race or going on a Ghost Tour bus – mainly because it's daytime on Saturday and the ghouls are probably having a lie-in.'

I giggle, although those dates sound perfect. Especially because I could have brought out my very best 'scared acting'. I could've jumped and slipped my hand into his – ('Oh my goodness! What was that?') – so it's a sadly missed dramatic opportunity.

'There's a restaurant in Clerkenwell that's pitch-black,' I suggest optimistically. 'It's called *Dan's Lenwah* and you can't even see your food.'

Jamie laughs. 'I'm sorry, it's called *what*?'

'*Dan's Lenwah*,' I repeat a little less certainly. 'I think it probably belongs to a man called Dan and Lenwah is, like, Portuguese or Russian for restaurant.'

'It's *Dans le Noir*,' Jamie chuckles, squeezing my arm. 'Which is French for *In the Dark*. Hope, you are *hilarious.*'

I beam. I wasn't joking, but I'll *take* it.

'But no,' Jamie continues as we walk up the steps. 'I have this weird thing where I like to see the face of the girl I'm dating. Especially when that girl has a face as lovely as yours.' Then he grimaces. 'Ugh, it's *me* that's the cheeseball. Can we please forget I said that?'

Literally never gonna happen.

A meteor will be heading towards earth and fires

will rage and the zombies will finally arrive and I'll still be here, hanging on to a lamp post and shouting, *HE SAID I HAVE A LOVELY FACE!*

'I don't mind,' I flush. 'Not even a little bit.'

'Good.' Jamie squeezes my arm and pulls me gently to a stop. 'Because I don't think I can play it cool with you, Hope. I don't like girls very often, so when I do . . .' He grins shyly. 'Sometimes I get carried away. I guess I'm just an old-fashioned romantic.'

I stare at him in wonder.

He's *me*.

This beautiful boy, standing by the River Thames, is *me* – only taller and Gemini and fully American and male.

And as we gaze at each other – bright blue eyes to dark brown – I feel a little warm click. As if something deep inside us has just recognised each other and waved.

Oh hello, I know you.

'I'm the same,' I tell him, so excited I'm struggling to get the words out. 'Exactly the same. I try to play it cool, but then I—' I throw my arms out. '*Kapow.* I burst out everywhere. Everything's too . . .

beautiful. It's like life is one big film, and I want it to be the most lovely, romantic, *happy* film it can possibly be.'

Jamie smiles and tucks a curl behind my ear.

'We're the same, you and me.' He grabs my hands and I can feel the warmth abruptly spreading through my fingers, up my arms, into my shoulders. 'So no holding back, OK? There's no right and no wrong. No rules. We'll be ourselves, as much as we want to be. Living life at full volume. Deal?'

I'm trying to breathe steadily, but it's impossible.

In my Director's Cut, I would infinitely extend this scene so I could keep it running forever.

'Deal,' I whisper.

And all the bits of life I don't like – the sad bits and the painful bits and the bits that should never have happened – I would cut without even looking at them. So I could spend all that extra screen time here, with him.

'Now.' Jamie spins me round until we're facing the London Eye. 'This is the start of our epic first date. It may or may not be number one on the London Tourist Guide to Romantic Dates. What do you think?'

Honestly, it doesn't matter where we are.

The soundtrack in my head has already started: lilting piano, violins, the romantic ping of some kind of percussion instrument. The sun is shining, my heart is swelling and the whole world is my movie set.

'I love it,' I beam at him.

'Good,' Jamie grins, taking my hand. 'Because this is just the beginning.'

19

HOPE and JAMIE stand in the queue for the London Eye. The sun shines, the water flickers with light. JAMIE is devastatingly handsome, in jeans and a T-shirt with a forest logo on it. HOPE is also ridiculously beautiful, in a black Chloé jumpsuit that is hers and fits perfectly.

A ROMANTIC SOUNDTRACK continues to play.

Every time the queue moves forward, JAMIE and HOPE get pushed together and his hand brushes hers and/or her shoulder touches his chest and the music gets louder.

HOPE's cheeks are warm. Her heart is pounding. Her stomach is fluttering. Every time she takes a breath, she can smell him: minty and sweet and somehow blue—

'. . . it was so weird, he just fell in out of *nowhere*. I was in the house, but some primal instinct kicked in. I ran out and jumped in and hauled him on to the grass—'

Another jostle. HOPE is pushed into JAMIE again.

His freckles are so cute, her head is dizzy, her breathing is getting faster—

'. . . but it was close. I mean, *real* close. Lucky I was there, you know? They think it was a heart attack.'

HOPE wonders what his lips taste like. Soft, sweet, like ice cream, or mango, or—

'What?' I blink. 'Who had a heart attack?'

'My boss.' Jamie smiles easily. 'I help out with this charity, building houses for disadvantaged people. The CEO – great guy, so inspirational – he fell in the pool without warning, so I . . .' He shrugs. 'Fate, you know? It puts us where we need to be.'

I stare at him, super impressed. *Charity work. Disadvantaged people. Building houses. Saving lives.* I was probably liking photos of dogs on Instagram when it happened. 'You're an actual hero.'

'Just in the right place at the right time,' he laughs. 'Although he was pretty grateful. Nobody tells you this but drowning people are kinda *heavy.*'

The crowd moves forward a few metres. Hope bumps into JAMIE's chest again and now backing singers have started the official JAMIE theme: *JAMIE da-da-da-da JAMIE ooh-ooh ooh-ooh JAMIE la-la—*

HOPE's breathing is getting even shorter. Her heart is pounding, her hands are trembling slightly. They're very nearly at the front of the queue.

JAMIE
I can't wait any longer. For some
reason, I feel a desperate desire
to kiss y—

'Any brothers or sisters?' Jamie asks.

'Umm.' I drop my pucker. 'There's f-four of us.
Two sisters, one brother. All older than me. You?'

'Only child.'

With a sudden wave of sadness, I squeeze Jamie's
arm: imagine being *just you*.

The crowd moves forward once more and
JAMIE hands over two tickets. HOPE
realises he must have bought them
online and is OVERWHELMED by his
romantic forward planning.

TICKET INSPECTOR
You two make such a lovely couple.
I can see that you are on a first
and very pivotal date, so let me
give you a private VIP pod all to
yourselves.

'Get a move on,' the ticket inspector snaps, wiping her nose on her coat sleeve. 'I don't 'ave all day.'

OK, this woman is *fired*.

'You're not scared of heights, are you?' asks Jamie. The pod opens up, the rope barrier is lifted and we're immediately swallowed by a mass of people crushing forward: kids, couples, old people, parents, tourists with neon backpacks. 'I never thought to ask.'

'Not at all.' I grin as an old man shoves me with his elbow to get to a window. 'I love heights. Little ones, big ones. Many sorts of tallnesses, and also widths depending on which way you're looking at them.'

JAMIE and HOPE easily make their way to the other side of the pod for the best view. They are completely and totally ALONE.

'MUM!' a little kid shrieks, stepping on my toe in her race to the pod door. 'LET ME OFF LET ME OFF I NEED TO PEEEEEE!'

OK, she's fired too.

The doors slide shut. Slowly, the wheel turns and the capsule begins to lift into the air.

Around them, LONDON expands and shrinks, flashing into miniature. Tiny boats chug silently down the winding river, the trees are tiny, the buildings are compact, and HOPE has run out of words for 'small' so everything is basically really little.

To the right, HOPE can see Regent's Park Theatre and the Globe and the Barbican and the West End and Leicester Square. To the left is Richmond, aka HOME.

Next to her is JAMIE. He takes a step closer to her and from the way he's looking at her somehow she just knows . . .

It's **KISSING TIME**.

Heart pounding, I hold my breath. When do I pop my foot out? Before, during or after the kiss? Do both my hands go in his hair, or just one of them? Will he put his hands on either side of my face? Do I need to bend backwards a little bit, but if I do will it topple us over?

Jamie takes another step towards me.

'I don't do this often,' he says softly, clear blue eyes matching the bright sky behind him. 'Dating, I mean. But I'm so stoked I took a chance with you.'

'Really?' The wheel moves steadily upwards and I'm starting to float with it. 'No offence, but you look like the kind of boy who dates *loads*. Like, all the time.'

He shrugs, obviously embarrassed. 'It's rare that I meet someone I like enough. And, every time I'm really into a girl, they turn out . . .' His face twists. 'I won't say *crazy* . . . But I seem to have really bad luck. Maybe I'm just drawn to broken people or something.'

I am literally never telling him where my mum has been for the past three months. 'Oh, Jamie. That's *awful* for you.'

'But there's something about you,' he continues, taking another tiny step forward. 'You're not like those girls, Hope. You seem . . . whole. Happy. Comfortable with being who you really are.'

He's getting so close I can feel his breath on my nose.

This is it!

I glance down and I'm pretty sure there's light coming out of my fingertips. Can everyone else see it too?

'I don't date, either,' I blurt as – I swear – the tips of my toes start hovering slightly off the ground. 'I mean, I've literally never dated anyone. Or been asked out by anyone. This is the first date I've ever had.' I take a deep breath. 'I've . . . never kissed anyone, either.'

Jamie smiles warmly. Then he takes one last step, puts a hand under my chin and tilts my face towards him, just like he did on the train.

'Yet . . .'

He hesitates long enough for me to feel like I've told the whole universe to pause. Like this moment will stand still forever.

Then JAMIE leans forward and the world starts moving again and the soundtrack explodes and HOPE's foot pops out and her heart bursts and there's glitter and lights and sound everywhere.

And he kisses me.

20

The next week is a glorious montage:

HOPE AND JAMIE standing on either side of the Changing of the Guard at Buckingham Palace in the rain, wearing fake moustaches and laughing.

HOPE AND JAMIE wandering down Brick Lane, hand in hand, eating bagels and staring in shop windows to point at interesting vintage items.

HOPE AND JAMIE jumping across the meridian line in Greenwich, then kissing with one foot on each side.

HOPE AND JAMIE sitting on the kerb

in Covent Garden, watching an acrobat and clapping.

HOPE, beaming with pride, watching JAMIE as he successfully rides a unicycle.

HOPE AND JAMIE playing the Beatles on a phone and dancing on the famous zebra crossing.

I give each date five stars.

In fact, if they were a film, I'm pretty sure it would be reviewed as Unmissable; a Critically Acclaimed Masterpiece; a Must-see For The Whole Family.

Day after day, all the way across London – just like Mum and Dad during *The Heart of Us* – until it isn't a stand-alone movie any more and it isn't even a sequel. This romance is a *franchise*, complete with branded T-shirts and a plastic toy version of us kissing forever.

Every morning, there's a *beep* on my phone.

Every morning, I wake up to read –

Good morning, beautiful! How did you sleep?
Tower of London today? xx

Or

I woke up thinking about you! Have you ever
been to Trafalgar Square? xxx

Or

I miss your face and it's only been twelve
hours :(xxx

And every morning I am so *happy*.

Happier than I've ever been before; happier than I even knew was possible. It's like there's a huge, warm well of joy inside me and it's so big it's splashing over everything, every time I move.

Covering the whole world with joy.

'. . . and he's got these little gold hairs on his hairline and he can speak Spanish and he never wears socks and he's a *really* good kisser and he only likes the best Colombian coffee and when he sneezes he goes *wwwhhhaaatcccchaaa* and there are freckles on his fingers and did I mention the gap between his front teeth and—'

'Take a breath,' Faith laughs from my bed. 'Or you're going to fall over and then you'll have a gap between your front teeth too.'

I lasted four seconds before telling her.

By the end of our first official date, I was so giddy I couldn't hold it in any more.

'Hey, how was your af—' said Faith and I exploded.

'OH MY GOSH, EFF, I'VE MET THE ONE AND HE'S PERFECT AND I'M SO HAPPY I'M GOING TO EXPLODE.'

Then I swore her to solemn secrecy.

I originally wanted to keep it all to myself, but Olivia, Madison and Sophia just weren't being enthusiastic enough so I had to tell *someone*.

'Isn't love *wonderful*,' I tell Effie, twirling round my room with the train book in my arms. I've been twirling all week: I am now a human fidget spinner. 'You never know when it's going to strike. It's so unexpected, so transformationalistic, so— *Look*.'

I shove the book triumphantly in Effie's face.

'Wow,' she blinks at the front cover. 'A book about

ancient steam trains. That's so . . . sweet. What does it mean?'

'Oh, nothing.' I beam at her. 'Just an in-joke. You know how it is with couples. We have our very own language that nobody else can possibly understand. It's basically code.'

Then I glide round my bedroom, straightening all my cute mementos of our dates on their shelf: Jamie's fake moustache, five train tickets, an empty coffee cup, a bit of dried grass, a flake crumble from my ice cream, a tiny crust of salted-beef bagel.

Then I look pityingly at my kissing poster.

Where is the *passion*? Where is the *soul connection*? Where is the *joonysaykwa*? I always thought they were so perfect, but now I can see they're just a poor imitation of how good a kiss can be.

'You're literally glowing.' My sister smiles, stretching her leg in the air and pulling on her toes with her hand. 'It's lovely to see you so happy.'

I beam. 'I'm not just happy, Eff, I'm Happy Girl Lucky. People have always said that's what I am, but I've never really understood the expression before . . . because why can't boys be it too? But now it truly capsules me perfectly.'

'It does,' Faith laughs. 'And I'm so pleased, Po. I mean, yes, it's all happening quite fast, but—'

I flash her a dark look.

'Not *fast*, as such,' she corrects hastily, putting her leg down. 'That's not what I meant. Just . . . intense, you know. Like *whoa*, *fireworks*. But I guess sometimes when you know, you know, right?'

'It's called a *whirlwind* romance,' I explain patiently, sitting on the bed next to her and patting her hand. 'Not a *light breeze* romance, Faith. It's *madly* in love, not *sane* in love. *Crazy* for someone. *Swept* off your feet. Love is supposed to be all at once. Otherwise, they'd call it . . . prodded off your feet or something.'

'Gently nudged.' Effie smiles. 'Elbowed into love.'

I stroke her arm sympathetically. 'Did you know straight away with Noah too?'

Faith wrinkles her beautiful nose, yawns and stretches. '*Nooooo*. I'm not sure I'm really a love-at-first-thing kind of person. For me, love's more like . . . mould. It grows slowly where it's happiest . . . In the right conditions. When it's getting what it needs.'

'Like a damp bathroom or an old sandwich.'

My sister grins. 'Exactly. I didn't really fancy Noah

159

when we met. He ended up writing this terrible love song and I told him I didn't like it.' She pulls a face. 'It was his first Number One so I guess my musical critiquing is no longer required.'

'Well,' I say, patting her shoulder reassuringly, 'don't worry, Eff. I'm sure not *every* great love story clicks straight away. It doesn't mean yours isn't *every bit* as good as mine.'

'Phew.' She smiles, then sits up straight and clears her throat. 'Po, baby . . . I know you thought Mum and Dad were going to be home after the premiere last Friday. I saw the breakfast you left for them.'

I flush. In all the excitement, I forgot to clear it away.

'Well, yes,' I admit in embarrassment, 'but I reckon Dad got totally caught up in Los Angeles with work. And Mum's probably not ready for a big party just yet – it would be way too much for her. Stupid me.'

Faith puts her arm round me and kisses my curls.

'You're not stupid,' she whispers into my hairline. 'But you didn't come to see Mum last weekend, either, and it's the first time you've missed a visit. Is everything OK?'

Honestly, I was trying to be sensitive.

The newspapers printed a blurry photo of Mum wandering around the grounds of the rehab place the next day, and she looked *terrible*. Frankly, if my mother was prepared to miss her own celebrity party and skip wearing mascara for the first time ever, she must be truly exhausted. The least I could do was give her a lie-in.

Although I did also send Dad a text on Tuesday that said:

WHERE WERE YOU I CANNOT BELIEVE YOU MISSED THE PREMIERE COME HOME NOW PLS xxx

But all I got back was:

Haha, bossy little mousebear, am on set, I'll ring again in the week, love you xx

Which is *not* what I was looking for.

'Mum needed sleep,' I say firmly. 'Her horoscope for the day pacifically told me that. So Jamie and I went to King's Cross, to visit Harry Potter's trolley.

Did I show you the photos of us with our scarves pretending to blow behind us?'

Faith laughs. 'One or fifteen times. He's very gorgeous.'

'Right?' I glow, patting her head. 'But don't you worry, Eff. Noah's quite cute too.'

My phone beeps and I jump up.

Counting down the minutes until I see you. :D
xxx

Alarmed, I glance at my watch.

I got so caught up talking about Jamie and thinking about Jamie and dreaming about Jamie and singing the Jamie song that I forgot I'm meeting actual Jamie in fifteen minutes.

'We'll continue this love chat about our guys later, Eff!' I shout, jumping up, grabbing Mercy's handbag and sticking on the neon trainers Faith just took off. 'I'm borrowing these, OK? Oooh, and I haven't told you yet how fast Jamie can run. Like, *super* fast. He's very talented and also kind and hot and interesting and funny.'

Then I bounce down the stairs.

'Hope?' Mr Gilbert emerges from the study with even fluffier eyebrows than normal. 'You haven't been in class all week. And I can't get hold of either of your parents, so could we possibly sit down and—'

'Later!' I call to him. 'I'll study later!'

Because life is here and life is now and YOLO: You Only Love Once.

So I'm doing it as hard as I can.

♋ Cancer: June 21–July 22

The moon is in Scorpio, leading to great emotional intensity for you today. Your mind is at its sharpest so enjoy the clarity of observation and perception!

This is now date eight.

Not including the three minutes when Jamie and I met, which I do actually include because that was the moment when both our lives changed forever. So that's nine dates. Plus, hours and hours of phone calls every evening, dozens of texts every day, Good Morning and Goodnight photos . . . that's at least an extra day: ten dates.

Obviously, I know what's coming next.

I've been steadily preparing for it all week, playing

every scene again and again – tweaking, editing, erasing, starting from the beginning with a brave eye for a fresh, endearing perspective.

Although honestly they're *all* so lovely. Maybe at the end I'll include the cuts that don't make it with a delightfully insightful commentary.

JAMIE
Hope, we've only technically known each other eight days, but it feels like we've never not known each other. So—

HOPE
Shhh -
She puts a finger on his lips.

HOPE (CONTINUED)
You don't need to say it, Jamie. I can always tell what's in your heart.

JAMIE
But I want to say it. I *need* to say it.

                    HOPE
        (*humbly taking her finger away*) OK
               then, go ahead.

                    JAMIE
        Will you be my . . . girlfriend?

A wave of giddiness soars through me – I just love
that! – then I pause.

Is it . . . *iconic* enough?

This is a one-shot take that won't be easily
repeated, so I need to make sure that it's going to
anchor this love story and immortalise it forever.
Such a huge shame we're meeting in Richmond Park
and not, say, on a moonlit bridge in 1943, but maybe
I can change the background later.

Let's run through it again.

                    JAMIE
        Hope, maybe it's too soon . . .

                    HOPE
                  (*firmly*)
        It absolutely is not.

                    JAMIE
          But there's something
          I need to ask you.
          Will you be my—

More direct?

                    JAMIE
          Please, Hope. Be my girlfriend.
          I can't live any longer if
                    you're not.

Kind of pathetic. How about something more
spontaneous?

                    HOPE
             (*makes funny joke*)

                    JAMIE
          Hahahahaha! I can't believe
          my girlfriend is such
                    a *dork*.

```
                  HOPE
        Did you just call me
              your . . .


                  JAMIE
              (smiling)
         Well, aren't you?
```

Bingo.

Then we'll have a snowball fight and he'll cram a snowball gently in my face. I'll pretend to be upset and then attack him back, and we'll fall over laughing before he wipes the snow from my face and kisses me tenderly.

It's not snowing so I'll have to do that in Special Effects too.

Grinning, I skip down the path.

As soon as it's all official, I'm going to launch an exclusive screening of *The World's Most Perfect Boyfriend* to Mercy and watch her face disintegrate with disbelief: it's going to be *awesome*.

'Good morning!' Jamie's standing by the entrance to the park, staring at his phone, and he looks so adorable in his STOP CLIMATE CHANGE jumper that I run the last few steps and fling myself round his neck.

'Sorry I'm late. I got caught up chatting to my sister about you. She's *so* excited for us. I can't wait for you to meet her.'

Then I kiss him, hard, on the lips.

When I pull away, my stomach spins with triumph: Jamie is distant and preoccupied. Obviously, he's deliberating over our next big scene too. It *is* incredibly momentous, pivotal to the entire shape of the plot (some might say).

Maybe I can nudge him sensitively in the right direction.

'Shall I tell you a good joke I heard recently?' I chirp, jogging him with my elbow. 'What do you call a warehouse that makes OK products? A *satisfactory*, hahahahaha.'

                    JAMIE
        Hahahahaha! I can't believe my
          girlfriend is such a *dork*.

Jamie smiles slightly.

'Very cute.' Then he takes my hand and kisses

my knuckle. 'You're looking extremely pretty today, Hope. Even prettier than usual.'

We start walking down a flowering path. There are yellow daffodils and white snowdrops and long waving grasses. Maybe I won't have to do much editing at all: add a few bluebirds and a couple of ducks and this setting could do quite nicely, thank you very much.

'It's luxury moisturiser,' I explain serenely. 'It's famous and it costs hundreds of pounds because it's got *actual* silver and *actual* platinum in it.' It's also Mercy's, but, until she works out how to lock her window, the contents of her room are a free-for-all as far as I'm concerned.

Jamie laughs. 'Your face is jewellery.'

'My face is *always* jewellery.' I give him a dazzling smile and a toss of my curls. 'Do you like my outfit?'

It's Mercy's black knee-length pencil skirt, a neon-yellow vest and pink trainers from Effie, and a Cartier gold necklace and earrings from Mum's room. You wouldn't think they go together, but somehow I've made it work because it's just a skill I have.

'You're gorgeous.' Jamie smiles. 'As always.'

There's a long silence.

'Oooh!' I say, abruptly reaching into my handbag. 'I nearly forgot! I brought you something . . .'

With pride, I hand him an orange rectangle. Every night this week I've come home from our dates and drawn a little cartoon on it: a bagel, a juggler, a moustache, an umbrella. I'm not really an artist, but I'm pretty sure you can see what they are apart from the unicycle.

'Hope,' Jamie says, turning it over. 'Is this the train ticket from the evening we met?'

'Yup. I drew your jacket in the corner. Look.'

'No way.' He closes his turquoise eyes briefly. 'This is the sweetest, most thoughtful thing any girl has ever done for me. Hope, I am falling in love with you so hard.'

I freeze, suddenly winded.

He's . . . *what*?

At best I was aiming for official girlfriend status, but this is . . . I didn't . . . I'm not sure I'm quite . . .

Taking a deep breath, I glance around where we're standing, trying to quickly recalibrate the scene again.

'I'm falling in love with you too,' I whisper because that's my line.

Jamie smiles, leans forward and gives me a soft,

sweet kiss on the lips. He lingers until my spotlight starts burning so brightly the entire park fades out.

'Which makes this much more difficult to say.'

'Ask,' I laugh as the light keeps spreading over the trees, down the roads, all the way through London. 'You mean more difficult to *ask*. I haven't said yes yet. You can't take anything for granite, not even me.'

'I mean,' Jamie continues distractedly, 'obviously, we've both known the situation from the start – there was no need to talk about it. And there was never the right moment, you know? It's all been so magical I didn't want to break the spell.'

I hold my breath. 'That's exactly the word: *magical*.'

'It was better to keep things organic, you know? But it can't be put off any more, so—'

This must be so hard for him.

'Don't worry,' I reassure Jamie quickly, grabbing his hands and squeezing them. 'It's not easy to get the words right, so any old way is fine. I'll be totally cool whatever.'

JAMIE
Hope—

HOPE
YES! YES, I'll go out with you
already! YES, YES, YES, YOU FOOL!

Probably.

'Wow,' Jamie breathes, visibly relaxing. 'You really are something else, you know that? I've never met anyone like you. You're so balanced, so awesome, so chilled. I never expected to connect with someone so fast.'

'Me neither,' I lie happily. 'Who saw it coming? Not me.'

Jamie touches my face and here we go, here we go, here we *go*—

'Hope—'

'*YES!*' Squeezing my eyes shut, I fling my arms round his neck and the foot's coming, the foot's coming, the foot's – *pop*. 'YES, I'LL GO OUT WITH YOU ALREADY. YES, YES, YES, YOU FOOL!'

'I'm really gonna miss you.'

There's a pause; we just talked over each other.

Jamie and I pull quickly apart, scene screeching abruptly to a halt.

Wait.

What?

Cut.

Cut cut cut cut cut cut—

'Wait. What? Where am I going?'

'Not you.' Jamie blinks twice. 'Me. I'm going home, back to California. Where I live. You know that, Hope. You've *always* known that.'

Cut. Cut. *Freaking cut.*

I stare at him blankly. 'No, I haven't.'

'You have. I told you I was Californian on the train, during our first-ever conversation. I have school to go back to. I'm only here on vacation with my parents. What did you think I was doing?'

I mean, I *didn't* think.

Obviously, I was far too busy falling in love to bother with logistics. I also kind of assumed that, if there was an imminent deadline for the credits rolling, I'd have been alerted to it somehow.

Otherwise, what was the *point* of this whole week? What have we been *doing*?

'I thought you'd left school already,' I say in a weirdly small voice. 'At sixteen, like we can in England. I thought you worked for that charity with the houses and the pool and maybe you moved over here to start the English head office. Or you had sick grandparents who happened to live in London, but would eventually die and I'd be very supportive, but you'd inherit and live here forever.'

'You made up a random set of rich Brit grandparents for me?'

'That's no more random than coming all the way to England for a break,' I bridle defensively. 'Why would anybody come to England out of choice? It's boring and rainy and not even the holidays.'

'It is in America, actually.'

'Oh.'

'Man.' Jamie breathes out. 'Hope, I've had the most awesome time with you. If I was staying here, or if you were in California, then things would be completely different. I'd date you in a hot second. You'd be my girlfriend so fast your head would spin. You're basically my perfect girl. I adore you.'

He's smiling, but my head is already spinning.

I'm trying to hold on to the fact that he just called me perfect, but all I can think is that I should have asked some smarter questions. Any at all would have been handy. Was I supposed to just *guess* we had an expiry date from the start?

'So you're *not* my boyfriend?'

Maybe this is a dream sequence. Maybe I'm in a coma, or it's an alternative timeline, or – or—

'I'm not your girlfriend? We're . . . nothing at all?'

My chest is starting to ache. *No no no no.*

'Hope. Listen.' Jamie puts two hands gently on either side of my face. 'We will *never* be nothing. *Never.* What we've shared, the connection we've had, the moments we've experienced . . . we will always have them. I'll never forget you. Never.'

My chin is wobbling out of control. 'But am I ever going to see you again?'

'Of *course*. I mean, I'm not sure when – can't imagine I'll be back in England any time soon, I've kinda done it now – but, if you're ever in America, be sure to look me up, OK?' He strokes my cheek softly. 'I can't imagine not seeing your lovely face again.'

My throat makes a weird little whimpering sound.

'Maybe,' I blurt as Jamie continues gazing at me with his electric-blue eyes, 'there's an alternative universe where there's a girl called Hope and a boy called Jamie who live in the same place. And, every time we look up at the stars at night, we'll see them, happy together?'

He smiles and kisses my trembling top lip. 'Exactly.'

'And maybe the universe has a plan for us that we can't see yet. It'll bring us back together when the time is right – we'll randomly bump into each other at, like, a party and we'll remember how much we mean to each other – it'll be like we've never been apart?'

'Yes.' Jamie kisses my nose.

'And we can still message each other and call and maybe send little gifts sometimes?'

'Of *course* we can. I'll always want to hear from you, baby.'

'But I'm still not your girlfriend?'

'Well.' Jamie grimaces. 'I can't really see how that would work, what with the distance and everything.' He smiles and strokes my hair. 'But who *knows* what the future will bring? I can't imagine never seeing you again, Hope. What a pointless life that would be.'

And that was all I needed: just a little bit of hope. Enough to hang my heart on.

'Don't be sad,' Jamie whispers as I close my eyes. 'It would break me to see you cry.'

Then he reaches forward and – with the sleeve of his jumper – wipes my dry cheek tenderly.

And it feels like I'm melting again. Except it suddenly occurs to me that actually melting probably isn't very nice. It would hurt and be confusing and afterwards there'd be nothing left of you at all.

Valentines Always Act With Class Valentines Always Act With Class Valentines Always Act—

'So,' I say, lifting my chin bravely. 'When do you leave? How much time do we have left?'

'None. I'm leaving for the airport now.'

23

And that's it.

The curtain's down, the reel has stopped running, the lights are off, the cinema is emptying.

My epic romance is over.

'Hope?'

I keep walking.

'Hope?'

And walking.

'Hope Valentine, it's a Saturday, but I insist that you take a lesson at some point this week. I'm in the paid employment of your parents, exams are approaching and I cannot impress on you enough the importance of education. Not only in preparing you for a rounded future but in arming you with knowledge and skills with which to—'

I blink and slowly turn towards the library.

At some point I must have said goodbye to Jamie and then walked through the park, down the road, through the electric gates, up the driveway, through the front door and into the hallway. Mr Gilbert is standing in the doorway – grey hair on end, eyebrows bushy and anxious – waiting for me to answer him.

'Sure,' I say numbly. 'Why not? Let's do some schoolwork.'

Without another word, I walk into the library and sit down.

'Ah . . .' Mr Gilbert looks startled. 'Oh. Now? Right! Let me just . . . ah.' He starts scrambling through a large pile of books on the table. 'Maths? History? Biology? Physics? What strikes your fancy, Hope? We've got quite a lot to catch up on so . . .'

I glance at my lesson books: dull and pointless.

Then I look up at Sophia and Olivia and Madison, but the chairs are all empty; there's nobody there because there never actually was.

'I don't care.' My voice is flat. 'You pick.'

'Oh.' My tutor blinks at my blank expression, then at the table. 'Well, last time you seemed quite interested in poor old Elaine, so why don't we . . .' Muttering, he grabs a poetry collection off the shelf.

'Ah . . .' He opens the book and scans it with a finger. 'In that case, why don't I quickly read her poem out loud, get us back into the swing of things?'

Mr Gilbert pauses anxiously and I shrug. 'Sure.'

'Then, uh.' He clears his throat. 'Umm. *The Lady of Shalott* by Alfred, Lord Tennyson. *On either side the river lie long fields of barley and of rye, that clothe the wold and meet the sky . . .*'

My eyes glide over my tutor's shoulder to stare blankly at the dark oily painting: her pale, closed face, her curled blonde hair, the scattered flowers.

What the hell am I supposed to do now, Elaine?

'*. . . There she weaves by night and day a magic web with colours . . .*'

Jamie's gone.

'*. . . And moving thro' a mirror clear that hangs before her all the year, shadows of the world appear . . .*'

One minute he's kissing me, the next he's disappeared.

One minute I'm happy, thirty seconds later I'm never going to see him again.

'*But in her web she still delights to weave the mirror's magic sights . . .*'

Although . . . maybe mine is the *other* kind of

romance. Maybe it's the tragic, star-crossed kind: ripped apart by circumstances beyond our control, joined forever by our hearts, pining for each other across oceans all our lives, never able to replace each other, never able to forget.

'*For often through the silent nights . . .*'

But I don't *want* that kind of love story.

I want a happy film: a boyfriend who lives in the same city and goes to the cinema with me at weekends. Who kisses me lots and makes me soup when I'm poorly. Who laughs when I tell jokes and who thinks I'm the most beautiful girl in the world.

'*. . . or when the moon was overhead, came two young lovers lately wed . . .*'

But now everything's going to go back to exactly as it was before.

Me, sitting here, waiting for my life to start.

'*"I am half sick of shadows," said the Lady of Shal—*'

Apparently, some people get the big love story and everyone else just has to sit and watch.

'Stop,' I say abruptly, standing up. 'Please, please stop.'

Mr Gilbert stops. 'Is everything—'

'No, it's not.' The centre of my chest hurts. 'I

don't want to listen to this. I don't want to hear a sad poem about a sad picture painted of a sad lady with a sad story who has a sad ending that makes everyone around her sad. Why can't we read something nice for a change? Something uplifting? Is that so difficult to find?'

I stare at the books around me, then at poor Elaine in her gloomy painting.

'All these extras,' I say, stabbing a finger at the poem. 'These knights and princes and whoever . . . They're constantly to-ing and fro-ing in front of the tower. Couldn't she have just gone with one of them? Like, once? Would that have been such a big deal?'

Mr Gilbert opens his mouth.

'But *nooooo*, she's only allowed out in her little death boat. Because you guys *won't let anybody have a happy ending.*'

I grab the book and slam it on the desk.

'Hope,' Mr Gilbert says as I open the library door. 'I'm not sure I totally understand what's—'

'I quit,' I finish flatly over my shoulder. 'Thanks for your hard work and stuff, but I'm out.'

Then I walk heavily out of the library and up the stairs.

My phone starts ringing – it's Dad again – so I hang up and put it back in my pocket.

'Po? Baby? What's going on?'

'Is she OK? Poodle. Poodle?'

'At least she's finally stopped twirling and sliding down the bannisters. That's something, I guess.'

Blinking, I push through my siblings.

Seriously. Months, years – *a decade and a half* – of begging them to hang out with me and now that I finally want some time on my own, here they all are. Lurking outside my bedroom, trying to get my attention.

Freaking *actors*.

'It's not Poodle,' I say, yanking open my bedroom door. 'It's not Po, it's not Poo, it's not baby. I'm not a child and I'm not a little *doll* for you lot to pick up and put down every time it amuses you.'

My siblings stare at me.

'You think because I try to be happy I don't feel sad. You think because I don't talk about something I don't *remember*. But you're wrong. So do me a favour: take your patronising poodles and stick them where the sun don't shine, along with your stupid heads.'

And I shut my door in their faces.

24

I'd like that last scene cut, please.

I'm not entirely sure what just happened.

I literally never lose my temper so I don't think that scene does justice to the direction of my overall character development. Also, I didn't flop on my bed, face down, and scream loudly into a pillow.

You can edit that bit out too.

'Hope?' Ten minutes later, my door squeaks open. 'Ba— Ummm. What other names have we got? Hoop? Hopeless?'

I put the pillow over my head. 'LEAVE. ME. A FREAKING LONE.'

'Well, we *would*, but you didn't lock the door and that means we *can't* actually leave you alone, according to sibling law. You know what it says in the handbook they give us at birth: no lock, no leave.'

'No bolt, no bail.'

'No barricade, no . . . lemonade?' They laugh.

'Hey,' Faith objects. 'At least mine kind of rhymed.'

My queen-size bed bounces and dips once, then twice, then a third time. After another sullen minute, I lift my head, feeling hot and crumpled. My brother is flopped across my feet like a big dog, Mercy is lying diagonally across the bed with one heel propped on top of the other and Effie has curled up to my left with her beautiful head on the small of my back.

Sighing, I roll over until she's resting on my stomach.

We all stare at the ceiling in silence.

'So,' Mer says after a few minutes. 'The American dumped you then, huh?'

I smack Faith.

'I didn't tell her!' she says earnestly, staring up at me with her huge hazel eyes. 'I promise you, Po, I didn't breathe a single word. Hand on heart.'

'It didn't take a genius to crack the code,' Mer sighs. 'You've been mooning around the house, making random speeches about love, disappearing every day and giggling noisily down the phone with a person called Jamie.'

'At one point you started humming the American national anthem while cutting a breakfast waffle into a heart shape and then covering it in little strawberries,' Max agrees. 'Also in heart shapes.'

'And your phone screensaver is you and a blond boy.'

'In a Lakers hoodie.'

'With ME AND JAMIE <3 <3 typed underneath in capitals.'

'Oh,' I say flatly, still staring at the ceiling. 'Well.' *Weird, I'm normally* much *more subtle.* 'Yes, it's over now, but Jamie didn't *dump* me. He had to go back to America, which he told me about at the beginning. I wasn't listening so it's totally my fault. Don't you dare blame him.'

Faith grabs my hand and squeezes it. 'I'm sorry, Po. He sounded lovely, but there'll be other guys, I promise. In the long run, this is all going to make you *so* much stronger.'

I scowl. What a terrible thing to say to someone. 'I don't *want* to be stronger. I want *Jamie*.'

My bottom lip pushes out.

'You'll be OK, baby.' Effie kisses my hand. 'It's your first break-up and it's going to hurt, but every day it'll get easier and before you know it—'

'Oh my God, it was a *week*,' Mercy snaps. 'Can we put aside the Instagram mantras and get a bit of perspective here? She met him *one week ago*. It's not exactly *Romeo and Juliet*, is it?'

'No,' Max says calmly. 'Because Romeo and Juliet famously knew each other for less than four days total and they're generally considered one of the greatest romances of all time. Maybe try looking at things from Hope's perspective, yeah, Merwitch?'

'Aren't you supposed to be at work?' Mer growls back, looking at her watch. 'Like literally *right* now?'

Max grins and yawns. 'Aren't you supposed to be worn out from all the shoe throwing you did at the paparazzi last night, according to page six?'

'Page seven, actually.'

'You're really starting to slip.'

I blink at the ceiling three times.

Then I suddenly sit up very straight. 'Oh my gosh, Max, you're right. That's *it*.'

'What's it? What did I say? Although of course I'm right, naturally.'

'The bit about looking from *my* perspective.'

I stare at the posters adorning my walls: the kissing one, the dancing one, the one where she's passed out and being carried out of flames. I look at my red velvet curtains and the gloves and the sword and the clackerboard. At a whole century of romantic movies all around mc.

This is a test.

I was so focused on casting my male role, I forgot that at some stage I'd have to audition for the heroine too. The universe wants to see what *I'm* made of and whether I'll fight for what I want. Whether I can be strong and remain true to who I really am.

Becausc I am *Hope Valentine.*

I'm a future legend in the making and I am not defeated by anything: not distance, not fate, not circumstance, not love, not heartbrcak and certainly not by myself.

What kind of leading lady am I anyway?

A *versatile* one, that's what.

'It's not over!' I leap off the bed and hold my hands out. 'I know I said it was a few minutes ago, but it was an error in my script. This is an unexpected plot twist and I'm going to roll with it because I am a *professionalist*.'

My siblings stare at me with wide eyes.

'Jamie loves me,' I explain happily. 'He told me so. And love ultimately triumphs – we all know that. It doesn't *stop* because of a bit of water and a few random miles here or there.'

Max coughs. 'I am deeply concerned by how big you think the Atlantic Ocean is, Poodle, and whether you're planning on building a raft out of cereal boxes.'

I run to the window.

This is a *classic* romance scenario – I can't believe I didn't see it immediately. We'll find a way. This is just the inevitable obstacle Jamie and I have to hop over for the sake of drama. The sun is still warm, the flowers are still glowing, the grass is still green and life is still full of happy endings.

'As they say, it's a doggy-dog world,' I tell the garden. 'Which reminds us that there are always dogs in the world, no matter how bad it gets. So, if there's love, you fight for it. You trust in it. You *find a way*.'

'Hope . . .' Faith says quietly behind me.

'That's my point,' I nod, turning round with a bright smile. 'There's always hope. Hope is who I am.'

I forgot it for a while back there, but I've remembered now. It's what I stand for and what's inside me – what has always been inside of me. And I'll never lose myself again.

'Don't worry, guys.' I smile, lying back on the bed and holding my hands up like a rectangle. 'We're taking a different direction, people. The curtain's up, the camera's rolling. Everything's going to be awesome.'

♋ Cancer: June 21-July 22

A triple conjunction of the sun, Venus and Pluto means it's time to make a decision that will turn a long-cherished fantasy into reality.

Take that leap and make it official!

WEDNESDAY MORNING: HOPE sits in the back of a large silver car, driving on a winding road through green fields. She has headphones in, and is watching a video on her phone.

The camera focuses in on the phone screen. JAMIE and HOPE are lying in a park, her head resting on his chest. JAMIE looks straight into the lens,

then leans over and kisses HOPE'S
nose. He freezes for a few seconds.

HOPE
(*tapping him and laughing*)
It's a video.

JAMIE
My bad.

He grins and waves.

JAMIE (CONTINUED)
Hey - my first big interview!

HOPE
(*holding out her hand as a
microphone*)
Tell us, Jamie Day, how are you
enjoying your cheese-fest in this
nation's great capital city?

JAMIE
It's awesome. Check out my co-star.

193

> Does it get any better than this
> girl? Look at that FACE.

HOPE beams up at him, adoration written all over her face like subtitles.

> HOPE
> So you like it, then? Is that what
> you're saying?

> JAMIE
> (*looking at her*)
> No. I'm saying I love it.

With a thrill, I move the cursor back for the sixty-billionth time.

> JAMIE
> Does it get any better than this
> girl? Look at that FACE.

Then forward.

194

                    JAMIE
        No. I'm saying I love it.

Then back.

                    JAMIE
          . . . I love it.

Back.

                    JAMIE
    . . . I love . . . love . . . love

'This is not a productive use of our congregated time,' Grandma says from the car seat opposite. 'Put that mobile device down, Hope, and learn to socialise appropriately.'

I glance up, still beaming.

This video has really helped every time I need a boost of positivity. I've been watching it every day, along with trawling through photos of Jamie and I, printing out the best ones and sticking them next to my bed. He's texted quite a few times already

– he's basically pining away without me – so that's helped too.

Unfortunately, my plan to make another little video for him today has been disrupted by the unexpected arrival of Genevieve and my grandmother in Full Battle Mode, followed by the marching of me and Eff into the back of her limo. It was supposed to be all four of us, but Mer and Max managed to hide in the laundry room until we'd gone.

'I'm just watching a short film I made last week,' I explain to my grandma happily, holding it out. 'You know, preparing for my future.'

'Valentines don't *make* films, darling.' Her eyes narrow. 'Valentines *are* the films.'

I glance at Effie and she flares her nostrils and wiggles her ears. Giggling, I look back at my phone.

After a lot of consideration, I've decided my favourite photo of Jamie and I is the one where we're snuggled up under a red-bus umbrella in Trafalgar Square. I'd just said something funny and we're both laughing with our eyes shut.

It's my new screen saver, obviously. Although I *might* change it to the one of us kissing in Covent

Garden, or maybe a cute one of Jamie sticking his tongue ou—

'Put. It. Down.' Grandma hits the floor next to me with her stick three times. 'And sit up straight, Hope. I require your full attention, both of you. This ridiculous situation with your mother has gone on quite long enough and it stops today.'

The limousine slows to a smooth stop outside familiar electric gates and I stare in surprise at Faith. She pulls an *I don't know* face. I was so busy with my phone, I hadn't even realised where we were.

But . . . it's not Sunday.

'Don't you *dare* ask for my passport,' my grandmother snaps as the tinted window rolls down and the security guard opens his mouth. 'I'm Dame Sylvia Valentine and you are not Spain.'

The rehab gates open immediately.

We park directly outside reception and Grandma opens the car door before the driver has a chance to. 'I don't have time for this *laissez-faire* attitude,' she tells the chauffeur. 'Stay in the car, please, Genevieve. This is an intensely private matter. I need to ensure there are no lurking media. Girls, with me, please.'

Faith and I jump out of the car – still staring at each other – and my grandmother hits the cottage front door hard with her stick.

It swings open smoothly. 'Good mor—'

'It is demonstrably not. A good morning would be spent drinking fresh orange juice and perusing a Henry James script in silence, not attending a facility dedicated to exploiting those who are desperate enough to let them.'

The receptionist blinks. 'I apologise if—'

'Don't apologise to me.' Grandma marches straight past him, me and Faith scurrying silently behind. 'As you can see by the fact that I am in control of my own agenda, I am not the one being taken advantage of.' She raps on Mum's door with her walking stick. 'Juliet? This is your mother. Open the door.'

There's a short pause while Effie and I stare at each other in terror. Then the door opens with a slow creak.

'Mum? What are you—'

'Putting an end to this nonsense.' Grandma bustles in and perches herself on the chaise longue, walking stick upright between her hands. 'This is quite enough. You are still a mother, Juliet. You don't get to hand the role over to an understudy when it gets too much for you to handle.'

Mum blinks a few times, pale and distant.

Then she lifts her chin coldly and stares out of the window. 'I am taking much needed *respite*, Mother. My work schedule over the last two years has been relentless. The last film was exhausting. I don't know what you're talking about.'

'Oh, yes you do. And you're coming home today. Now. This little scene you're making is over.'

My phone has just buzzed. Turning subtly away – nobody has noticed that Effie and I are here anyway – I slip it out of my sleeve.

I really miss you. :(xxx

My heart bounces into my mouth, and a jaunty piano solo kicks in: *Jamie da-da-da Jamie-da-da Jamie—*

Glancing over my shoulder, I quickly type:

I really miss you too. But it'll be ok, I know it will. xxx

Then I turn back.

'Juliet—'

'My schedule is already arranged,' Mum's saying in a faraway voice. 'I have a chiropractor appointment this evening – he's doing wonders for my back. All those late nights on set . . . I really do need a professional on hand to—'

'Juliet.'

'And then there's music therapy. I've started a course that's actually proving very—'

'*JULIET. STOP.*'

You can say what you like about Dame Sylvia Valentine, but she certainly knows how to make herself heard.

Grandma stands up slowly.

'My darling, nobody said this would be easy. God knows if it's not the hardest thing in the world. But you *have* to be stronger than this. If not for yourself, then for—'

My phone buzzes again. Twisting quickly, I duck behind a giant vase of white flowers and click on it.

I wish you were here in LA with me. xxx

200

I kiss my phone. Then – *wait just a minute*. Quickly, I glance to the side. Grandma's still monologuing – I've got time. As fast as I can, I click on my horoscope app and read Cancer a little more carefully. *Triple conjunction yada, decision yada, long-cherished fantasy into reality yada.*

Take that leap today and make it official!

Effie tilts her head at me so I hold one finger up. Then impulsively I click on the voicemail Dad left for me at some point last week. I forgot to listen to it because I was very preoccupied with finding and then losing my soulmate: it's been a busy week.

'Hey, sweetheart.' Dad sounds rushed. 'I've been trying to get through, but we keep missing each other. Call me when you can.' Someone says something in the background. 'Tell him he can take the cheque or walk. I don't have time for his bull— Sorry, Po. LA is madness. I gotta go. Love you.'

Frowning, I click on Jamie's text again.

I wish you were here in LA with me. xxx

Then I turn slowly to face the room.

'I don't have to listen to this,' Mum is saying,

201

gazing rigidly out of the window. 'I have a shiatsu massage in twenty minutes; there are knots in my neck and you're making me *very* tense.'

Grandma's mouth tightens.

'If that's not enough to persuade you, Juliet, consider your own personal career and the reputation of the Valentines, now in tatters. Or, if *that* no longer means anything, I'll add that from this moment forward your behaviour will no longer be *supported*.'

'Fine,' Mum snaps, still facing the other way. 'Don't.'

I glance at Faith – she's flushed and wide-eyed – and at Grandma: steel and fire. Then I stare at Mum's poor skinny back: brittle and pale and unhappy.

This can't go on. None of the massages and acupuncture and yoga and eye-movement desensitisation sessions seem to be working. Everyone said they would, but it's been fourteen weeks and nothing's changed.

Mum's not getting what she needs because the man she loves, her chosen life co-star of nearly twenty years, is not here. She needs *love*. And, the longer this temporary separation drags on, the worse she's going to get.

Mum doesn't have the hope inside her that I was born with.

She doesn't have the strength.

'It's going to be OK,' I say suddenly, running over and wrapping my arms round her waist. 'I'm going to make everything better, Mum. Just you wait and see. I am going to *fix* everything.'

Mum blinks, puts a pale hand on my head for a moment and gently kisses my hair. 'You can't, little one.'

Then she straightens her back and extricates herself to stand by the window once more.

'It was *such* a pleasure to see you all today,' she announces, clearing her throat. 'But I'm afraid I have auricular acupuncture in a few minutes and it's far too late to cancel. It would be terribly impolite, I'm sure you understand.'

Grandma's face goes purple. Without a word, she marches out of the room. You can hear her walking stick rapping all the way down the corridor.

'I'll see you on Sunday,' Faith says gently, kissing Mum's blank face. Then she glances at me with large, pained eyes and leaves the room. For a few seconds, I watch Mum's tensed back in silence.

Then I make a decision.

'Bye,' I whisper, because I know what I have to do, for me and for her.

I have to be enough hope for both of us.

26

'Hey there. This is Michael Rivers. If your call is work-related, try my agent at First Films. If not, go right ahead and leave your message after the beep.'

Beep.

'Hey there. This is Michael Rivers. If your call is work-related, try my agent at First Films. If not, go right—'

'Hey there. This is Michael Rivers. If your call is work-related, try my agent—'

'Hey there. This is Michael Rivers. If your—'

'Hey there. This is M—'

'Hey th—'

'Hey—'

'Hello? Hello? *Hope?*'

I pause – oh, hang on. 'Dad? Is that you?'

'Yes, of course it's me, sweetheart. You've just rung my mobile eight times. What the hell is going on? Is everything all right? Has something happened? Are you OK? Your sisters, your brother—'

Wow, parents can be *so* dramatic sometimes.

'No, no,' I say quickly. 'Everything's fine. I just wanted to talk to you, Dad.'

There's a silence.

'Hope,' Dad says in a measured voice. 'Baby, I love you very much, but I just shut down an entire shoot so I could take this call. I stopped my actor halfway through his scene. Do you know what that costs?'

'*Oooh.*' I think about it for a few seconds. 'A hundred pounds? No, it's American. Three hundred dollars. Per second or per minute? How long have we been talking? Wait, let me set a timer.'

Dad laughs. 'It's a lot of money, Po. So, in future, if it's not urgent, like *actually* urgent, you have to leave voicemail and I'll call you back, OK?'

'OK.' I nod happily. 'That seems reasonable.'

Then I stare around my bedroom.

As soon as Grandma dropped us off – still silent with metallic fury – Effie left to see Noah and I raced upstairs, plonked myself in Dad's director's chair and made the call.

Calls.

Eight calls.

There is no longer time for any more of my famously nuanced subtlety.

'You know, I *have* been trying to get hold of you all week,' Dad points out in a warm, deep voice. 'How are your lessons, little one? Are you studying hard? What about your siblings, are they behaving?'

'Uh . . .' *I fired my tutor, Max keeps skipping work and Mercy's all over the newspapers.* 'Faith's being pretty perfect.'

'Obviously. And Mer? Is she OK? You're all looking after her, aren't you?'

The British gossip pages obviously haven't reached America yet. I think the people who need *looking after* are the ones my sister targets on a nightly basis. 'Mmm-hmm.'

'What about your mom? How's she doing?'

I glow triumphantly at my dancing couple poster. 'She's going to be fine, Dad. Don't *worry*. She's just very tired. And she needs you. Are you still not finished with this stupid film yet?'

'Hope.' There's a long pause. 'Not quite, sweetheart. It's turning out to be a lot more complicated than we thought. The budget's gone to hell, my lead's being a nightmare . . . I need to be here, on set. I'm sorry.'

I nod. That's what I figured he'd say.

Which means it's time to shift roles. It's not manipulation or lying because I am an artist. It's just me performing the *truth* with creative conviction.

'*Mike!*' somebody yells in the background. '*We're gonna need you back here now, please! Or you-know-who is going for an extended break!*'

'Hope,' Dad says quickly. 'I know you're disappointed, but I really have to g—'

Taking a deep breath, I make my voice wobbly. I don't need to bother with tears: he can't see them.

'But I *miss* you.'

'I miss you too, baby, but—'

'*Please*, Daddy.' A little bit more wobble. '*Please come home.*'

'*Michael, come on!*'

'All right!' Dad yells. 'Calm your pants!' Then he says patiently, 'Po. Look, I'm snowed under . . . but wherever I am is always your home too, OK? So, when your exams are done and things have calmed down, maybe—'

Jackpot.

'Great,' I say brightly, dropping the wobble. 'Now, please.'

'What?'

'Now. I'd like to visit now. Tonight.'

'What?'

'My visit. I've taken you up on your very kind offer and I've decided I shall leave right now. With the time difference, I'll be there yesterday. Although I'll have to leave very soon or I won't be able to catch up with tomorrow.'

Admittedly, I'm not entirely sure how international time zones work.

'Hope,' Dad says slowly. 'I didn't mean—'

'Well, you said your home is my home so I'm coming, bad luck. Also, I *happen* to have a holiday from school so it's perfect timing. Otherwise, I'll have too much time on my hands and it'll feel like I'm just adding for night'em.'

'You'll be adding for *what*?'

'I'll be adding for night'em. You know, where things go on for so long that it feels like you're up all night, doing maths. I've never been sure where the *em* comes from, but I guess it's from the olden days when people were super polite.'

A boom of laughter. 'It's *ad infinitum*, which is Latin for *to infinity*. What on earth is Mr Gilbert teaching you?'

Literally nothing as of yesterday. 'Well, I obviously can't speak Latin. I've never even been to Italy.'

'Italians speak *Italian*.'

'Italian, Latin, potato, potato.'

'Hope,' Dad says when he's finally stopped chuckling. 'Little one, it's seriously boring out here. There's nothing for a teenager to do. It's LA. You can't drive so you'll be stuck in the middle of nowhere, without any friends, without anything to do—'

'I'll love it,' I reassure him chirpily. 'So you'll send the tickets over in half an hour, yeah? I'm super excited, I can't *wait*.'

'Hope—'

'You're the best. Thanks, Dad.'

'Hope.'

'Good question, thanks for asking. Actually, I reckon a night flight is best; it'll give me the chance to rest on the journey.'

There's a silence, then Dad breathes out.

'Fine. You win. I'll email the details over when it's booked.'

'Private jet or First Class?'

Dad laughs again. 'Don't push your luck, kiddo. You're hanging right on the edge as it is.'

Once he's gone, I stretch smugly.

That's the really great thing about being a superb actress: your skills can be utilised at a moment's notice.

If Dad won't come back for Mum, I'll just have to go to Los Angeles and get him for her. We'll prove the papers wrong, stop the rumours, collect Mum from rehab and make everything go back to normal.

Meanwhile, Jamie will see how *jet-settery* I can be. Long-distance, schmong-distance.

Once he realises how little the miles between us really matter and how much we mean to each other, he'll have no choice but to make me his official girlfriend. Romance will triumph because it always does. I just have to follow my stars and make that very first leap.

After all, two birds always find it much easier to pick up a stone together than the one that's stuck alone in the bushes, etc. etc.

This way we *all* get our happy ending.
Beaming, I type:

I wish I was there with you too. :) xxx

Then I press SEND and grab a pen.

Effie, there's a triple conjunction of the sun,
Venus and Pluto so I've gone to LA to get Dad
and see Jamie. Take care of Mum and don't let
Mercy in my room until I'm back — I WILL
KNOW.
   Love you, Po xxx

I slip it under her bedroom door.

I return to my bedroom and settle back in my director's chair with a triumphant grin. I think we can agree that I followed my destiny, leapt over my obstacles, controlled my narrative, rose to the challenge and — with the help of my father's credit card — I became the heroine we all need.

Hollywood, here I come.

27

HOPE sashays into the arrivals area of LAX airport. She looks surprisingly radiant and uncrumpled after an eleven and a half hour flight.

JAMIE is standing by the barrier, holding flowers. His expression is nervous but excited.

HOPE sees JAMIE and her face lights up. She drops her one small yet efficient suitcase and runs to him, jumping into his open arms.

JAMIE swings HOPE around, laughing.

                    HOPE
What are you doing here?! I didn't
expect to see you until tomorrow!

                    JAMIE
As if I'd miss a single second of
                seeing you.

                    HOPE
   (*laughing and putting her hands
            over his eyes*)
              Like this?

                    JAMIE
            Exactly like that.

They KISS.

Wait, I can do better.

Take Two:

HOPE is pulling her one very compact
suitcase through LAX arrivals,

shockingly beautiful after such a long
journey. Suddenly, she hears SHOUTS.

SECURITY 1
Where are you - what are you— STOP
THAT BOY!

SECURITY 2
This is a breach of protocol! Sir,
you must not go beyond that line!
It is against the official rules we
have for our American airports!

(sound of commotion)

JAMIE
Hope! HOPE! Where are you, HOPE?

HOPE
(shocked)
Jamie? Is that you?

JAMIE hurdles a security barrier, runs
through an electric monitor, skids

round a security person and races towards HOPE with his arms out. He PICKS HER UP and SWINGS HER IN THE AIR.

                    JAMIE
        I couldn't wait another second
         to see my beautiful girlfriend's
                     face.

                    HOPE
                  (*amazed*)
            Your . . . girlfriend?

                    JAMIE
                  (*smiling*)
        As if I could ever truly let you
                      go.

They KISS.

Security people, racing towards them both with tasers, realise what's happening and stop in their tracks.

                    SECURITY 1

Awwww,   what   kind   of   monsters   would
we   be   to   break   this   iconic   moment
                       up?

                    SECURITY 2
                  (*wistfully*)
I   remember   being   young   and   in   love
             like   that   once   . . .

OK, that is just *adorable*.

Maybe I can make the second security guard a
prominent secondary character: give him a backstory,
a painful divorce; he's lost his belief in love, but
seeing us together makes him—

There's a loud crash.

A porter with a little black cap is trying to push
a trolley with my five large suitcases on it, along
with a laptop bag, make-up bag, separate case for
shoes and a couple of sunglasses boxes balanced on
top. I only had one evening to prepare my entire
Wardrobe and Props Departments so I shoved in
everything I could find, then upgraded myself to
First Class so they'd let me take it all.

217

Entire films have been known to *rest* on the styling.

'Oops,' I say, helping him pick a few bags off the floor. 'It's difficult to know what you need for an epic romance, right?'

A large neon quilted jacket of Faith's topples off.

'Skiing gear,' I add cheerfully as I pick that up too. 'And boots. You know, just in case there's a chalet scene.'

Then I skip along next to the trolley.

Jamie doesn't know I'm coming yet. I played out all the options – tweaking and editing – before realising that the most epic romantic gestures are always unexpected.

So I've been sending cunning text messages like this:

It's very rainy in London! Just off to my first lesson in London. :(xx

And

I hate being stuck in England without going anywhere at all. xx

Unfortunately, this *does* also render my airport fantasies impossible unless Jamie happens to be here on unrelated business:

JAMIE
(*amazed*)
Oh my goodness, Hope? I was just randomly standing in airport arrivals, thinking about how much I miss my girlfriend—

HOPE
Your . . . girlfriend?

JAMIE
(*smiling*)
As if I could ever truly let you go.

I've put on red lipstick, just in case.

'Hope?' There's a short lady standing by the barriers, smiling shyly at me. 'Hope, is that you? It's Roz.'

Roz is Dad's secretary; she sent through my flight

details by email late last night. I also got an extremely long email from Dad, which had handy emergency credit-card details attached. Obviously, I used them immediately.

'Hello,' I say, holding my hand out. 'I'm Hope Valentine. Thanks for sorting everything out for me at such short notice, Roz. It *did* feel like opening a panda's box of trouble, didn't it?'

Roz laughs and takes my hand. 'Indeed, but we got there in the end. I'd forgotten about the whole British hand-shaking thing. How am I doing?'

'Perfect!' I think she just broke one of my fingers. 'You're a natural!'

She's got rosy, round cheeks and glasses. I like her already.

'Then I'll put it on my résumé asap,' Roz smiles, turning to the porter and handing him twenty dollars. 'Please let me take this. Thank you for your help.' She pushes her glasses up her nose with a finger and – with noticeable effort – starts pushing the overloaded trolley towards the airport doors. 'Hope, I've heard *so* much about you. Your father just talks about you all non-stop.'

I beam at her. 'He does? Even on set?'

'Of course! I'm so thrilled you're here. Your father works far too hard, and I'm hoping it'll force him to take a break.'

'Exactly!' I thought it through on the journey, and I reckon I should be able to get him to fly home and sort things out by the end of the week, ten days max. 'And what do you do exactly, Roz?'

We push through the exit and warm, thick air smacks me straight in the face. With a flush of happiness, I tilt my smile towards the Californian sunshine.

'Well.' Roz wheels the trolley across the road. 'You know how it is, Hope. Mainly they talk and I listen and write it all down.'

'But do you ever get to go to Dad's studio? Have you seen films being made? Any huge stars? Who were they? What did they say? Did they mention that they might need an understudy at some point in, say, four or five years?'

I should have completed my RADA training by then.

'I don't go into the studios themselves, no,' Roz laughs. 'And I can't tell you what they say, I'm afraid – that's top secret.'

I nod. This is one high-class movie secretary. I'd be outside the gates every morning, handing out cups of coffee nobody asked for and borrowing scripts out of handbags to look for my perfect role.

'Do you have any plans for while you're here?' Roz flicks a glance across at me. 'Your father says you've never been to Los Angeles before, so is there anything you'd particularly like to do? Anything on your wish list?'

I smile secretively, turning my phone on. Within seconds, there's a *beep* and a video of Jamie appears, waving and wearing the world's cutest athletic track kit.

A glow radiates from my stomach. He is so *adorable*.

'Mmm?' I say, beaming and putting my phone back in my pocket. 'Oh, I've got a few bits and bobs in mind, yeah.'

'Any chance you can squeeze in a quick hug with your old papa first?' a deep voice says from behind me. 'Or is your social calendar fully booked already?'

A snap of happiness crackles through me.

'Dad!' I whip round and jump as high as I can, but still only just manage to get my arms over his shoulders. I forgot how *big* he is. '*You're here you're here you're here you're here—*'

My father laughs, a big booming laugh.

'Baby girl, where else was I going to be?'

28

This is where I belong.

Richmond is where I grew up, but Los Angeles is in my heart, running through my veins, passed down the generations, tied to my future, woven into my fate, lining the path to my—

'LOOK! LOOK! SOMEONE FAMOUS!'

A bright red sports car is driving past us with the top pulled down. The driver has mirrored sunglasses, silver hair blowing in the breeze, a deep orange tan and a—

'Nope,' Dad chuckles, glancing over. 'Sorry, sweetheart. That's an accountant, or a lawyer, maybe a restaurant owner. Most people in the business don't drive cars that showy.'

I nod in disappointment at our big, black, boring sedan: a *little* bit of show here or there wouldn't go amiss. Although I do love the way Dad says *The*

Business as if movies are literally the only profession in the world. Grinning, I prop my feet on the dashboard.

The roads are total chaos: six lanes of important, glamorous people who clearly have even more important, glamorous places to be. There's beeping and accelerating and sharp braking and a general vibe of impatience. Every five minutes, Dad sighs, 'Oh, *what* is that idiot doing?' and, 'You're not getting there faster by being a jackass!' as a silver car dips round us, gleaming in the sunshine.

We've also spent an hour lodged in this fast-moving traffic.

I've really had time to inspect my new surroundings: the sprawling flatness, the squat buildings crouched beneath enormous roads, the violet sky, the glittering sea in the distance and the dusty hills on either side. Green palm trees line the roads in rows – spiky and tropical and cinematic – and my excitement is starting to steadily build.

My future lies in Los Angeles. I can *feel* it.

This is literally where the Valentines started. My great-grandmother Pauline changed our name from Plumb when she arrived here from York via a boat to New York in the 1910s, and thus our dynasty began.

As soon as I've established my dramatic talent in England, I'll move here to add class to their biggest blockbusters with my British charm.

Just *three months* until that journey starts.

'Sweetheart,' Dad says as we eventually leave the traffic and drive up a quiet winding hill. It's completely dark now, so all I can see is the headlights bouncing off bushes. 'I'm afraid I have a *lot* of work to do. I'll try and see you whenever I can, but Roz has very kindly offered to help out with anything else you need in the interim.'

I twist towards his secretary. She's been sitting so quietly in the back seat that I'd totally forgotten she was there.

'Thanks, Roz.' I beam at her.

'You're welcome,' she smiles, nudging her glasses up her nose again. 'Anything you want, Hope, I'm here. It's important you have a lovely holiday. I remember my first time away from home – it was just the biggest adventure.'

Dad grins. 'Not *too* big this time, though, right?'

'Oh no,' Roz agrees. 'A sensible, appropriate

amount of adventure for a sixteen-year-old I'm partially in charge of.'

Thrilled, I sit up straight and push my chest out.

'Fifteen,' Dad corrects firmly. 'Hope's not sixteen for another three and a half months.'

Dammit. I thought he'd forgotten.

Roz winks at me – 'Sure thing, Mike' – and I giggle and wink back. I knew I would bond with movie-industry insiders immediately.

Slowly, the car pulls to a stop and Dad presses a button. An enormous black metal gate between four-metre-high hedges whirs and starts to slowly swing open. My father pulls through the gates and parks up next to a yellow Lamborghini, a shiny red Corvette and a blue Porsche.

I flash him a pointed glance.

'They're not mine,' he laughs, climbing out and opening the boot so he can start unloading my suitcases. 'Jeez, Po, did you bring all of Richmond and half of the Alps with you?' He pulls out the ski boots and flashes my pointed glance straight back at me. 'At least I don't need to worry about how you'll handle the SoCal snow.'

I shrug – one day I'll explain *props* to my father

– then stare guiltily at the tiniest house I have ever seen. It's a grey cement rectangle, one storey, no windows, surrounded by bushes, like a garage.

'Oh, Dad.' I flush, grabbing his elbow. 'I'm sorry. I didn't realise . . . I didn't think it through . . . I can *totally* sleep on the sofa. I'll just get a few cushions and—'

Dad booms with laughter as there's a blue flash and a soft *beep*. 'We'll manage, Po. You're quite small so I'm sure we can fit you in. Tuck you into a laundry bag maybe.'

Then the door opens and it's like origami.

The house unfolds from nothing at all into a huge white marble hallway with a tinkling fountain, then unfolds again into an enormous living room with a shiny grand piano and a gold cocktail bar and the palest cream leather sofas.

I drop Mercy's new handbag on the floor.

A few steps later, the house unfolds again into *another* room, then a gigantic kitchen lit by several cut-glass chandeliers. Breaking into an excited jog, I speed into a glass conservatory with a wood-burner, then a bedroom with a bed that has a television literally built into it. A bathroom – the bath is in the floor! – and another bedroom.

Another bedroom, a gym, a cinema room, a courtyard . . .

'Not bad, huh?' Dad is following me through the house, chuckling at the *ooooh* sounds I'm making. 'I called in a long-standing favour to live here while I'm filming. Let's just say that fifteen years ago I pretended not to notice that the owner of this place couldn't act, and the rest of the world has been pretending ever since.'

Oh, just *wait* until I show Sophia and Madison and Olivia this luxury swank pad. Hang on a second! I need to ship them over from England first.

Yup, they're here now.

'Mike?' Roz chirps as my friends immediately hold their thumbs up and then start rummaging through the kitchen cupboards. 'I'm going to head home, give you time to catch up. Hope, is there anything you'd like to do tomorrow? I could take you for a newbies tour, a nice breakfast, or—'

Ooooh, mini-spa!

'No, thanks,' I say over my shoulder, clicking a

button. *Rainforest shower!* 'Can you collect me tomorrow mid-afternoon, though? And bring some nail files. Maybe some nail varnish? Blue Trumpet by Chanel is my favourite.'

Delighted, I screw open a little pot. *Black earbuds!*

'HOPE!' Dad booms. 'THAT IS NOT HOW YOU TALK TO ROZ – SHE IS NOT YOUR PERSONAL ASSISTANT.'

'Oh.' I blink in surprise. 'She's not?'

'Don't be silly,' Roz laughs as Dad glowers at me. 'I'm happy to help. You can't survive LA with a chipped manicure – I'm not a monster! Have fun, you guys.'

She's gone before I can even put the lid back on. Dad shakes his head.

'What? What did I do?' I protest.

'Come on.' Still shaking his head, he starts walking towards the back of the house. 'I want to show my mini-diva daughter something before I strongly consider grounding her just hours after she landed.'

Quickly, I grab my phone and type:

That video is so cute! Richmond which is
where I am is so boring without you! xxx

Scene *set*.

Then I scamper after my father through the lounge and between two huge glass walls to an enormous bright turquoise infinity pool surrounded by plush sunloungers and palm trees and tropical flowers.

I hadn't realised quite how high up we are. We're perched at the top of a steep hill. Below us is a view that stretches miles, to mountains on one side and the sea on the other. The soft breeze is warm, the sky is a deep, smoggy ink, scattered with stars, and below it Los Angeles twinkles. Down there, people are laughing, talking, dancing, loving, dreaming, living.

I breathe deeply. *Hello, world. It's me, Hope.*

Somewhere, one of these lights must be Jamie. I bet it's the brightest one.

'Happy?' Dad asks, putting an arm round me.

Smiling, I look around and feel the fluttering sensation that anything is possible. It's going to be pretty difficult to tear my father away from this beautiful location and send him back to a spot just outside the M3, but I'm going to do it anyway. Maybe I'll start tomorrow.

'The happiest,' I beam, resting my head against Dad's arm.

'Welcome to Hollywood, little one.'

29

HOPE wakes late the next morning (tight frame round her eyes). Confused, her eyes widen. THE CAMERA pans out as A SLOW SMILE spreads across her face. She remembers.

SHE IS IN LOS ANGELES.

Grinning, HOPE yawns and spreads out luxuriously across an enormous bed covered in cream silk sheets.

'Computer,' I say loudly. 'Open the blinds.'

With a click, the room fills with warm yellow sunshine. 'Computer, play some Californian music?'

'*Now playing "Wouldn't it be Nice" by the Beach Boys.*'

A cute guitar starts plinking.

Beaming, I swing my legs out of bed and wiggle my toes. 'Computer, warm the floor up and switch the shower on?'

There's the sound of running water.

'Computer?' I pad across the marble floor to the bathroom. 'Why is it called an on sweet? Is it because when you're finished showering you're cleaner and sweeter?'

'*Checking for definition,*' Computer says in a melodious female voice. I wonder who got that acting job. '*It is French for then, later or next.*'

'Didn't really answer the question but thanks!'

Dad synced me up and showed me how to work the Smart House last night. As far as I'm concerned, this morning I am an A-list movie star just before Oscar night and this house is my obsessive fan. I'm going to make it do *everything*.

'Computer,' I say, poking my head out of the shower. 'Turn on the coffee machine, warm up some towels and make me a croissant? With butter and jam. Ooh, and some orange juice.'

'*Demand not recognised.*'

'Computer, please?'

'*Demand not recognised.*'

'Toast?'

She ignores me.

So I dry myself, make my own breakfast and get dressed all on my own. I've got a *lot* to do today and would ideally have saved my energy and focus for more glamorous matters, but whatever.

'Computer?' I say when I'm ready. 'Sorry if I was rude earlier. Could you please tell me the largest UK hit single of 1997?'

'*The biggest UK hit single of 1997 was "Candle in the Wind" by Elton John.*'

I clap, delighted. 'Computer, please program "Candle in the Wind" to play every morning in Bedroom One at six am.'

'*Music set.*'

What else? 'Computer, please start playing *The Heart of Us* on the television in the living room at nine every evening.'

'*Film set.*'

Quickly, I unzip one of my five overstuffed suitcases and tug out Mum's favourite printed silk Liberty dressing gown. I hang it gently on the back of Dad's bathroom door. A blue scarf she loves is draped on the sofa, her favourite white linen shirt on the dresser, a gold heart necklace over a mirror.

Beautifully framed family photos go on top of the piano and the coffee table in the living room, also on the kitchen worktop and outside by the pool. I found an insanely cute Polaroid of Mum and Dad kissing each other on my director's chair in the nineties, so I stick that on the fridge.

Finally – stroke of sheer genius – I spray Mum's signature scent heavily on Dad's pillow. Everyone knows that memories are stored in our sense of smell, so this should definitely make him pine for home.

Done.

Now it's *my* turn for romance.

'Computer,' I say, flinging myself on to my bed in a star shape. 'What's the horoscope for Cancer today?'

'*A Mars–Jupiter rendezvous at twenty-four degrees of Scorpio results in an extremely positive encounter. The lunar twilight zone causes a brief pause while we wait for a friendly Libra moon to arrive. Good news – life's on your side!*'

I beam at the ceiling. Obviously it is.

'Computer, can you send a text message to Jamie Day, please?'

'*Yes*,' she replies, very politely considering I'm holding my mobile in my left hand. '*What would you like the message to say?*'

I'm here I'm here I'm in Los Angeles and we're going to see each other again isn't this the most romantic gesture ever made by anyone ever SUURRRPPPRIIIISSEEE!

'Umm . . .' I consider thoughtfully. 'Write— No. Don't write umm. Wait, I don't want you to send—'

'*Sending* umm right no don't right umm wait I don't want you to *to Jamie Day*.'

Oh *shoot*.

My phone beeps almost immediately.

LOL what are you talking about? xx

Haha oops I sat on my phone here in England where I am right now! xx

Good evening, beautiful. It's morning here. You're so far away. :(xxxx

Grinning all over, I squeak and kick my legs on the bed.

Not as far as you think, Jamie Day.

So what are your plans for today?? I'll imagine I'm there too instead of England where I actually am. x

Finish school at 3 then heading to Dogtown. xx

Have a fun day! I guess I'll just be right here, staying in London all day, as per usual. x

Wow, I am so good at pretending. There's no way the poor boy can suspect I'm anywhere other than London.

Overwhelmed, I roll over and squeak into my pillow. Then I hop off the bed. Hair, make-up, styling, lighting, soundtrack, transport, lines . . . I've got less than three hours to prepare my star for the biggest romantic scene of her entire life.

And that star is me, so I'd better get a move on.

30

FADE IN . . .

A BEAUTIFUL GIRL'S HIGH HEEL appears out of a banana-yellow convertible Lamborghini. Background extras stare curiously to see Who It Is.

HOPE VALENTINE appears, more flawless than she has ever been before. She is wearing matching black satin trousers and a black satin camisole. Her make-up is perfect and her posture is even better than normal and frankly it was pretty good to start with.

Behind her, DOGTOWN shines: glamorous and sophisticated.

As the car zooms away, HOPE strolls through the shiny crowds of Hollywood agents who all want to sign her, but she is too focused and humble to notice.

JAMIE is ... doing something in DOGTOWN, maybe drinking a milkshake or shopping or whatever. He is lost in thought, doing whatever that something is.

SOMETHING makes him stop and turn round.

HOPE and JAMIE stare at each other in silence, cheeks flushed, hearts beating in harmony.

Then JAMIE'S FACE LIGHTS UP. He drops his milkshake. Wordless, they run towards each other.

SWELL OF MUSIC.

HOPE JUMPS and JAMIE CATCHES HER. He swings her into the air as she laughs, sun sparkling behind her. Then he puts her down, slowly.

JAMIE
(*holding her face in his hands*)
I can't believe it. I thought I'd never see you again.

HOPE
Oh, Jamie. I never doubted us for a single second.

JAMIE
I never should have. I never will again.

JAMIE leans towards her slowly, tenderly brushing a single stray hair out of her face.

HOPE
I thought about you all the time we were apart.

                    JAMIE
    I was a fool. A fool, I tell you.
    Hope, we can make this work. I know
                    we can.

                    HOPE
       Distance means nothing when our
           hearts are joined together.

THEY K—

'Hope?'

THEY KI—

'Hope?'

THEY KIS—

'Hope, are you OK? Have you got period pains?
There's Tylenol in my handbag.'
    Frustrated, I spin towards Roz.
    *No, Roz, what I have are people who keep ruining
my best kissing scenes with body-function-related images.*

'I'm fine, thank you.'

'Um . . . you were muttering to yourself and holding your face in your hands.'

Oh dear, she clearly doesn't understand dramatic process, despite being in The Business.

'I have a very intense inner world,' I explain. 'My imagination is always on the go – twenty-five seven. It's well known that creative people function in a way that others find confusing.'

Roz smiles. 'That *is* well known.'

I'm trying to be as gracious as I can about Roz's dusty grey Ford, but my big entrance would really have been enhanced by the Lamborghini.

'Now.' Roz frowns and pulls into a smaller road lined with vivid painted buildings. 'Are you sure you meant Dogtown, Hope? You definitely want to visit *Dogtown*? Not . . . a spa in Santa Monica or shopping on Melrose Avenue?'

I nod enthusiastically.

'Dogtown, please. I am a *huge* fan of dogs. Dalmatians, Labradors, Boston terriers, Boxers, those little curly ones. Any dog, really. I firmly believe that it *is* a doggy-dog world and we should celebrate them all.'

Roz smiles, glances at me, then back at the road.

'You know, I just had a thought. Why don't I come with you? We could rent a bike, ride down the—'

'Umm.'

HOPE and JAMIE and ROZ cycle along together, wind blowing romantically in their hair.

'No. Thank you, but I would very much like to be a tourist on my own today, without reuniting with anyone I've met before in my life.'

Roz glances at me again.

'And the dogs,' I add because she just frowned. 'Obviously.'

'*Okaaaaaaay*,' she says slowly, doing the glasses-nudge. 'In that case, do me a favour? Stick to the boardwalk, don't talk to strangers and don't wander the backstreets alone. I'll pick you up here at six before it gets dark. Sometimes *Los Angeles* is a bit of an ironic name, if you catch my drift.'

I nod. *Los Angeles* is French for the City of *Angles* because in Hollywood it's very important to get the right angle for a shot. Also to find the best angles for your face when you're in front of a camera. And you can get very lost in angles because they point everywhere.

Oh, Roz. So cautious. So sensible.

Although the roads are kind of dirty here and there's graffiti everywhere. The rubbish bins are overflowing and I can see a woman wearing tinfoil on her head and pushing a shopping trolley full of mannequin heads down the pavement. Maybe I will follow Roz's suggestions for a bit, see how it goes.

Roz drives up another small road and I'm relieved to see a beach. *That* must be where the dogs are.

'And you're definitely going to be comfortable in this lovely outfit?' Roz says, putting the handbrake on with a loud crunch. 'It's very hot out there. I've got a clean gym kit in the trunk you could borrow?'

I glance down at my black satin trousers and camisole. It's Mercy's and Stella McCartney and beautiful. Lace-trimmed, thin little straps, wide breezy legs and very, very flattering.

'Black reflects heat,' I remind Roz patiently. 'Plus, you've got to live your best life, put your best foot forward. There is no dress rehearsal. And yes, you can reshoot, but it's really expensive for the production team so it's generally best to get it right first time.'

She smiles at me. 'I see.'

Beaming graciously, I flick my hair and step out of the car. I'm immediately hit by a blast of heat so intense my entire outfit sticks to me like shiny, burnt chicken skin. My high heel wobbles on the scorching pavement, but I quickly manage to find my balance.

Valentines Always Act With Class.

'So you've got my number and I'll see you at six, OK?' Roz is leaning out of the window, chewing her lip. 'Six o'clock on the dot. Call me whenever. Walk to the *right*. Don't buy anything. Use the money I gave you for water. And, if you see a dog, just . . . don't touch it.'

'OK! Thanks! Bye!'

Buzzing all over – Jamie is close, so very close! – I wait patiently until the dusty Ford putters slowly out of sight. Then I pull my shoulders back, lift my chin, neaten my hair, reapply red lipstick, pull down my sunglasses and try to face in whichever direction the sunshine is most flattering.

This is my moment, and I'm not taking a single second for granite.

And 5 . . . 4 . . . 3 . . . 2 . . . 1 –

Action.

31

HOPE VALENTINE sashays down the boardwalk. To her left, the sea glitters blue, and around her are Hollywood agents who—

'EEEEEEEEEYYYYY, HOTSTUFF! LOOK AT YOU AND YOUR FANCY-FANCY! YOU WANNA BUNNY? I GOT BUNNIES, A BAG FULL OF BUNNIES FOR YOU – BUNBUNS FIVE DOLLAR.'

A man in a pink romper suit with orange wellies is waving at me. In one hand is a sack, in the other a kicking rabbit.

Get out of my big scene, mister.

'Umm.' I wave back. 'No bunnies for me today, thanks very much! Maybe another time!'

HOPE VALENTINE recommences sashaying down the—

PAUSE.

Sweat is making my trousers stick to me so I quickly bend down and roll the legs up, then take both my earrings out, pierce the fabric and stick the backs on the inside. I'm now wearing satin shorts.

Then I stand up again: nice save, Wardrobe Department.

And . . .

Roll.

HOPE VALENTINE sashays down the boardwalk.

"T-SHIRT? YOU WANNA T-SHIRT?'

To my right is a row of scruffy but colourful buildings covered in graffiti, weird paintings and tiny items hanging from strings. There are tattoo parlours, pizza takeaways and sunglasses stalls. A

man with a Mohican is holding up a pink I LOVE
VENICE BEACH!!!! T-shirt.

'No thank—'

'Mind!' A glistening, topless man swerves past me
on a bike so I take a step backwards.

'Watch it!' A beautiful girl on roller-blades dips
round me.

'Lady, you wanna head? I got any kinda head,
small, big, medium, extra medium, tiny . . .'

To my left a man is holding up painted skulls.

Next to him is another Day-Glo stall stacked with
paintings of demons eating hamburgers, then one
festooned with bamboo pipes and dreamcatchers;
another with hundreds of pin badges and miniature
skateboard key rings, one selling bracelets and
necklaces made from feathers. A few more steps and
there's a stall piled high with tiny dolls and aliens
wearing neon bandanas and YOUR NAME ON A
GRAIN OF RICE.

A man with electric-green hair is playing a guitar
and singing while a bald lady snores next to him in
a rainbow deckchair.

But I can't see *any* dogs. Like – none. And where
on earth is Jamie?

HOPE VALENTINE pauses by a skateboard park and watches guys shooting into the air and twisting round, but JAMIE is not one of them so she keeps walking.

There's a group OF VERY HOT SURFERS in wetsuits standing with boards under their arms, but JAMIE is very unfortunately not one of them so she keeps walking.

Then she walks past a small outdoor gym and glances at the very big and veiny muscled men pumping iron and grunting. Obviously not Jamie.

A handsome, ripped blond boy jogs past. HOPE spins optimistically, but it is still not JAMIE.

OK, this is getting ridiculous.

This is exactly why you hire professionalist location scouts. I can't do everything by myself.

Sweat collecting on my top lip, I get my phone out.

Did you make it to Dogtown in the end?
What are you doing there today, pacifically?
xxx

Then I press SEND and wipe my face.

I'm going to need to reshoot this entire scene: my make-up's dripping, my clothes are soaked in sweat. My feet are slipping in my heels so my sashay is getting a little more dramatic than it's supposed to be.

Next time, I'm going to get a research assistant to find out a little more detail before I head out to my set. This lack of preparation is shocking – I'm considering having myself fired.

Lifting my sunglasses, I squint at the beach on my left. It's the largest, deepest beach I've ever seen: a sweeping expanse of golden sand with surfboards, sunbathers and little painted guard huts dotted here and there, and the sea is a dark blue shimmer in the distance. Except, surely if Jamie was there he'd have just said *I'm going to the beach*, right? Also, it's gonna ruin my heels.

I peer optimistically ahead, hand shading my eyes. There's a massive silver playground at the edge of the path: gigantic climbing frames with hoops, ropes, horizontal poles, monkey bars. Half-dressed people are hanging from it – swinging, climbing, bouncing, balancing, swaying.

On the grass next to it is a small group. Some of them are lying on the floor or standing in squats with their legs bent; the others are balancing precariously on top of them, sprouting from their shoulders, thighs or backs.

I squint at them curiously. What the holy horoscopes are they doing? Then my heart jumps so hard it hits my teeth.

Jamie?

He's standing at the side, arms crossed casually, wearing red board shorts with his top off: shining gold in the sunshine. Even from this distance, I can see the dazzling white of his teeth as he laughs, the glitter of his blue eyes, the spark of platinum in his hair. He's never looked more Californian.

And I'm hit by a wave of overwhelming tenderness. Just look at him, so happy and shiny in his natural habitat.

Oh wow, I've *missed* him.

My heart is pounding, my hands tingling, my cheeks flushing, and before I can even get the cameras working I'm running towards him. Cue music, lights, sound and happiness—

Any second now—

SOMETHING makes him stop and turn round.

Now—

SOMETHING makes him stop and turn round.

Now, Jamie.

With a frown, he reaches into a pocket, pulls his phone out, looks at it, then puts it away again.

SOMETHING makes him stop and turn—

I'm standing directly behind him.

'Jamie?'

'Jamie?'

'*Jamie?*' I tap him on the shoulder.

Then Jamie jumps and spins to face me. I light up and the soundtrack explodes and it's just me and it's just him and it's just everything.

Then his whole face hardens.

'Hope, what the hell are *you* doing here?'

32

HOPE AND JAMIE stare at each other in silence, cheeks flushing, hearts beating in unison.

It's fine.

It's fine it's fine it's fine it's fine – he's happy to see me happy to see me he's happy . . .

JAMIE
(*holding her face in his hands*)
I can't believe it.
I thought I'd never see
you again.

'Like, seriously. What are you doing in California?'

HOPE

Oh, Jamie. I never doubted in us
for a single second.

'I . . . uh . . .' I stick my hands out. '*Surprise?*'

JAMIE

I never should have. I never will
again.

'Well, yeah, obviously.' Jamie glances at his friends, still balancing on top of each other behind us. 'I don't understand – I thought I'd never see you again.'

Hold up – that line didn't have the right emphasis. The stress should be on *see* not *thought*. Maybe I should ask him to do it again.

'I'm just . . . visiting my dad. For a holiday. You know, he's working out here. I missed you. And you . . . said if I was ever in Los Angeles to look you up. So here I am . . . I did.'

But Jamie's face hasn't changed; there's tension in his jawline, as if he's carved out of stone.

Silence.

'I-I didn't think it through,' I continue quickly, starting to feel a bit nauseous. 'I'm s-so sorry, Jamie, I should have warned you I was coming. You're busy with your friends. I should have called—'

Jamie suddenly smiles brightly and puts his arm round me.

'Hey, I'm just *surprised*! You should have told me you were coming.'

My entire body is suddenly so slack with relief it's an effort not to lie down flat on the ground with my face in the grass. 'You're not . . . mad?'

'Why would I be mad?' Jamie grins widely. 'So unexpected, though! I thought you were thousands and thousands and *thousands* of miles away. Wow, check out your outfit! Only *you*, Hope, would wear black satin to a beach. What have you done to your pants?'

I look down awkwardly.

'It's . . .' Why have I got earrings stuck in my trousers? Who made that dumb decision? 'They're not— I wanted to . . . Look nice . . . But I got hot and— I probably look a bit silly, don't I?'

I've never looked silly in Mercy's clothes before.

258

Jamie laughs easily as I quickly bend down and unpin them. 'You're gorgeous, as always.' He shakes my shoulder. 'Now, why have you gotten shy?'

I flush. 'Not sure really.'

'Don't be! Come meet my friends. We're just doing Acroyoga or Y-basing – we do it after school most days. Here's the Base – they're the ones on the ground – then the Flyers – they're in the air – and the Spotter, that's what I was doing.'

Starting to relax – I wanted to surprise him and I really did! Target achieved! – I smile and wave at them. One very pretty blonde girl in a yellow leotard and grey leggings is in an impressive, bendy, upside-down circle, grabbing her ankles with her hands while she balances on the feet of a really muscled boy in an L-shape.

'Hey!' she shouts from the air. 'Jay! Stop hitting on girls and get over here! I wanna try another plank on plank, but you're the only one strong enough to do it with.'

Jamie laughs. 'Bet you say that to all the guys, Abi.'

'You bet your red board shorts I do.'

They're both giggling so I giggle with them. 'Can

I have a go too?' I step forward. 'It looks really fun. I mean, just something really simple? Like—' I look round the acrobatic group. '*That* one?'

A guy is kneeling on the ground and a girl is balanced on his thigh with her left leg out and one arm in the air.

I mean, how hard can standing on someone be?

'That's not safe,' Jamie frowns. 'We've been doing this for a really long time and you're not *trained*. It requires pretty decent muscle tone in the legs, so it's best if you watch us do it.'

'Oh!' I look down at my legs. 'OK. Sure!'

I perch myself on the grass and watch Jamie do a push-up with Leotard Abi balanced in an identical push-up on top of him, facing the other way.

'Don't wiggle!' She laughs, one arm in the air. 'You're wiggling!'

'You're dripping sweat on me, dirtbag!'

'I am totally not!'

'*Soooo*.' A ginger guy stands up from where he's been lying on the ground with his legs in the air. 'You're a new buddy of Jay's, right? We go to school together. He's the best, right? Such an awesome dude. Everyone *loves* him.'

'Oh yes.' I nod emphatically as Jamie pops Abi on to his shoulders. 'He's amazing. I *guess* you could call us "new buddies", hahaha.' I make ironic little bunny ears with my fingers. 'I'm Hope.'

I say it humbly, like *yes, I'm THAT Hope, the one he's been talking about constantly, but let's not make a big deal about it, OK?*

'Yeah? Cool. Jay's gotta lot of new buddies. Popular guy, that one, haha. Where are you from then?'

I stare at him. 'England.'

'But where from *originally*?'

' . . . Richmond.'

'Well?' Jamie hops over energetically while I'm still staring at the guy in shock. 'What did you think? Pretty ace, huh?'

Blinking, I nod so hard my head hurts. '*So* ace.'

All I really want is to go for a stroll with Jamie while the sun goes down, hold hands, kiss and make our relationship official – maybe pat a few dogs together – but I suppose watching my nearly-boyfriend spin a semi-dressed girl in the air comes a close second.

'Jamie?' I ask instead. 'Where are all the dogs?'

'Huh?' He waves at a girl walking past. 'What are you talking about? What dogs?'

'You said you were in Dogtown. So I thought—'

His friend laughs. 'We're in Santa Monica, dude. Why're you telling cute girls we're in Dogtown? That's right down that way with all the skaters. You can't even skate.'

'Can so.' Jamie scowls at him and pulls on a T-shirt. 'And it's *basically* Dogtown here.'

'It's not. Not even close. Nice try, though.'

The muscle in Jamie's jaw is twitching again. I think it might be time to get this scene back on track.

HOPE JUMPS AND JAMIE CATCHES HER: swinging her into the air as she laughs, sun sparkling in her hair. Then he puts her down, slowly.

Beaming, I hop towards Jamie.

Then I fling my arms in the air, wrap them tightly round him and try to lift both feet up so he's catching me. Except . . . Jamie stares at me without moving his arms so instead I'm just dangling round his neck.

Slowly, I let go of him and clear my throat.

                    HOPE
    I thought about you all the time
              we were apart.

'Jamie, I thought about you all the time we were
apart.'

                    JAMIE
    I was a fool. A fool, I tell you.
    Hope, we can make this work, I know
              we can.

'Cool.' Jamie nods. 'That's cute of you.'
    I blink.

                    HOPE
    Distance means nothing when our
         hearts are joined together.

'Distance means nothing when our—' OK, that just
sounds weird now. 'Ah, never mind.'
    I stand on my toes and lean up to him.

THEY K—

'Come on,' Jamie says, turning away and tugging my hand. 'Let's go play on the monkey bars.'

33

HOPE AND JAMIE are immediately in sync. They astonish everyone in the outdoor-gym-thing-hoopy-thing with their athletic prowess. They are the ULTIMATE COUPLE.

Standing under the huge steel poles, I rub my hands together. I might not be as sporty as Effie, but I'm pretty strong and bendy. It's important, when you're a movie star, to be able to do your own stunts – it makes filming cheaper for the producers, which is just respectful.

Gamely, I clap and jump up hard.

The hoops are way too high. My fingertips graze one of them and send it bouncing away.

'Jamie, could you give me a leg-up?' I squat and

spit on my hands to give them more grip. 'A little boost to start off with?'

He frowns. 'It's deceptively difficult. Watch.'

In seconds, Jamie has leapt into the air, grabbed a hoop and is hanging there confidently, tensed arm muscles gleaming in the sunshine. 'See?' He rocks backwards and forwards aggressively. 'You've gotta get a *swing* going. Momentum, you know?'

I nod. 'Ah. So then do I—'

But he's gone, swinging powerfully from hoop to hoop, letting go in the middle of a swing, flying gracefully through the air and then – just as it looks like he's about to fall – grabbing another and soaring into the sky again.

Hoop after hoop, until he's twenty metres down the park.

He twists elegantly with a little mid-air spin and then starts curving back towards me. My stomach flutters: he's so *cute*. I mean, who even knew that there were monkey bars for people over the age of six? Not me, that's for sure. And who would have thought that so much enjoyment could be squeezed from jumping and swinging and being upside down for no reason? In England, people complain if there's nowhere to sit on a train.

'Amazing!' I say, clapping my hands. 'You're brilliant! Now if you can just show me how to—'

Nope, he's gone again.

So I sit down and make myself comfortable on the ground while I watch Jamie swing to the other end. When he gets there, he leaps off – landing with his hands in the air – and heads to a horizontal bar, grabbing it and doing thirty pull-ups. Then he finds a rope and starts climbing it with incredible agility.

When he's down again, he gets on the ground and starts doing push-ups, grunting slightly and doing little claps in between. Push-up, grunt, clap! Push-up, grunt, clap! Then he hops up and does a few star jumps. I think maybe he's working out for real now. So I get my phone out of my bag to check for messages.

I
AM
GOING
TO

YOU

I frown. Oh wait, another text just arrived.

KILL

Ahhh.

Hey Mer! How's it going? Hope xx

I wait a few seconds, then:

**DON'T YOU HOW'S IT GOING ME YOU
LITTLE BUMCAT WHERE ARE ALL MY
CLOTHES**

Oh my goodness, she's so dramatic. I didn't break into her room the morning I left and take *all* of her clothes. Just the nice ones that looked good on me.

Calm down. I only borrowed a few items. Why do you always wear black, Mer? It's very limited and not always flattering. Bring a bit of

colour into your life! I can help beatificate you
if you want xx

Beep beep.

OH MY GOD AND MY NEW GUCCI
HANDBAG. WHY DO YOU NEVER HAVE
ANY RESPECT FOR OTHER PEOPLE'S
THINGS!!! OPEN YOUR DOOR AND GIVE
THEM BACK RIGHT NOW OR I SWEAR
THE NEXT THING LEAVING THIS HOUSE
IN A BAG WILL BE YOU.

I blink three times.

Wait – does Mercy think I'm in England? Does
she think I'm still in my *bedroom*? I left yesterday
morning – are you seriously telling me nobody in
my house has noticed I'm no longer in the
country?

Quickly, I type:

Effie, did you not get my letter? xx

A few seconds later:

> What letter? It's midnight – why are
> you awake? Come sleep in my bed if you
> want xxx

I smack the phone lightly on my forehead.

Just how invisible am I, on a day-to-day basis? How little of an impression do I make? When I'm a famous person, kidnapped and held to ransom, it's going to get really awkward: nobody at home will notice and the kidnappers will have to give up and send me back with an apology note.

'Were you watching?' Jamie appears in front of me. 'Or were you on your phone even though you *asked* me to show you?'

Flushing, I stick my phone back in my bag.

'I was watching,' I say, jumping up and clapping. 'It was great, Jamie! Super impressive.' What else can I say? 'And . . . how . . . long . . . have . . . you . . . been . . . swinging from things?'

'Oh, since I was a kid. I've been coming here for years, even though I live on the other side of town in Pasadena. But I'm not *that* strong, you know. Loads of people are better at it than me.'

Then Jamie grins radiantly, puts his hand in mine

and tugs me towards him. A flush of joy ripples through my body.

'Hope,' he says quietly, cupping my face with his hands. 'I really did miss you, you know.' He's gazing at me softly with his turquoise eyes. 'I'm stoked you're here, for however long I have you.'

I sigh happily and relax against his chest. 'Me too. I just want to make the most of it.'

'Absolutely,' he beams, stroking the top of my head. 'Let's do that, baby. Let's treasure every single second we have together, while we still have them.'

Then, slowly, he tilts my chin and kisses me.

And it's exactly the same as it was in London: the soft warmth of his lips, the mint, the feel of his thumb brushing my jawline, the gorgeous fluttering in my stomach. We fit together so perfectly, as if I'm supposed to be here, like we're part of the same—

OK, it's over.

We start walking back towards his friends, hand in hand.

JAMIE
Guys? This is my girlfriend, Hope.

271

Your . . . girlfriend?

(*smiling*)
Well, aren't you?

'So,' I say chirpily as Abi waves at us and I wave back. 'What do you fancy doing tomorrow? It's Saturday, so I was thinking maybe we could—'

'Whoa.' Jamie stops walking. '*Tomorrow?* Hope, I gotta surfing trip planned with the guys.'

I blink. 'Oh! But you just said—'

'Well, yeah, but I didn't know you were coming, did I? If you'd given me some *warning*, then maybe I could have rearranged, but I didn't know you'd be here until, like, an hour ago.'

Dammit, why do films never tell you that romantic gestures can be irritatingly inconvenient? I should have sent some kind of Save the Date.

'Sorry.' I squeeze Jamie's hand apologetically. 'Of course. You're right.' Then I laugh. 'Keen-bean over here, as per usual. Although . . . *ooh*, maybe I could come too? Surfing sounds really good fun and I actually brought my sister's wetsuit with—'

'*WE'VE JUST SPENT ALL AFTERNOON TOGETHER.*'

'. . . But you literally just said you didn't know I was here until an hour ago.'

'Don't be obtuse, Hope, you know what I *meant*.'

Jamie's face is stone again and the muscle in his jaw is pulsing in and out.

'I . . .' My chin wobbles. 'I'm s-sorry, I didn't mean—'

'Oh, baby,' Jamie says, abruptly kissing my cheek. 'Don't get upset. It would break me to see you cry. You know, I guess I'm used to doing whatever I wanna do. But of course I can spend time with you instead.'

I blink. 'Th-thanks.'

'I mean,' he continues breezily, 'you're only in California on vacation, right? Like, how long are we talking? A week? Ten days max?'

I nod and he brightens further.

'In that case, I'll be mostly at school anyway. So . . . why don't we spend all tomorrow together doing whatever *you* like? You choose.'

'Really? Are you sure?'

'Absolutely.' He's so gallant. 'Tomorrow I'm *all yours*. I'll put aside the awesome trip *I* wanna do and we can do whatever *you* wanna do instead. How does that sound?'

Erm, now I just feel guilty.

'Jamie.' I grab his hands. 'That's so sweet of you. I'm sorry, I didn't mean to pressure you. I've got *loads* of other things to do. I'll hang out with my dad and talk to the computer house and—'

Jamie stops me with a finger on my lips.

'Hope,' he says softly. 'Stop worrying, baby. There's *nothing* I'd like more than to spend my spare time with you.'

34

TAKE TWO: HOPE wakes the next morning (tight frame round her eyes). Confused, her eyes widen. THE CAMERA pans out as A SLOW SMILE spreads across her face. She remembers.

SHE IS IN LOS ANGELES.

Grinning, HOPE yawns and spreads out luxuriously across an enormous bed covered in cream silk sheets.

'Computer,' I say loudly. 'Open the blinds.'
    With a click, the room fills with yellow sunshine.
'Computer, play some Californian music, please.'
    'Playing "California Dreamin'" by the Mamas and the Papas.'

A guitar starts playing.

Grinning, I swing my legs out of bed and wiggle my toes. 'Computer, warm the floor up and switch the shower on.'

There's the sound of running water.

Yesterday didn't go *quite* as well as hoped: wrong outfit, poorly memorised lines, inappropriate location, no research and my poor co-star wasn't even prepared for my arrival. So I've decided to reshoot the entire scene from the beginning.

I mean, you can't expect to get *every* scene in one take. Editing is all part of the cinematic process. And now I know exactly what I'm doing.

Singing along, I take a long shower, then carefully select Mer's black denim shorts and Effie's neon crop top. From what I saw yesterday, this outfit is typically Californian. With skilled hands, I expertly tie my hair into an I-don't-care-how-my-hair-looks knot (it takes forty minutes) and apply outdoorsy, glowing make-up, as if I've just been swinging from something very recently.

'Computer?' I say, carefully examining my legs for strength in the mirror. Olivia, Sophia and

Madison give me the thumbs up. 'What's the horoscope for Cancer today?'

'*Here is your horoscope: a Mars and Saturn transit causes an increase in passion, and the Virgo moon in your third house of communication results in easy conversation. Find your happy place and everything will make sens*e.'

I beam at the walls. 'Thank you, that is *excellent* advice. I really appreciate the support.'

Then I glance back at the chair in the corner of the bedroom. Mum's stuff has been washed, ironed and put there in a neat, fragrant pile with the gold necklace carefully placed on top.

Sighing, I redistribute everything around the house again.

I was hoping to have a long conversation with Dad last night, but he didn't get back from the studio until I was asleep. And he's already gone again this morning. Maybe if I make this place *really* messy he'll get fed up and come home to Richmond just to get away from it.

'Computer?' I frown. 'What other films starring Juliet Valentine do you have on file?'

'*Films featuring Juliet Valentine include* The Hurtful Ones, A Thousand Years, A Pair of Blue Eyes . . .'

'Stop.' I clap my hands. Mum is *so* beautiful and young in that last one, even though her eyes are quite clearly grey. 'Please play *A Pair of Blue Eyes* this evening at seven pm, just before *The Heart of Us*.'

'*Film is set.*'

Beaming, I unroll a poster of Mum styled as a sixties mod, perched on the back of a scooter in a miniskirt and knee-high boots (she wasn't born then, but it was a very cute era).

The more subtle reminders of Mum I leave lying around, the less real work I'll have to do when I finally talk to Dad. It's like sending him the script early.

Then I pick up my phone.

'Hope!' Roz says after one ring. 'Are you OK? How did you sleep? Did you get the dinner I left for you? I put some breakfast in the fridge too. Your dad usually grabs something on set so I wanted to make sure you didn't starve.'

The food was all green and leaf-based so I feel about ten per cent more Californian already, but also starving. 'It was delicious, thank you! Can you pick me up in twenty minutes? I need to get to Hollywood.'

I can now hear my father yelling at me in my head.

'Please,' I add quickly. 'Thank you, Roz. Also please. You're not *my* personal assistant – I know that. Thank you.'

'Hope,' Roz says slowly. 'I'm sorry, but I'm kind of at . . .' There's a pause. 'You know what? Sure. No problem. It should take me about forty to get to you, but I'll leave right now.'

'Cool.'

We'll have to drive pretty fast. Jamie's meeting me at ten for our Start Again Date and I don't want to be too late to record over yesterday's performance.

'Are you going to be OK on your own again?' Roz sounds concerned. 'Because I can always—'

'No, thank you,' I say quickly.

HOPE and JAMIE and ROZ stare into the sunset together, eating their ice creams.

'I've got plans. More touristing for me. All by myself. No boy-based activities whatsoever.'

There's a long silence.

'Sure,' Roz says finally. 'I'll be there as soon as I can.'

Jamie's already at his mark and is waiting for me.

As we pull up, he's sitting on a little metal barrier outside a convenience store in a car park just off Sunset Boulevard. Today he's wearing a white T-shirt with SAVE THE WHALES written on it in huge letters, and blue jeans. He's texting on his phone and his hair is shining in a scruffy white-gold quiff. He's so beautiful a bright happy light whooshes through me until it hits my face with a wallop. I can literally feel my face glowing.

'Do you know that blond boy?' Roz asks abruptly as she puts her car into park. 'Hope, is this where I'm dropping you?'

'No,' I say, averting my eyes seamlessly. 'Huh? What? Why would you ask me that? That is *such* a weird question to ask a teenager in a strange country in a strange town full of strange strangers she's never met before. And um . . . yes, here's good.'

Flawlessly done, Hope. Bravo.

'You know.' Roz thoughtfully nudges her glasses.

'I'm pretty easy to talk to, Hope. So, if you wanted to tell me anything, I wouldn't necessarily pass the information on to your father. It would be just between us. I mean, that's kinda my job, right?'

Umm, her job is to literally tell my father everything. And I do *not* like the word 'necessarily' there, thank you.

My eyes flicker impatiently to Jamie again.

'It's much more important that you're safe and happy,' Roz continues slowly. 'And . . . dating can be complicated at any age. I mean,' she screws up her mouth, 'I guess I'd know, right?'

Smiling, I pat her shoulder in sympathy.

It must be so hard to find The One once you're old and all the decent ones have been taken. Maybe if I get some extra time this week I'll give her a makeover and set her up on an online dating site for those who've lost hope.

'True love isn't complicated,' I explain gently, opening the car door. 'Trust me, *finding* The One is the hard bit. Once you've tracked him down, the rest is easy.'

Jamie's got his head lowered – texting again – so

I grab my phone out of my pocket in case any of them are heading in my direction. None as yet.

'Well,' Roz says as I step carefully out on to the pavement: back straight, posture excellent. 'I'm still here if you need me. Six o'clock pick-up, OK?'

'Eight?'

'Six.'

'Seven forty-five?'

'Six, Hope,' Roz laughs. 'We don't get to negotiate on what time the sun goes down. That's kinda determined by a rotating earth.'

Stupid planetary curfews.

Impatiently, I wave goodbye as Roz slowly putters away with sporadic bangs. Once she's finally gone, I flex my neck and give my knuckles a tiny crack. Then I frown, click all the spotlights in my head on, cue my intro music and focus the cameras.

Research: done.

Script: learnt.

Co-star: ready.

And – *shoot.*

As the yellow Lamborghini zooms away, HOPE strolls across the car park, strong legs toned and clearly powerful, even from a distance.

JAMIE pauses from texting.

SOMETHING makes him stop and look up.

Jamie pauses from texting and looks up.

HOPE and JAMIE stare at each other in silence, cheeks flushing, hearts beating loudly.

We stare at each other, cheeks flushing, hearts thumping.

Then JAMIE'S FACE LIGHTS UP.

Jamie's face breaks into a grin.

Wordlessly, she runs towards him.

I run.

HOPE JUMPS AND JAMIE CATCHES HER,
swinging her into the air as she
laughs, sun sparkling in her hair.

I jump, laughing, and he catches me and spins me
round.

Then he puts her down, slowly.

Slowly, Jamie puts me down.
   'Good morning, beautiful,' he says with a bright
smile. 'How about we start again?'
   Then he leans towards me.

THEY KISS.

And *that's* more like it.

35

We kiss until the world fades out.

Until the car park blurs into soft focus and it's just me and Jamie, wrapped round each other in a cloud of technicolour. And, for a brief moment, I kind of want the credits to roll.

That's it – you can go home now.

The End.

'So.' We finally pull apart, lips tingling. 'Hope, what's the big plan? What are we doing *here*? Because I have to tell you –' Jamie grins – 'a convenience store in downtown Hollywood is not the heady height of what California has to offer.'

Laughing in excitement, I grab his hand.

I spent all night thinking about it, and suddenly remembered – romantic films always have a kind of circular plotline. They reference themselves and loop backwards constantly. The beginning is the end, the end is the beginning and so on. Everyone knows love goes round and round in circles.

And that's what I'm going to do with us too.

'Now,' I beam as I start leading us to the left, 'I'm afraid all of my plans are going to seem super touristy to you. But do you want to explore this magical capital with me?'

Jamie blinks. 'Los Angeles isn't our capital, Hope.'

'No,' I say quickly. 'I know it's New York.'

His eyes widen. 'The capital of America is *Washington DC*.'

'Oh.' I giggle. 'Yeah, I knew that. Obviously. I was *joking*.' Although New York is cooler and prettier so maybe they could take a vote and transfer it over or something. 'It was just that was what you said on our first date.'

Jamie's staring at me blankly, so I try again.

'What I'm saying is *Camembert* cheesy,' I say pointedly, then pause for a few seconds. 'Swiss cheese cheesy.' Another pause. 'Parmesan cheesy. Uh—' Some of these are his lines. 'Manta Ray Jack cheesy?'

'What are you talking about?' Jamie frowns. 'What are we doing today? Going to a farmers' market?'

Oh, forget it. Instead, I beam again and open my hands.

'Ta-da!'

In front of us – two doors away from the convenience store – is a little office with a dozen people milling around outside it. Above it is an enormous red, white and blue sign that says:

★ MEGA HOLLYWOOD TOURS! ★

Tour homes of MOVIE STARS and CELEBRITIES with us!! 5 STARS!

Number Two Tour of HOLLYWOOD!

Spontaneously, I start clapping.

'Do you see?' I'm hopping up and down, that's how proud of myself I am. 'We're going to do *all* the Los Angeles touristy stuff, just like we did in London! It'll be exactly like our romantic British montage, except we've shifted it across the Atlantic Ocean! How cute and heart-eyes is *that*?'

Also – not gonna lie – I'm *so* up for this.

I've finally *made it to Hollywood*. And yes, I know

it's only for a quick preview before I have to go home again, but while I'm here I want to see everything the movie capital of the world has to offer.

I want to stick a straw in and suck this city *dry*.

'Hey there, lovebirds,' a cheerful man says, emerging from the office. 'Are you coming on the ten forty-five with us?'

'Oh *yes*, please.' I'm so exhilarated my mouth has stuck together. 'I booked online last night! And I've brought water to keep hydrated and a few snacks and my phone and my camera and another camera just in case!'

'We can't promise you'll see anyone you recognise,' he laughs. 'But, fingers crossed, we'll spot a celeb. There's quite a few milling about this town, haha! Can't get rid of 'em!' Then he hands over a pair of neon-red baseball caps that say MEGA HOLLYWOOD TOURS and matching T-shirts. 'These are yours, kids! We'll be leaving any minute so get yourselves kitted out!'

Thrilled, I take my topknot down, pop my cap on and wedge it with some difficulty over my tight curls. Then I throw the enormous T-shirt over my crop top and shorts, thus transforming it into a Mega Hollywood Dress.

Beaming, I hold out Jamie's cap and tee for him. And it's only then I see his face: cold, stiff and completely shut down.

My smile drops. 'What? What's wrong?'

'You. Have. Got. To. Be. *Kidding me.*' His voice is weirdly flat. 'I am *from* Los Angeles, Hope. I was *born here*. I *grew up here*. This is my *home*. Why the hell would you bring me on this . . . clichéd *tourist tat*?'

I stare at him in bewilderment. 'Because . . . erm . . . that's kind of . . . the point.'

Like riding a red double-decker bus without a destination, and going on the London Eye, and visiting the Changing of the Guard at Buckingham Palace. And illegally feeding pigeons in Trafalgar Square, and eating fish and chips, and riding a unicycle in Covent Garden, and wearing I HEART LONDON sweatshirts and taking photos of ducks in Hyde Park, and enjoying a long, rainy boat trip down the Thames.

The cliché is what makes it *romantic*.

Otherwise – let's be honest – it's just a really

expensive way to spend a week in London. Does Jamie think we Brits do that on a daily basis? That British people are all wizards who live in castles and make calls from red phone boxes? That we wear top hats and monocles, and read Shakespeare every morning, and say 'blimey' every three minutes?

OK, that last one's true but still.

'You want me to wear *that*?' Jamie points at the MEGA HOLLYWOOD TOURS cap and T-shirt. His mouth is a thin, straight line. 'IRL? In public? In front of people I might *know*? What if I'm *seen*?'

'What if you are?' I say in surprise. 'Who's going to care?'

His eyes narrow. 'Well, that's very nice, isn't it? No need to get nasty, Hope.'

I blink. 'That's not what I—'

'But *sure*. Riding around in a free loser cap and T-shirt while staring at the houses of privileged strangers all day is *so* much better than going surfing with my mates in Mexico. Hope, driving is my favourite thing. I could have just *driven* us if you're this keen on seeing where rich people live.'

We stare at each other in silence.

Who did he think lived in Buckingham Palace

two weeks ago if not a privileged rich stranger? He took, like, *fifty* photos.

'IS THIS THINK ON? HELLOOOOO, DARLINKS! I'm goink to be yourrr tour maestrrrro for the day – it's true! Yes! So strap in and getting your best view because today is going to be the toppest notch day of your lifes. I'm not doubting about it!'

A woman has pulled up next to us in an open-top MEGA HOLLYWOOD TOURS van. She has long, straightened, bleached hair down to her waist, enormous pillowy lips, voluminous round breasts and brown, crinkly-yet-stretched skin, a bit – and I'm not trying to be rude when I say this – like an old leather car seat that's been sat on quite a lot.

She could be thirty or a thousand; she's obviously immortal.

'Get in, DARLINKS!' she calls cheerfully, beeping the van horn and waving with a wireless microphone dangling from her left ear. 'I'm Dominika *with a K* and we have no time to waste, no, no! These celebs, we've got to hunt them like tiger! Careful and quiet and speed! Haha!'

Jamie and I go back to staring at each other.

'What do you want to do?' I say finally as my stomach starts twisting. 'If you're truly going to hate this, we can do something else. I won't mind.'

I will mind very much.

But I'd much rather waste our tickets and go elsewhere than be scowled at all around Hollywood by my nearly-boyfriend for the next two hours.

'You're really selfish, you know that?' Jamie pulls his MEGA cap on and tugs it hard over his forehead so I can't see his face. 'Come on. Let's go *tour* or whatever.'

36

You're expecting me to freak out around about now, right?

Wrong.

Luckily, I've seen enough classic romances to know that every couple needs at least one big fight to ultimately bring them closer together. It helps them bond and understand each other better, and also appreciate each other more when it's all over.

And *hurray*! This is our very first one!

Jamie's properly mad – he's got his arms folded, the cap pulled down and his back turned – I can only imagine how gorgeous the make-up scene is going to be. Holy horoscopes! Mars and Saturn are right on cue, as always.

An Increase of Passion *indeed*.

'Now, darlinks!' Dominika calls as the MEGA HOLLYWOOD TOURS van pulls out into the sunny, bustling streets of Hollywood. 'You know this building? You see it before! You have! Yes! This house is Julia Roberts's in *Pretty Woman*! Fire escape right here!'

What's my next line, though?

'Here is the super-famous church, you know, you seen it, lots of nuns, singing, haha!! Take all your photos!'

Honestly, I'm not super skilled at fighting. Everyone knows that Cancerians tend to avoid confrontation whenever possible – we're nearly as passive as Pisces.

'And over here! We have hotel Janis Joplin died in! You see? They keep room the same. How nice, no?'

Maybe we can hop straight to the making-up part?

'And yes! You take photos, many, many photos! After, if you want, I give you home address of celeb's house! You ask, I have list! Anyone you want! You want Leo, I have him, you want Tom, I have him, you want Ryan, I have him . . .'

In fact – oh my goodness – this might be a really perfect opportunity to show Jamie what a brilliant, understanding and easy-going girlfriend I'd be.

I'm a *fool* if I don't take it.

'I'm sorry,' I say genuinely, grabbing Jamie's hand. 'You're right. It was selfish of me to bring us on this tour. I promise I won't do anything like it again.'

'Well,' Jamie sighs, visibly softening, 'I guess we're here now. We might as well *try* and enjoy it, right?'

I nod, delighted. 'Thank you.'

Then I beam at him softly, tilt my head at an angle and give him a quick kiss on the lips underneath his cap: making-up session complete, bonding done. It was over very fast, but we're just that little bit closer now, I can feel it.

The van has turned off the main streets and is starting a much slower drive up a small, pretty, secluded, tree-lined hill. Behind towering hedges and walls to either side of us, we see tantalising glimpses of roofs, garages, a window here or there, a flash of shiny cars in between gated entries. Excitement is steadily growing.

With every pointed roof, every giant gate, every flash of sunshine through the trees, my heart lifts a few more notches. Just *think* of the cinematic history, the fascinating lives going on behind these massive walls, the movie stars, the *stories*—

'And thissss is Beverly Hills!' Dominika cries into her microphone. 'Thisss is where much of the biggest and most famousest people in the world are living! You have the money, you are living here, for sure. England! What you think of it?'

I blink at the other people in the van – there are at least twelve of us, mostly young, mostly American, a few couples – and they all slowly spin round.

Wait, is she talking to me? Am I *England*?

'It seems very nice,' I say as clearly as possible from the back of the van. 'Very green and quiet.'

'*Yesss!*' Dominika nods enthusiastically. 'Celebs are my friends. So nice. They are waving at us, and we are waving back sometimes! Charlize, she lives over there . . .' She points to her left. 'Over there, we had Keanu. In the distance you see Johnny and, if you look right, you see where Jen and Brad are happy together once, so sad.'

All I can see is terracotta wall and an electronic gate – nothing else is visible – but, if I stare hard enough, I can just imagine their fascinating conversations, the laughter, the romance . . .

'This is ridiculous,' Jamie sighs, slumped down in his seat with his cap pulled down. 'We can't see anything. We're paying to look at chimneys. And why would we *want* to see anything? Who gives one about these people? They're no better than me.'

I look at Jamie in surprise. 'Nobody said they were.'

'Yes, they did. The implication is that they're better than me. We're staring because the entire world believes that the rich and famous are somehow *superior*. They're just ordinary people. In their big houses. Probably pooping or something.'

'Of course they are.' I laugh loudly. 'Nobody's found a way to outsource that yet.'

Jamie rewards me with an unexpected smile.

'I'm just *saying*,' he says, relaxing slightly. 'There's an enormous divide between rich and poor. There's no difference between *me* and *them*, and yet somehow they get the swimming pools. Where's the fairness in that?'

'Very true,' I agree. 'It's not fair.'

The van drives further up the hill and more giant walls and tiny slivers of roof are unveiled: Katy, Orlando, Kurt, Al . . .

'Except,' I add, turning back, 'I guess we *choose*

to elevate them like this, and we choose *who* to elevate. We're voting with our fascination and our money. So it's probably more of a systemic societal problem that needs to be addressed universally rather than targeting individuals, right? Especially when making and enjoying art is generally accessible to everyone and therefore relatively democratic.'

Huh, where did *that* come from? Ooh, I wish Mr Gilbert could hear me right now. If I hadn't fired him, he'd be *so* proud.

Jamie smiles. 'OK, it is *so cute* when you try to sound clever. Did you get that off the internet?'

I blink. 'No?'

The tour van has turned a corner and now we're at the top of the hill. A gorgeous vista of beautiful sunlit countryside is expanding around us: dry and beige, with pops of bright green and fluorescent flowers. Below us Los Angeles is sleepy and dusty.

'Darlinks!' Dominika trills as I stare at the incredible view of Hollywood. 'To our right we have super-special house, design by big sixties architect, name not important, but this house belong to A-list, major actor we know from films like—'

There's an intake of breath from almost everyone

in the tour van. With a simultaneous movement, they're suddenly tense and buzzing and craned towards one side.

I lean too.

'Ooooh! Getting your cameras ready, spotters! The gate is opening! We have a celeb sighting! I am telling you, this is number-two tour in Hollywood! We see famous all the time!'

Except . . . Hang on. Where exactly are we?

I recognise that gate. I recognise the hedges on either side of it. I recognise the tiny gold postbox and the gold water hydrant on the road outside. And I *definitely* recognise the big black sedan nudging slowly out into the road.

'It is!' Dominika cries triumphantly. 'It's Mister . . . Wait. No. This is not actor! It's . . .' She gets her binoculars out and peers more closely. 'Yes! This is his friend, fame black film director, Michael Rivers! You know him! Everyone – quick! Wave!'

Dad and Roz are in the front seats, talking animatedly. Slowly, they stop talking and turn to stare speechlessly at the red MEGA HOLLYWOOD TOURS van.

Dominika has haphazardly parked and is standing

299

on the driver's seat, waving vigorously while her passengers wave and take photos excitedly.

'*Coooool*,' one girl sighs, looking at her phone. 'Michael Rivers? Oh my God, I *love* his movies. What a *legend*.'

Eyebrows raised, Dad lifts his sunglasses up and leans forward with a deep frown to stare directly at me in the back of the bright red van.

I'm waving too, obviously; it would be rude not to.

His mouth falls open slightly.

'Tourists! You may know,' Dominika exuberantly announces, 'my boo Mikey is currently divorcing megastar British actress wife Juliet! You know her from *Hearts of Us*. She is crazy now, in England. Locked away, haha! Too old, I think. Maybe not enough care of yourself, you lose your man. Rumours that he is having affair and *thissss* must be his mistress!'

Umm, *excuse me*?

'I'm sorry,' I say loudly, standing up and putting my hand in the air. 'I don't want to be rude, but that's straight-up rubbish. Juliet's not crazy or locked away. She can get out any time she wants – it's *voluntary.* His name's not *Mikey* – it's either Michael or Mike – and he's not having an affair. That's his secretary, Roz.'

Everyone turns to stare at me.

'Which is . . . what I read on the internet,' I clarify vaguely, sitting back down again and continuing to wave. 'TMZ. Big fan. Mega.'

Everyone refocuses on the black car once more. There's a brief pause, then Roz pokes Dad and starts waving at us. With a completely shell-shocked face, Dad waves too.

'Yess! Wave, guys! What am I telling you? Celebs, so nice!' Dominika pushes her chest out. 'And Mikey baby is *super* hot-cake, no? Mmmm. My type, for sure. Maybe if he's looking for new girlfriend I will meet him, you think?'

I will jam that microphone into a nostril if this woman comes within a five-metre radius of my father. Also calling my dad a *hot-cake* is horrifying.

'OK! Everyone sit!' Our van starts pulling slowly away again. 'That is result! What did I say? I am great, great friend of many celebrities.'

I mean, I *had* kind of hoped we'd see a celebrity who I wasn't already related to coming out of a house I didn't currently live in with the woman who didn't drop me off half an hour ago, but just look how *happy* everyone else is.

'Seriously,' the superfan in front of us sighs tearfully, scrolling through her photos and kissing her phone. 'That's my entire life basically made. *Michael Rivers just waved at me.*'

Smiling, I turn to Jamie. 'See? Look how much pleasure people get from films and—'

His entire face is a series of big circles: eyes huge, nostrils flared, mouth open.

'Hope,' he says slowly. '*Is your mother Juliet Valentine?*'

It's not that I didn't tell Jamie.

I merely avoided the topic of mothers so it never really came up. And I never mentioned my surname, maybe because for once in my entire life I wanted something that wasn't handed down to me by my family.

For once, I wanted something to be *mine*.

'Yes.'

'Your mother is the movie star Juliet Valentine?' Jamie's eyes are getting rounder. 'Oscar-winning Juliet Valentine? *Millionaire* Juliet Valentine?'

Multimillionaire. 'Yes.'

'The woman on the front of that magazine right there?'

He points to a shiny gossip rag poking out of a handbag in the seat in front of us. Mum's pale face is pictured gazing bleakly out of the rehab window.

In big letters underneath, it says **MORE HEARTBREAK FOR THE VALENTINES**.

The media's at it again. Poor Mum.

I nod.

'But—' Jamie's visibly spinning out. 'We've just been riding around in a van that says MEGA HOLLYWOOD TOURS on it, taking photos of houses and walls that belong to your friends and *neighbours*. Don't you have any pride at all?'

'Of course I have pride,' I say indignantly. 'I'm incredibly proud of my family. But their achievements are not *my* achievements. I haven't earned any of it. And the people who live here aren't *my* friends; they're friends of my parents. I haven't seen any of them for years and years. I genuinely don't think they'd even remember me.'

There's a sudden memory of a glorious party at our house in Richmond. Music playing, soft lighting, giant orchids and lilies everywhere, a white marquee in the garden, waiters with silver trays of delicious tiny vollyvonts. Mum and Dad with their arms round each other, laughing and dancing; the rooms filled with beautiful, sparkling people I recognised from the big screen.

All five of us children giggling at the top of the stairs.

Being sent firmly back to bed by Maggie before sneaking out again to listen, to watch, to inhale every second of the glamour.

A lifetime ago . . .

'Hope,' Jamie frowns. 'You're literally Hollywood royalty. Why the hell did you tell me your surname was Rivers?'

'I didn't. I said my *dad's* surname is Rivers. But in my family the Valentine surname gets passed down, what with my great-grandmother and Grandma already being so famous. And when you said that you didn't like films . . .'

'I've heard of *the Valentines* – I don't live under a rock. Although . . .' Jamie peers at me more closely. 'I suppose I can see a similarity between you and Juliet now I'm looking for it. Same eye shape.'

I glow at him. 'That's so kind of you.' I lean forward to kiss him gently. 'Thank you.'

Then my phone beeps, and I pull it out.

DID YOU STEAL MY NEW STELLA
MCCARTNEY PYJAMAS?

Mercy always knows how to ruin a moment.

> By 'pyjamas' do you mean 'black satin
> two-piece'???? Hope x

A few seconds later, a *beep*.

> NO, I MEAN THE PYJAMAS I WEAR IN
> BED, YOU TOTAL DOUCHE-BAGUETTE.
> WHAT IS WRONG WITH YOU? KEEP
> THE DOOR LOCKED BECAUSE THIS
> IS WAR.

Oh, for the love of— I was running around Dogtown in *sleepwear*? No wonder Roz was reluctant to let me out of the car. Maybe I shouldn't have been so harsh about the Bunny Bag Man and Tinfoil Head Woman; they were probably thinking the same thing about me.

There are also three unread messages from Faith:

> Baby, if you need me I'm just across the
> corridor, OK? F xxx

Leaving food outside your door. EAT
HEALTHY. Your heart needs to HEAL. F xxx

Getting anxious. No boy is worth this. Text
back. F xxxxx

Frowning, I consider my options.

I mean, I *could* tell them where I am . . . as a team, we could definitely persuade Dad to come home immediately.

But . . . nope.

I deliberately put the phone back in my pocket. A bit of worrying won't do them any harm. It might make my sisters appreciate me more when I'm actually there. Also, their observational skills are shockingly bad. They should definitely never be allowed pets.

'OK, *darlinks*!' The tour van pulls to an abrupt stop at a light. 'And here we have Walking Fame! It is over two thousand six hundred stars on the floor. So you are hopping out here, I think! Today we have seen our celebrities. You can leave review on website, and also big tip in pocket, haha!'

With a flush of delight, I swivel in my seat. I didn't realise the tour ended up here.

The Hollywood Walk of Fame.

Without a second's delay, Jamie clambers out and tosses his red cap back into the van; it whacks me in the stomach by accident.

I take off my cap and shrug off my MEGA HOLLYWOOD TOURS T-shirt, then cram it into Mercy's Gucci bag.

'Thank you very much,' I say with decidedly fluffy hair, handing Dominika forty dollars of the Emergency Cash Roz gave me. 'You are an extremely talented guide. I wish you much success with men who aren't my father.' Then I hop out on to the pavement.

'Come on.' I grab Jamie's hand and smile encouragingly. I've had an excellent idea. 'There's something very cool I want to show you.'

38

I know what I'm looking for.

I'm just not entirely sure where it is, so I hold Jamie's hand and together we wander slowly along the crowded Hollywood Boulevard. We stare down at each of the engraved bronze stars set in red marble on the pavement.

Halle Berry . . . Bruce Willis . . . Charlie Chaplin . . .

To our right, Spider-Man and Snow White are flirting, giggling and winking at each other. Indiana Jones and Han Solo are eating hot dogs together. Superman is standing by a cash machine, clearly trying to remember his pin number, and Cinderella is handing out gym membership flyers. Marilyn Monroe is pulling faces at children, who scream and hide behind the Terminator while Fred Astaire sits on the kerb, blowing his nose.

It's as if the sky has been zipped open and all the stars have tumbled out.

'HEY, BABY!' Donald Duck yells as we pass. 'NICE BOOTY! YOU WANNA—'

Not him, he doesn't count.

Hearts thumping, we walk across the stars – over Bugs Bunny, Morgan Freeman, Audrey Hepburn and Winona Ryder – until we find a slightly quieter stretch of street.

'Here!' I exclaim with joy, pulling on Jamie's hand. 'Here they are!'

Directly below my feet is a plaque that says:

To the right of it is another star:

And to the left is:

Three generations of Valentine women, immortalised forever. I can't help wondering how they managed to get their stars gathered together. Maybe it's a bit like a graveyard – you can apply for some kind of family plot.

With an unexpected tightness in my throat, I bend down.

The tips of my fingers touch each star, hot and glowing in the sun. *Hi, Mum. Hi, Grandma. Hi, Great-grandma I never met.*

It's easy to forget how hard they must have worked; how much talent they had. What kind of determination and courage they've shown. A burst of pride whips through me. *I am part of this dynasty of incredible women.*

And Dad. He should have a star too.

Although – I glance up the pavement – there are only three blank stars left, so once my father has nabbed one it's going to be a race between Mercy, me and Max to see which of us is immortalised. Effie's obviously a dead cert.

For a brief second, I can hear Mercy's voice in my head.

'Just try it, Poo-face,' she snaps. 'I'm the talent, that's my star and I will bite your grabby little fingers off.'

'Shut up,' I tell her. 'And please go away – you're totally gatecrashing my brain.'

Then I let myself picture my name on the pavement:

And I see the red carpet; the paparazzi gathered; the cameras flashing; the cheers as my plaque is unveiled; my humble yet poignant speech; the delighted faces of my loved ones all around me; Mum's joy, Dad's pride. And Jamie's there too, gazing at me with unabashed admiration: he's stood by me throughout the whole journey; he believed in me from the start; we faced the trials and tribulations of rising fame together . . .

That star is mine. I *know* it is.

Feeling deeply emotional, I stand back up.

'You know, this really is my deepest dr—'

'Hmmmm?' Jamie's staring at his phone. 'Man, my buddies are having the best time in Mexico.' He scrolls down the screen. 'Abi just wrote the funniest thing about guacamole. Seriously, she's such a character.'

Wasn't it supposed to be a boys' trip?

Also Jamie's feet are plonked directly on top of Grandma. If she ever finds out a boy stood on her, she'll hunt him down and beat him to death with her walking stick.

'How is this girl not snapped up already?' Jamie chuckles, typing. 'She's so cool. We've got so much in common. *Great* legs.'

I look down at mine. Then I swallow hard as something over Jamie's shoulder catches my eye. It's an enormous, oriental-style theatre, glowingly white, with huge red pillars and spiked black dragon heads, a tall, narrow green roof and an enormous carved stone dragon plaque in the middle. In front of it, I can see handprints, shoeprints and autographs in the cement pavement . . .

Oooh. It must be Grauman's Chinese Theatre!

I have *always* wanted to come here. It's the most famous cinema in the entire world! It's where *Star*

Wars and *The Wizard of Oz* premiered, where multiple Oscar ceremonies have been held! I'm pretty sure it's even where that old red-carpet photo of Mum with Grandma was taken.

Then I look up. Hanging from the wall is the most enormous film poster I've ever seen. Nine metres tall, a backdrop of pale blue skies and towering mountains, with PINNACLE sketched lightly across the snow in footprints in the foreground.

My stomach lurches. The universe knew we were coming; it has *always* known.

Find your happy place.

'What?' Jamie sighs, finally glancing up. 'What are you looking at me like that for?'

This is exactly what we need. A classic romance to inspire us – true love triumphs! We can defeat the odds! Confirm our relationship status so I know where I stand! Plus, maybe a little bit of darkness to hold hands and kiss in.

                    JAMIE
              (*leaning over*)
    Hope? I don't want you to leave.

                    HOPE
                  (*sadly*)
               Neither do I.

                    JAMIE
               We'll find a way,
                  won't we?

                    HOPE
               Of course we will.

She kisses him.

                 HOPE (CONTINUED)
Now *shhhh*! It's really rude to talk
     during a film. We should be
              respectful.

I look at my watch.

'Do you fancy seeing a movie?' I ask with a
sudden bolt of optimism. 'It's Mum's and I haven't
seen it yet, but it's supposed to be *amazing*. I
know you said you don't really like films, but
maybe you just haven't been watching the right
ones.'

316

Jamie looks at his phone again, then blows air out through his mouth. 'Fine.'

Yessss! Before he can change his mind, I run as fast as I can to the box office and buy two tickets. It's going to be in 3D and high definition and everything: it'll be like we're actually there!

I grab Jamie's hand and we walk into the enormous, ancient theatre. Then I hold my breath. It's like an old Technicolor film, bright and rich and gleaming. Hundreds of deep red velvet seats face the biggest IMAX screen on the planet, shrouded in a red velvet curtain embroidered with golden palm trees. Immense marble columns engraved with trees and shrines and birds and blossoms tower upwards.

The ceiling is a jewel box: sapphire and ruby and emerald and gold. It's carved in a round, intricate rose shape and there are tiny dragons chasing herons, and horses cantering around and castles painted in oil above us.

Around the edges of the theatre, tiny Chinese lanterns glow rosily, like miniature red orbs. The whole room smells of . . . *Hollywood.*

This is where we gather – the famous and the unknown, the wannabes and the nearlies and the one-days – just to be part of something bigger than ourselves; to take a seat in cinematic history, set among the stars.

I turn to Jamie with lit-up eyes.

'These chairs look uncomfortable,' he frowns. 'Do they even tilt back properly? Where am I supposed to put my drink? How long does this film last again?'

Come on, movie: time to work your magic.

Grinning, I put my black-rimmed plastic three-dimensional glasses on and hand Jamie his pair. He scowls at me but puts his on too.

We're barely seated before the lights go down and music suddenly swells: trumpets and violins, a full orchestra. I'm tingling all over and there's a lump in my throat.

Quickly, I grab Jamie's hand and squeeze.

Here we go here we go here we go here we—

With a glorious swish, the red velvet curtains open . . .

FADE OUT.

39

`. . . FADE IN.`

`HOPE stumbles out of the auditorium.`

`What the—`

`How could she—`

`Why did they—`

`THAT WAS NOT A ROMANCE.`

Numb, I lean against a marble pillar in the foyer.

Happy happy stay happy happy happy—

'Well,' Jamie says, staring at his phone again, 'that was OK, wasn't it? Still not my kinda thing, but yeah. Not bad, I guess. Could've been worse.'

Why did nobody warn me?

'I always thought your mom was overrated, but she wasn't terrible. Though I'm not sure I totally bought the *concept*, you know?'

There was no love story in that film *at all*. Like, *nothing*.

I kept looking, but once an hour had passed, and no hot guy of any kind had shown up, I realised I'd been conned.

'So she went all that way and didn't even find her daughter? What was the point, then? Good special effects, though. That avalanche was awesome.'

Why would anyone make a film like that? What possessed my mother to take that role in the first place? What's wrong with girl meets boy, girl loves boy, girl overcomes obstacle, girl ends up with boy? I mean, they're classics for a reason.

'What happened at the end, though? I was watching my buddy getting totally worked by a wave on my phone so I missed it. Did she get back or not?'

It's just a film, Hope. Just a film just a film just a film just a film—

I blink at Jamie, the foyer still spinning in circles around me.

'I don't know. I shut my eyes.'

'Oh. Well.' Jamie grimaces and looks back at his phone. 'Guess we'll never know, then. Never mind. Hahaha! Have a look at this wipeout. It's *hilarious.*'

I stare at the video of roiling waves without seeing anything.

No *wonder* Mum's exhausted. Making that film must have completely drained her. My father really must go home right now. Juliet Valentine needs all the love and affection she can get. And I'm her hope so it's time for me to *focus.*

'I was thinking,' Jamie continues, finally putting his phone away. 'The personal *profit* from a movie of that scale must be immense. You guys must be loaded. Does your family do much charity work? You really should. You know, I've started up a new sea conservation project because the ones already running just weren't doing enough. What do you think?'

He points and I blink at his SAVE THE WHALES T-shirt. Next time I see a film, I am getting a *written guarantee* that it's not heartbreaking before I buy a ticket.

With an effort, I pull myself together. I am Hope

Valentine – movie star in the making – and sadness is *not* in my narrative.

'Ch-charity?' I shake my head hard. 'Wh-what do you mean? *Oh*. Well. Mum and Dad built a school in Nepal about a decade ago. They go out most years, I think.'

'That's good.' Jamie nods. 'But what about *you*? What are *you* doing? Personally?'

I stare at the floor, flushing. 'Not . . . that much.'

'Well.' He stretches his arms out and cricks his neck. 'That's not ideal, is it? I could show you some projects you could get involved in, maybe get a donation from your—'

I'm trying to listen, really I am, but my eyes start to drift round the foyer.

It's very similar to the auditorium – ornate and carved and red and gold, like another smaller jewellery box – and there's an old-fashioned popcorn counter and large glass display boxes filled with memorabilia. Oooh! There's the green curtain dress from *Gone With the Wind*, Marilyn Monroe's gold dress from *Gentlemen Prefer Blondes*, Dorothy's apron from *The Wizard of Oz*—

I inhale quickly. Is that—

'*Mum?*' I take a few quick steps forward. 'Oh my gosh. Jamie, that's my *mum.*'

She's on the other side of the room, soft rosy lights glinting off her platinum hair, skin flawless, eyes huge and grey. The famous Valentine nose – the one Mercy inherited – is large and noble, her wide mouth is crooked in a smile, and she's a lot curvier than the last time I saw her. She looks haughty and imperious in long grey satin.

She also looks about ten years younger. The fine lines round her forehead and mouth are completely gone, and there are no dark shadows under her eyes.

It's freaky how *real* she looks. In many ways I can't quite put my finger on, this waxwork looks a lot more alive than my mum did last week.

'Wow,' Jamie murmurs as we reach her, leaning right into her face with narrowed eyes. 'That is *creepy.* You don't look much like her after all.'

Honestly, it's overwhelming. I know she's basically a giant candle, but all I want to do after seeing that film is tell Jamie to give my mother some personal space and then wrap my arms round her tightly.

'Umm,' I say instead, holding out a hand with an awkward laugh. 'Is it too soon to introduce you to my parents? Jamie, meet my mum. Mum, meet Jamie.'

Jamie stares at me. 'That's just weird, Hope.'

'. . . I was joking.'

'You're not even vaguely funny.'

'Sorry.'

'Anyway . . .' He starts walking towards the exit, phone in hand once more. 'So some of my other friends are having a beach barbecue later.'

I nod, pleased Jamie hasn't missed out on everything because of me.

Then I give Mum's waxwork one last glance before turning to the doors. I've really got to talk to Dad as soon as possible. Maybe if I get up super early tomorrow I can drop a few more subtle hints, casually bring up the topic of the Olden Days, maybe low-key place a few photos of Mum on the—

'Hope? Are you listening?'

'Course I am!' We push back into the bright sunshine and I smile. 'So barbecues . . . actually, I know how to make really delicious halloumi kebabs. Maybe I could bring some with the—'

'Well . . .' Jamie taps on his phone. 'This has been fun.'

'Oh.' I frown. 'Am I not . . . coming with you?'

I swear it's as if his face has just been bricked up like an abandoned house. His jaw goes stiff, his mouth hard and flat. 'We can't spend *all* our time together,' he hisses. 'Is that what you want, Hope? To be with me *constantly*? Do you want to glue yourself to my side or something?'

I stare at him, suddenly cold.

'N-no, of course not! It's just that you said we'd spend the day together so I assumed that—'

'*The day's basically over now. My entire life isn't about you, you know. Why are you so needy?*'

What on earth is happening?

'Sorry. I'm sorry!' *Erase erase erase.* 'It's just that . . . I love spending time with you, that's all.'

There's a long silence.

'You know, Hope,' Jamie's eyes are like hard blue marbles, 'when you say things like that, it's *really* unattractive.'

'S-sorry.'

'Stop saying sorry all the time,' Jamie sighs. 'It's getting annoying.'

I stare at the floor. What did I do? And, once I know, how do I fix it?

'Look.' My forehead is unexpectedly being kissed and a golden arm goes round my shoulder and squeezes it. 'I've gotta go to this barbecue because it's all arranged and I'm busy tomorrow. But I'll call you, OK? We can work something out.'

I nod. 'O-kay.'

Then I look at my watch. It's only two pm, which means Roz isn't due to pick me up for another four hours. I suppose I could go watch Mum's film another couple of times, but it would have to be on my own.

"Umm," I say instead. "Is there a bus I could maybe catch back?"

"A *bus*?" Jamie shakes his head and smiles brightly. "We don't really *do* public transport in LA, Hope. I'll drop you home on the way. It's not safe out here on your own. There are *way* too many weirdos.'

40

You see the problem, right?

It's all well and good ad-libbing on set, but too much improvisation and the narrative arc gets confused. And this script is now starting to veer off course dramatically and needs recalibrating.

I glance over at Jamie.

He's driving with his eyes narrowed. He hasn't said a single word in twenty-five minutes. It is definitely time for me to step in and get this story back in the right lane.

Giving my head a quick shake, I clear my throat.

And lights, cameras –

'You know,' I say casually, leaning against the car door, 'Gemini is ruled by Mercury, which is the planet of *communication*. While Cancer is led by the moon, which is all about *emotions*.'

Jamie continues driving.

'So Gemini tend to be more *go-go-go*, hopping from one new thing to another, while Cancer is much more of a homebody, into familiarity and creature comforts.'

Still driving.

'Cancerians often struggle to . . . uh . . . *express* themselves, while Geminis really don't.' I turn towards him slightly. 'We Crabs are more *intuitive*, you see, more sensitive and kind of instinctual, while you guys like clear *verbal* connection. It's a really good combination, because we totally balance each other out. Air and water. Water and air. Which, everyone knows, make . . . bubbles.'

More silence.

'But bubbles need to be looked after, otherwise too much water and too much air and the—'

'Do you have a point?' Jamie snaps tiredly. 'Or are you just chattering again?'

I flinch. 'Please tell me if something's wrong.'

'Nothing's wrong.'

'Are you sure? Because . . . The sign of Gemini is twins, after all, so it's completely normal that there are two sides of you. It's just . . . is everything OK? Are you stressed about something at school? What can I do to help?'

'*I* don't need help,' Jamie snaps, still focused on the road. '*I'm* not the one who believes in *horoscopes*. Next you'll be telling me you believe in unicorns too.'

My cheeks go very hot. He was *supposed* to tell me he's got a lot on at the moment – an overdue project or something – and I'd ease his mind, offer a solution and make everything better again.

'Of course not!' I laugh, shaking my head. 'But why *wouldn't* the planets affect us? The moon causes tides and periods and everyone knows that's actual science. So maybe the location of the *entire universe* affects us all just a little bit?'

'No.' Jamie's still staring at the road. 'It doesn't.'

'Maybe?'

'Nope.'

'But . . . if fruits and vegetables are seasonal, couldn't humans be seasonal too?'

'Jeez,' Jamie says, glancing to the side. 'You really are something else, you know that?'

Again, that line does not seem to have quite the same positive inflection it did in London. Although I shouldn't be surprised: Geminis never believe in horoscopes, which is kind of ironic if you think about it.

Jamie's small green Toyota finally pulls up outside my gates. There's a long silence.

'Umm,' I say, just in case it's my cue. 'Thanks for the lift, Jamie. Really appreciate it.' Then I open the car door.

Honestly, I'm not sure how much longer I'll be in Los Angeles, but at this rate I won't be Jamie's girlfriend for *months*. Maybe I should drop a hint, bring up the—

'Hope?'

My heart lurches and I spin round. 'Yes?'

'Give me a smile?'

I smile.

'Give me a kiss?'

I give him a tentative kiss.

Then Jamie leans his forehead against mine, and stares into my eyes. I can feel it: the tension building, the excitement rising, our souls connecting, *it's happening it's happening it's finally happening*—

'Hope, I need to ask you something.'

Happiness rushes through my arms, racing across my chest, warming my face. *Finally finally finally yes yes yes yes yes*—

'Will you . . .'

'Oh my gosh, yes!' I shout, throwing my arms abruptly round Jamie and kissing his cheek. 'Yes! Yes! Of course I will!'

'. . . pass me my sunglasses case? I left it in your passenger door.'

Aaaargh, did I just jump my cue *again*?

'Umm, of course I will!'

Move with the direction, Hope.

'Here!' I reach into the door. 'Here are your sunglasses! Oh my gosh, yes! Here you go!'

Then I hand them over and breathe out in relief. *Seamlessly done, Hope. Bravo.*

'Cool. Laters?'

Honestly, I have no idea what my next line is.

                        HOPE
        See you soon! I'll miss you.

Needy.

                        HOPE
                   Call me!

Demanding.

332

                    HOPE
                  Call me?

Desperate.

                    HOPE
    WHEN AM I GOING TO SEE YOU AGAIN
     BECAUSE I HAVE NO IDEA WHAT OUR
    RELATIONSHIP STATUS IS AND WE ARE
           RUNNING OUT OF TIME.

Definitely not that.

My phone starts buzzing, so I grab it.

'Cool,' I repeat, as breezily as possible. 'Laters.'

41

Three days.

It took my siblings *three whole days* to notice I was no longer in the house with them. So much for the telepathic bond between family: paper *bunting* has a stronger connection.

'Po,' Effie says as I hit the green button on my phone. 'Baby, what's going on? Is everything all right?'

Yeah, my sisters have suffered enough. I turn the camera on.

Faith's beautiful face appears – crumpled and anxious – and my stomach twists. Did I *really* have to put the people I love the most through this drama? The worry they must have felt when they finally realised I was gone, the sleepless nights—

'She's just sulking,' Mercy snaps from behind Faith. 'We can *hear* you, Poodle. You may have locked the door, but that whiny heartbreak music has been playing on repeat for days. I swear if you don't give me my stuff back right now I'm going to kick the door down and get it for myself.'

'Shut up, Mer.' Effie knocks on my Richmond bedroom door, then lightly rests her cheek on the wood. 'Po, we're *so* sorry you're feeling sad. I should have realised you weren't really OK even though you said you were. Open the door, baby? Please?'

I stare at my phone. Three days and they still haven't noticed?

OK, I no longer feel guilty.

If I really was in there, I'd have starved by now and Mercy would have had to rip her precious Gucci handbag out of my skeleton hands.

'For the love of—' I say in frustration. 'I accidentally left the music on my computer running on loop. So go ahead, Mercy. Knock yourself out. Neither me nor your clothes are actually in there.'

'*Told* you,' Max crows cheerfully, poking his grinning face into the frame. '*Told* you she'd run away. I bet she's living in an ashram in India. Or under a pile of furs in a cave somewhere in the

Arctic. You guys need to start giving me credit for being the visionary I actually am.'

'Oh, please.' Mercy rolls her eyes. 'As if. Where would she go? Who would she run *to*? She's still in there, hiding out with a week's worth of canned food like a crazy little squirrel.'

She kicks my bedroom door hard.

'Time to face the music, Poodle McDoodle. Out you come. And wear a padded pair of knickers, you little thief, because I'm gonna *kick* your *butt*.'

'Mercy,' I say, shaking my head, 'squirrels don't have can-openers so you're just being dramatic. And I don't own padded knickers because I don't need them. There's a spare key in the vase on the hall table so go have a look yourself.'

Faith immediately runs off, grabs the key and opens my bedroom door. Through my phone I watch as they walk in, bewildered.

'The cupboard?' Mercy says less certainly. 'Bathroom?'

'I'm not hiding under a pile of towels, I'm in Los Angeles.' A triumphant grin lights up my face. 'With Dad. In *Beverly Hills*. We have a turquoise pool and a computer that runs the whole house and marble

floors and an amazing hilltop view and a mini-spa.'
I hold my phone up so they can see it. 'A *mini-spa*,
Mercy. With black earbuds, which, as we all know,
are the swankiest type.'

Max laughs loudly. 'She's got a point, Mer. Look
at you and your basic ear cleaning.'

I've never seen Mercy speechless before: it is *deeply*
satisfying.

'No,' my oldest sister says finally, crossing her
arms. 'Nuh-uh. You can't be in Los Angeles. No
way. If anyone in this family deserves to go to
Hollywood, it's me.'

'Because you're The Talent,' Effie sighs loudly.
'We know, Mer. We get it. Repeatedly.' Then she
leans towards the screen. 'That's so cool, though,
Po! Is Dad looking after you?'

'Yes!' Which reminds me: 'Is Mum OK? Have
you seen her? How's she doing? Is she holding up
all right?'

'She's fine,' Faith smiles. 'Another feature came
out in the papers yesterday, but I'm sure she didn't
see it. Pretty sure anyway. At least, I . . . hope not.
It was feral. But you're having a great time, Po?'

Now I just feel guilty. Here's me, living the

Hollywood dream in glorious sunshine, but Mum's still in rehab being ripped apart by the media.

I need to speak to Dad asap and get him out of here.

'Erm, well, California's unbelievable,' I nod enthusiastically. 'It's sunny all day and everyone smiles all the time. It's the happiest place in the world, *scientific fact.*'

My siblings look at each other.

'That's actually Norway,' Max points out. 'Or Disney World, depending on which posters you believe. But what we're really asking is how's the *boy*? You know, the Californian one who just so *happens* to live in the same city you're in now, by *complete coincidence*?'

'Jamie is . . . *great*,' I confirm, even though I'm pretty sure Max is being sarcastic. 'I've actually met some of his best friends already, and they're all *lovely* too.'

'Stalker,' my eldest sister says, leaning towards the screen. 'On which note, Poodle, you won't *believe* who rocked up at the house yesterday looking like a total—'

'Let's focus on Hope's adventure, shall we?' Faith

pokes Mercy in the arm. 'Everything good? Jamie everything you hoped for?'

'Eff, we're like the perfect romance. We even had our first fight!' Faith frowns so I quickly reassure her. 'Don't worry, the making-up was great too.' I clench my fists to my chest. 'Nothing can pull apart what is supposed to be together. Love is all that really matters. It's what lies at the heart of us.'

My siblings look at each other again.

'Will you stop doing that, please?' I say in frustration. 'I can see you! You're not doing *secret, invisible face code.*'

'Hope,' Faith says gently. 'It's just . . . they're Mum's lines. From her film. What's going on, baby?'

'She's probably screwing everything up by being too keen,' Mercy snarks, lifting a pot off my dressing table. 'Is this my best moisturiser, Sticky Fingers? And where is the lid, you grubby little—'

I flush. 'I am *not too keen.*'

'Sure you are.' Mer nods. 'You probably told him he was your leading man.'

My cheeks are on fire. 'No, I did *not.*'

'Oh, *Jamie,*' my big sister simpers, fluttering her eyelashes and clasping her hands together. 'My hero, my knight in shining armour, my Californian dreamboat—'

'That's not—'

'My life would be nothing without you. Why don't I follow you across the world like a total loser—'

'I didn't—'

'I'll take anyone, as long as they show me the tiniest bit of attention—'

'I wouldn't—'

'Love me, love me, somebody please love me—'

Something explodes in my chest.

'SHUT UP! JUST SHUT UP, MERCY! SHUT UP SHUT UP SHUT UP! YOU DON'T KNOW WHAT YOU'RE TALKING ABOUT! YOU'RE A STUPID COW! I WILL NOT BE UNDERMINDED CONSTANTLY BY YOU ANY LONGER.'

Bang bang.

'YOU KNOW WHAT? IF I'M TOO *DUMB* TO HAVE A SINGLE THOUGHT IN MY WHOLE FLUFFY EMPTY *HEAD* – IF I'M A *WALKING CLICHÉ* – THEN MAYBE YOU SHOULD GET THE HELL OUT OF

MY *BIMBO* FANTASY WORLD AND JUST *LEAVE ME TO IT.'*

Faith's face has gone a funny colour. Even Mercy has frozen.

'AFTER ALL.' Why are my hands shaking? 'Maybe I don't *pass the Bechamel test as a human being,* but if that means being like *you lot* then maybe I don't *WANT TO.'*

'Wait,' Max says in confusion. 'Are you *yelling,* Po? I've literally never heard you yell before. What the shizzle is going on? Why are you comparing yourself to a lasagne?'

'Po.' Effie grabs her phone back off Mercy. 'I don't know how you . . . where you heard that. But it isn't true; none of it is true. We *love* you, you're our baby sister . . .'

'Hope,' Mercy says in a low voice, snatching the phone back. 'I'm sorry. I was being a cow. I can't help it. I can't . . . control myself. But I didn't mean any of it.'

I shake my head, blocking them out. Because I'm in a lovely place and I'm having a lovely time. And I'm going to keep having a lovely time no matter what anyone says or does to try and stop me.

'I'm in Hollywood,' I finish, cheeks blazing. 'And you guys are not. And you know how we're all just biding our time until we can go our separate ways? Well, I got there first, so . . .'

'What?' my sisters say.

'BITE ME.'

♋ Cancer: June 21–July 22

Cancer is one of the zodiac's key 'fixers', and your nurturing needs are on high alert today. As the sun in Capricorn clashes with Uranus, you're going to feel a new burst of energy!

Enjoy the wave of enthusiasm and make sure you point it in the right direction!

Good morning Jamie! How did you sleep? Thanks for yesterday, I had a lovely d

Delete.

Good morning! I had a nice day yesterday. Thank y

Delete.

Hi! Yesterday was fun! :) What are you up to?
x

Biting my lip, I delete the kiss and search for a suitable emoji instead. Maybe an . . . avocado. They're officially funny, right?

'Computer?' I say, pouring two glasses of orange juice and putting them next to each other on the outdoor dining table by the pool. 'What's the most popular emoji right now?'

'*The most popular emoji worldwide is the face with tears of joy, expressing an emotion between sobbing and laughing.*'

'Thanks,' I say, adding it, then sprinkling granola into two bowls. 'Computer, what's the best text to send a boy that is not needy or annoying and doesn't make them mad at you?'

'*I'm not quite sure how to help you with that.*'

Carefully, I put a cafetière of coffee down too, then a plate of egg whites I'd burnt and covered with ketchup.

'Computer, how do you make a boy ask you out officially?'

'*I'm not quite sure how to help you with that.*'

Ugh. Useless technology.

I turn to Olivia, Madison and Sophia, lying on sunloungers on the far side of the swimming pool. I don't want to sound ungrateful, but they've basically been lying there since they arrived. Sometimes it feels as if they're treating this place like some kind of hotel.

'Any advice, guys?'

Olivia lowers her sunglasses, looks at me over the top of them and shrugs. Then she goes back to sunbathing.

'Helpful, thanks so much.'

Giving up, I add a balloon emoji – that seems suitably Gemini air-like – and press SEND.

I finish my preparations for today by putting two towels, two sets of headphones and two books (OK, one book and one fashion magazine) on the nearest sunloungers. I then run through my most subtle conversation starters about how to make a marriage work.

Then I sit down to patiently wait.

And wait.

And wait.

And—

'Dad!' A full fifty minutes later, my father finally appears on the terrace, urgently patting his jeans. 'Come! Sit down! We haven't spent any real time together since I got here. But we've got a whole day of *chatting* ahead of us, hurray! Just, you know, talking about life, how great Richmond is, people in England we might miss or—'

'Po,' Dad says, frowning and scratching his head. 'There's a problem with one of the scenes, some kind of continuity issue. It's difficult to fix post-production – in fact, it's a total disaster. Baby girl, I've got to head back in.'

'*Now?*'

'Fifteen minutes ago.' He scowls and pats his jeans pockets again. 'Car keys, car keys . . . Where's my bag? I need those script notes. Did Roz move them? Where the heck did I—'

Then he looks up and sees my expression.

'Oh, sweetheart.' Dad rubs his face guiltily. 'I'm so sorry. Why don't I take us out for dinner tonight? We could get all dressed up, head to Chateau Marmont, do a bit of celeb-spotting . . .'

I brighten considerably. 'Can I take my autograph book?'

'Mmm-hmm.' Dad picks his car keys out from under a beautiful photo of Mum that I intentionally dropped over them. 'Sure.'

'Although . . .' I stand behind him, excitement building. 'Could I come with you now? To the studio? I promise I'll be really helpful with all the props and—'

Oh my gosh, this is *such* a good idea.

Imagine it: *me, on a real-life Hollywood movie set.* Maybe the star of the movie quits just as we arrive, there's a huge panic – the film is ruined! – but then—

                    HOLLYWOOD PRODUCER
                    My God, that's her.

                           HOPE
                           Me?

                    HOLLYWOOD PRODUCER
          Our new leading lady. You have an
          indescribable film-star quality. I
                    can't explain it.

HOPE

But I'm only fifteen and I have to go
    back to England soon . . . I'm not
    trained. I've never acted before—

HOLLYWOOD PRODUCER

It doesn't matter! We'll make it
    work! I know star quality when I
                  see—

'No,' Dad says, grabbing his bag from the corner.
'Sorry, Hope, but I can't get you past security at
this late notice. I'll be back before you know it.
Promise.' Then he yawns widely.

'It's the weirdest thing,' he adds, rubbing his left
eye. 'The house computer must be broken. I keep
being woken up by Elton John. It's like being in my
twenties again. Man, I hated that song *then*.'

Quickly, I stare into the distant hills. 'Oh my
goodness. Wow. That is *so* weird. What a *crazy* thing
to randomly happen to you, Dad. You should call
in a professionalist to look into it.'

Dad pauses, hand on his wallet. 'Hope?'

'Mmmm?' I stare at the pool. 'Dad?'

'Hope?'

Now at the decking. 'Dad?'

'*Hope*. Look at me.' I reluctantly look at him. 'Do you happen to know anything about reappropriated seventies piano ballads being blasted into my bedroom at six in the morning?'

'Absolutely not.' I look him straight in the eyes. *Be the Orange, Hope.* 'Maybe your subconscious remembers that pacific music and you're programming it in your sleep?'

'Right.' Dad's nose twitches. 'One more time, Po, it's *specific.* The Pacific is an ocean. And the only memory I have of *Candle in the Wind* is your mom screaming MARILYN IS ROLLING IN HER GRAVE at the radio.'

I beam at him. Not quite the romantic image I was aiming for, but I'll take it.

'1997,' I nod wisely. 'The year you and Mum met. Must have been a pretty *memorable* occasion, even though it was so very long ago, huh?'

'It's not that long ago.' Dad frowns, looking through his bag. 'And we met in 1990. At the studio I'm working at now, as it happens. Where are my sunglasses?'

Oh, for the love of—

'Hey, Bimbo.' Mercy's inside my head again. 'Haha, you put all that musical effort in for literally *no reason*.'

'And, Hope?' Dad adds, fishing out his sunglasses and heading towards the sedan. 'Will you please clean your stuff up after yourself? I keep finding your clothes and jewellery scattered in every room of this house. It is *not* a hotel.'

He leaves and I run inside to my bedroom.

Mum's kimono, her shirt, her necklace, her scarf, a pair of her monogrammed slippers, her silk gloves . . . all folded and neatly piled on top of the chair again. Which means literally nothing I've done since I got here has worked. I'm still not Jamie's girlfriend, Dad's still here and Mum's still in rehab. I might as well have stayed in my bedroom in London.

Blinking, I sit down abruptly on top of Mum's stuff.

Am I being . . . too low-key?

Are my famously delicate performance skills actually working against me this time? Maybe I need to be *more* obvious. *Less* artful. Oh, this is so typical of my star sign: we're always tackling things sideways instead of head-on, like the little Crabs we are.

And now I can hear Jamie's words from our very first date.

I usually can't stand casual people. Why pretend you don't care if you do? It's like living your whole life with the volume turned down.

And . . .

Sometimes I get carried away. I guess I'm just an old-fashioned romantic.

And . . .

So no holding back, OK? There's no right and no wrong. No rules. We'll be ourselves, as much as we want to be. Living life at full volume. Deal?

Suddenly, I know how to Fix. It. *All.*

'Computer,' I say, jumping up and clapping my hands. 'Call me a car to Melrose Avenue immediately.'

'Completed. Your car will arrive in ten minutes.'

'Computer? Find me the phone number for a car-insurance company in Beverly Hills.' Then I grin widely. 'One that specialises in yellow Lamborghinis.'

43

Dressed in a black catsuit, HOPE carefully surveys the massive walls of PARAMOUNT STUDIOS. It looks easy, but only because her breaking-in skills have been honed through many years of borrowing stuff from her sister.

Pulling a mask down over her face, HOPE starts to quickly scale the boundary wall. She is startlingly flexible, agile and determined. Also her legs are very strong and her posture is excellent.

HOPE

(*to herself*)

All I need to do now is drop behind that security guard and jump/roll behind that bush.

Falling nine metres, she lands silently and elegantly behind him.

SECURITY GUARD

(*turning*)

Wow. That was impressive. I am now under your spell and will do whatever you ask of me.

HOPE

Your first mistake was turning round.

She hits him in the stomach with her hand.

HOPE

Your second mistake was being under my spell.

With the speed of lightning, she puts him in a headlock.

HOPE

And your THIRD mistake was—

'You here for the two o'clock tour?'

I stare at the uniformed man standing next to the massive wall I've been surveying carefully. 'Sorry?'

'The Studio Tour. We've got one starting in ten minutes. You here for it? Because you're gonna get mighty hot dressed like that – just saying.'

I look down in exasperation at Mercy's black catsuit.

It's not quite as invisible as I'd hoped, given that it's the middle of the day and thus we're in blazing sunshine. Also, the wall outside Paramount Studios is a pale peach colour.

Maybe the leather gloves and skullcap are slightly unnecessary, but they just make the outfit look more put together.

'This tour of which you speak.' I'm deliberating thoughtfully. 'Does it get me into the studio?'

'Yeah. Because, as I said, it's the Studio Tour.'

'Where I might perhaps see movies being filmed

and prominent directors fixing last-minute set-continuity problems?'

'Probably not, because it's Sunday, but . . . sure.'

I now have two options: scale the impossibly high peach wall, hit the security guard in the stomach, headlock him, shout and then jump-roll behind a bush.

Or—

'There's a little cart,' the guard adds.

'Like a golf buggy?'

'Yeah. It makes a *wheeeee* sound when it drives.'

'Done. Please lead the way.'

I've *finally* learnt my lesson.

I fired my old assistant (me) and got a new one (also me). On the drive over here, we did all the necessary research: scouring IMDb and Wikipedia for any films in 1990 that might have involved both my mum and my dad.

And I found it: *The First Butterfly*. It has a two-star rating, my mum is listed as 'frowning New Yorker girl' and Dad was an unpaid movie-runner.

I've been freaking out about it ever since. Because it means that not only did my parents not meet on

The Heart of Us – so watching it five billion times was unnecessary – but they actually met when they were teenagers, which is even more romantic.

They fell in love across a crowded set.

Dad, a young, ambitious lad from America – so tall, so handsome, such a go-getter! – and Mum, a beautiful young rich girl from London, following in her famous family's footsteps. They connected immediately during one beautiful week, yet circumstances tore them apart because that's exactly what circumstances do.

But – after years of thinking about each other, of sending letters and faxes or whatever – they finally found their way back to each other, got married and had us.

Proving that true love *always* triumphs. And also proving that Mum was fifteen when she had her first role in a movie. A point I will obviously be taking up with Grandma when I get home.

'So,' my guide, Patrick, says as a group of us climbs into the golf buggy with laminated passes round our necks. 'This is the second oldest surviving film studio in America and the only original studio still based in Hollywood.'

I get my phone out and smooth back my curls. Just because I'm here for a pacific reason doesn't mean I can't take photos of any celebrities or maybe get spotted by a director for a main role in five years' time. Mum would be so proud of my multitasking!

'There are twenty-three stars over the mountain logo,' our guide continues as we zoom down a neat little road. 'Each star represents one of the original contracted actors, such as Gloria Swanson, Mary Pickford—'

Oooh! There's the famous iron gate through which they once walked full-grown elephants!

'Douglas Fairbanks, Wallace Reid, Pauline Frederick—'

Just imagine walking through these gates, knowing that your set is waiting for you. You've learnt your script, your costume is ready—

'Marguerite Clark, Pauline Valentine—'

I spin round in shock. 'Pauline Valentine was one of the original stars of this studio?'

'She was!' Patrick looks delighted to have such a keen-bean on board. 'Fun fact: Pauline was originally a waitress from York in England. She worked part-time in a chocolate factory before she jumped on a boat over here and landed her big break in the silent-movie industry.'

'I know,' I beam proudly. 'She was the leading lady in sixty-seven movies and has a star on the Walk of Fame.'

My great-grandmother was a *legend*.

The tour buggy keeps whizzing down tiny streets. 'To the right is Stage Eighteen,' Patrick continues, pointing at a vast hangar. 'It's big enough to fit a plane inside, and you can control everything: light, warmth, sound, air . . .'

A man walks out but it's not Dad. We keep driving.

'This is a parking lot, but it can be turned into an enormous wave pool. It holds nine hundred fifty thousand gallons of water and has been used for films like *The Ten Commandments* . . .'

I put my hand up.

'Um, I think it's time to repaint the background,' I suggest politely, gesturing at a giant muddy-grey wall with little grubby clouds puffed across it. 'It looks a bit faded and dirty.'

Our guide laughs. 'It's supposed to. The Californian sky is so blue and cloudless it doesn't look like a

358

real sky on film. They have to make it less perfect to make it more genuine.'

He's right: the sky behind it *does* look like a sapphire sheet. So blue it's unreal.

With another loud *wheeeee* – I was not oversold – the buggy-cart whips round the corner. Suddenly, life-size brownstone townhouses appear out of nowhere, complete with rusty fire escapes, basement windows, curved doorways and bright red fire hydrants.

'New York,' Patrick explains cheerfully. 'An almost perfect replica, slightly smaller than in real life. Look.'

We all hop out of the buggy for a closer view.

'They're not actual houses,' he continues. 'They've got printed plastic bricks stuck on the front. And if you open a door . . .' He pushes open the nearest front door. Behind it is thin plasterboard coated with small ripped squares of wallpaper, just enough to show from outside the window. 'It's called a *facade*, which is French for *fake front*.'

I follow curiously behind.

'And . . . umm . . .' I get as close as possible. 'What about *The First Butterfly*? Do you know much about that film? It's a really old movie that was filmed here in 1990, and it's set in New York. I'm doing a – uh – school project on it.'

'Yeah.' Patrick considers for a second. 'I think I know it. A lame romance, some really bad acting, but a minor cult classic. Some of the scenes were shot in fake Greenwich Village, I think.'

I frown. *Ooh*, that could work.

'Hop in, folks!' Patrick climbs back into the buggy and we all dutifully follow. 'While we're driving past the Technicolor Building, I'll tell you a story about Katharine Hepburn . . .'

I stare around, fascinated. One day, this is where I'm going to be, wandering from my trailer, getting my make-up done, learning my lines, grabbing a coffee before my first take of the mor—

I sit bolt upright. A very tall man has just walked out of one of the vast hangars, talking animatedly on his phone. I'm now hanging off the back of the buggy.

'Dad! Dad! DAD!'

'Ma'am.' Patrick's head swivels. 'Ma'am, please sit down and keep your head inside the moving—'

Too late – I've already gone.

As *if* my legs aren't strong enough.

They certainly have enough power to send me zipping down the empty street and out of the clutches of Patrick, who is pegging it desperately after me.

'Ma'am!' he's yelling. 'Get back in the car! You were *distinctly told* at the start of this tour to *stay in the cart and to respect the working privacy of film-studio staff—*'

I just run faster.

Dad must recognise the sound of my pounding feet, because he suddenly freezes and spins round.

'I'm so sorry, Mr Rivers,' Patrick calls from behind me. 'I *did* tell the guests to stay in the cart, but this one wouldn't—'

With a *thud*, I wrap my arms round my father.

'It's OK,' Dad tells Patrick over my head. 'Thank

you, but I'm afraid this particular little rule-breaker happens to be mine. I got this.'

We wait for a few moments until the guide's gone and the little buggy has whizzed away, then my father bends down. 'Hope, baby, what's going on? What are you doing here? Why are you wearing a black catsuit and leather gloves when it's eighty degrees?'

Intense relief is rushing through me: *finally*, we're getting somewhere.

Don't worry, Mum. We're coming home.

'Dad,' I say quickly into his T-shirt, tightening my grip. 'Please don't be angry with me. I know you said I couldn't come, but you don't understand how important this is. There's something I have to show you, so you need to come with me right this minute.'

Without delay, I start pulling on his hand towards fake Greenwich Village.

I'll work out how to be subtle when I get there. Maybe I can get them to turn on the street lamps and play some violin music or something.

'Hope.' Dad hasn't budged and he's six foot five so I'm basically just walking on the spot while tugging on his fingers. 'Sweetheart, what are you talking about? Go where? Calm down and explain.'

Maybe it's time to stop scuttling sideways like a crab. I'm just going to say it . . .

'We're going back to the place where you first met Mum,' I explain impatiently. 'To the exact set. And then you'll remember in a sudden rush of intense romantic memories how much you miss her and how much you love her. Then you'll wrap up this film you're making and come home and Mum will leave rehab and she won't be sad or crazy any more and the newspapers will shut up and the family will be just like it used to be and nobody will leave and we'll all have our *happy ending.*'

We're *so* close. In fact, if I work really fast, Dad can probably leave this afternoon and get back in time for Mum's visiting hour yesterday.

'Please,' I beg, still tugging as hard as I can. 'Please, Dad. Let's go – let's go— We can—'

Without a word, I'm suddenly being wrapped in an enormous hug. Silently, Dad tightens his arms. Then he pulls away and bends down to look at me.

I can't work out what the expression on his face is. It doesn't seem angry or irritated or surprised or overjoyed or impressed or any interesting and complex mixture of the above.

'Baby,' he says quietly. 'Sit down for a minute.'

Then he slowly lowers himself on to a very familiar bench – taking up most of it – and pats the space next to him.

My eyes open wide. 'Is this—'

'Forrest Gump's bench?' Dad smiles with one side of his mouth. 'One of them, yes. Tom Hanks got all dressed up after the film had wrapped and sat here with a box of chocolates as a prank. Nobody at the studio even noticed, bless him.'

I sit down impatiently and glance at my watch. As fascinating as this insider information is, we don't really have time for another tour. I've already done one; we'll have to come back for the special extras at a later point.

'Hope,' Dad says slowly. 'The clothes and bits of jewellery, the ones scattered around the house every morning. They're not yours, are they?'

I nod in exasperation. '*Obviously* not.'

'And . . .' My father frowns. 'The smell . . . That weird smell on my pillow . . .'

'Mum's iconic perfume,' I explain in a *duh* voice.

'I see.' Dad smiles slightly. 'But Juliet has never worn that perfume, Hope. She was the official face of it, but she thought it stunk of old socks and used it as poop spray in the bathroom.'

Oh, for the love of—

'My God, the *song*.' Revelation has just hit my dad's face. 'Elton John. Did you think that was our song? Mine and your mom's?'

This is like pulling teeth. Why is it so difficult to trigger any of Dad's romantic memories?

'The year I thought you met,' I explain extremely slowly, as if I'm talking to a preschooler. 'Dad, why didn't you *tell* me you actually met Mum when you were fifteen?' I can feel my eyes lighting up. 'I want to hear the *whole* story, the romance, where did you first see each other, what did you say, where was your first kiss, how did you feel, what happened when the movie wrapped—'

I bet it was on a step in fake Greenwich Village, and my dad brushed away one of my mum's tears and said—

'Hope,' Dad says quietly, taking my hand. 'We've made a mess of this, and I'm sorry. We're *both* so sorry.'

I stare at him. 'Well, there's no need to be *dramatic*, Dad. You can just tell me the big love story now, but make sure you start right at the beginning because the meeting is always . . . the . . .'

I crunch to an abrupt silence. Because I suddenly know what the expression on my father's face is: it's sadness.

'So,' I say, quickly turning away and picking at one of the armrests. 'What do you mean by *one* of the benches? How many were there exactly, because—'

'Look at me, Hope.'

Reluctantly, I lift my gaze.

'At me, sweetheart. Not at my left ear lobe.'

'Whatever you're about to say,' I interrupt quickly, 'just consider how tired you are, and how hard you've been working. You know, you've *both* been tied up on these intense films in different countries, and that kind of stress can put a lot of pressure on—'

'Hope, your mother and I are getting a divorce.'

I blink. 'Nu-uh.'

'We are.'

'No, you're not. That's just what the papers say, Dad. You can't let the media rip you apart; you can't listen to them. They're just jealous singletons who are terrible at their jobs and—'

'Those *fool* journalists,' Dad sighs, rubbing his face. 'We weren't going to say anything until both the films wrapped. The plan was to sit down and explain it to all of you together, as a family. But this one ran over and the story got out before we were ready.'

I shake my head, looking down at the bench.

'So, when you say Tom Hanks got dressed up, do you mean the full cream suit with the blue tartan shirt and the socks, or the—'

'Po.' Dad's eyes get even sadder. 'I know you're very adept at shutting out the reality you don't want to face. You're exactly like your mom in that way. But you can handle the truth, sweetheart. You have to.'

'No, I don't.' I fold my arms. 'Because the *truth*, Dad, is that nothing can pull apart what is supposed to be together. Love is all that really matters. It's what lies at the heart of us. So, when you find it, you hold on to it.'

'And when you lose it,' he says gently, 'you let go.'

I stare at him.

This is crazy. This is madness. This is—

367

'You're wrong,' I say, standing up. 'All relationships have ups and downs – that's how love goes. They all have obstacles you have to overcome. That's part of the narrative. You've just lost hope, that's all. Same as Mum. But that's what *I'm* here for.'

Dad closes his eyes briefly. 'Sweetheart—'

'Don't worry, Dad. Everything's going to be fine.'

45

TUESDAY AFTERNOON: HOPE lies on her
bed in LOS ANGELES, watching a video
on the giant flat-screen television.

The video is of JAMIE and HOPE lying
in a park, her head on his chest.
JAMIE looks straight at the camera,
then leans over and kisses HOPE'S
nose. He freezes for a few seconds.

                    HOPE
        (*tapping him and laughing*)
            It's a video.

                    JAMIE
             My bad.

369

He grins and waves.

                    JAMIE (CONTINUED)
          Hey - my first big interview!

                         HOPE
          (*holding out her hand as a*
                  microphone)
          Tell us, Jamie Day, how are you
          enjoying your cheese-fest tourist
          adventuring through this nation's
                great capital city?

                         JAMIE
          It's been awesome. Check out my
          co-star. Does it get any better
          than this girl? Look at that FACE.

HOPE beams up at him, adoration written
all over her face like subtitles.

                         HOPE
          So you like it, then? Is that what
                  you're saying?

                        JAMIE
                  (*looking at her*)
              No. I'm saying I love it.

I grab the remote and rewind.

                        JAMIE
          Does it get any better than this
              girl? Look at that FACE.

Then forward.

                        JAMIE
              No. I'm saying I love it.

Then back.

                        JAMIE
                  . . . I love it.

Then I open my messages.

   It's been two days now and Sunday's message to
Jamie has two blue ticks: read but unanswered.
Although the balloon *was* very vague.

Plus Jamie's been at school, so he's obviously very busy. He must have got caught up in all the barbecues and whatever else he did yesterday. Maybe he read my text in his sleep, but *forgot* he'd read it, or thought he'd replied but hadn't. Or maybe he was so impressed with my use of emojis that he's still working out what to send back.

Deliberating, I lick my lips. Maybe I should send a different colour balloon?

My stomach flips. At the top of my phone screen it says *Jamie is online*. I stare at it for a few minutes: *Jamie is online Jamie is online Jamie is online*. Then I impulsively search 'cat' in GIFs, find an adorable tabby kitten falling asleep and toppling over, paste it in and press SEND.

The ticks go blue, then *Jamie is no longer online.* Oh God, no. What have I done?

Haha! I wasn't being passive aggressive! It was just a cute kitten! Not annoyed you haven't replied to my message from two days ago! LOL xxxx

Seconds later: *Jamie is online.*

Ticks go blue, then *Jamie is no longer online.* And, for a second, the cinema screen in my head splits in two and I can see me on one side – clutching my phone four centimetres from my nose – and him on the other side with that hard, stony expression on his face.

Which is ridiculous. He's probably just on the toilet or something.

Or, you know, mid-lunge.

Having a good day? :) Hxx

Impulsively, I press SEND.

Then I put my phone firmly down on my bedside table and wander through the silent house. Dad's gone to work already. He's attempted to talk to me a million times since he drove me home on Sunday, but I've kept my headphones in and/or faked being asleep/mid-imaginary-phone-call.

I've written a Post-it note that says:

Remember that time you were having a really bad day at work so Mum kept pulling silly faces while filming a scene until you laughed even though it took seventeen takes.

And another one:

Remember that time Mum made her entire Oscar speech about how much she loves you and how you're her rock and literally everybody in the film industry cried.

I've stuck them in Dad's leather script bag so he can find them throughout the week. At this rate, I reckon it'll take two days to break my father: we'll be home by Friday.

Remember that time Mum took you for an ice cream in Hyde Park and you told her for the first time that you loved h

My phone beeps.

Dropping the pen on the floor, I leg it into my room.

Yup. x

A kiss from Jamie – hurray! Then another *beep.*

Ha cute cat

All I need now is to subtly Segway into the right topic.

How was your bbq? How's your car doing? Is
it good? x

Jamie is typing Jamie is typing Jamie is typing Jamie
is typing Jamie is typing Jamie is typing Jamie is
typing Jamie is—

What?

OK, the groundwork is laid.

Just wondering if you're free after school some
time this week? xx

Possibly Thursday. If I don't have track.

Great! I can do Thursday! Come over when
you're done? Hxx

Jamie is typing Jamie is typing Jamie is—

Jamie is offline.

I stare at the empty screen for six or seven minutes.

Then I go to the bathroom.

Make myself a snack.

Finish writing the note to my dad.

Wander outside. Olivia, Sophia and Madison are lying by the pool again, headphones in, magazines strewn everywhere, and I try not to look too irritated.

Finally, there's a *beep*.

Sure

Relief pulses through me. Kissing my phone, I run back into the bedroom and hit *play* so the video's screening once more.

HOPE
So you like it, then? Is that what you're saying?

JAMIE
(looking at her)
No. I'm saying I love it.

Because I suddenly remembered.

Right at the beginning, Jamie said that he's an old-fashioned romantic. And that he wanted me to be myself, as much as I want to be: to live life at full volume.

So that's exactly what I'm going to do.

46

THURSDAY AFTERNOON: HOPE stands by the
infinity pool, wearing a red silk dress.
She stares wistfully over Los Angeles,
sunshine in her hair, posture, etc. etc.

There's a noise behind her.

> HOPE
> (*turning*)
> You came.

> JAMIE
> How could I not?

> HOPE
> You should know that I am a modern
> girl from a family of strong women.

There's a question I want to ask
you.

JAMIE
I already admire your sparkling
spirit.

BEEP BEEP
I blink.

HOPE
(*turning*)
You came.

BEEEEEEEEEEEEEEEEEEP

JAMIE
How could I not?

BEEP BEEP BEEP BEEP BEEP BEEP
'One second!'
As fast as I can, I grab the big wicker basket I
found in the laundry and run to the front door in
Mum's white shirt and Faith's denim shorts.

379

HOPE

(opening door)

You came.

'Are you coming or what?' Jamie shouts out of the window of his Toyota. 'I've been sitting here ages.'

'Sor—' I start, then bite my lip. *What's another word for sorry?* 'Umm, Jamie? Please can you get out of your car?'

'What? Why?'

'It's just . . .' I shift the weight of the basket. 'I've got a surprise for you.'

'Can't you give it to me in here?'

'Please?'

Scowling, Jamie switches off the engine, climbs out and frowns. 'What is it? You look pretty today, by the way.'

Glowing, I close my eyes and lean up for a kiss.

Our lips touch gently.

But it feels kind of rigid – like making out with a rock or a wall – so I open one eye. Jamie's staring over my shoulder with the glassy, blank expression fish have when they're lying on a bed of ice.

A sudden chill runs across my shoulders.

'*Soooo* . . .' I pull away and focus on revealing my surprise. 'I wanted to do something *really* special with you, a date that neither of us would *ever* forget. Something *full volume*. And I came up with something pretty awesome. Can you guess what it is?'

'I dunno . . . Shopping? Trying on lipstick? Me carrying your bags?'

'No, no!' I flinch slightly. 'You're going to *love* it, Jamie, I promise!' My hands are shaking. Nervously, I pull a set of car keys out of my shorts pocket. Then I stand on tiptoe, put my hands over his eyes, spin him round and pull them away again. '*Ta-da!*'

Jamie blinks at the yellow Lamborghini in front of us.

'I borrowed it for you,' I explain breathlessly. 'It's insured for the whole day. You s-said that you loved driving, that it was your favourite thing, so I th-thought we could take it down the Pacific Coast Highway. I've packed a picnic—'

Quickly, I hold out the laundry basket.

'We've got *all* your favourite foods,' I continue, searching through it and holding up items. 'Grapes, avocados, quinoa, kale, coconut water. I thought maybe we could drive to a nice spot, eat a picnic dinner, do whatever you want to do – and—'

Jamie's turquoise eyes haven't moved from the car in front of him.

My stomach turns over.

Why are my hands shaking?

'The car belongs to my dad's friend and it was just sitting in the garage so—'

'For me?' Jamie says slowly. 'To drive?'

I nod. 'Uh-huh.'

'For the whole afternoon?'

'Mmm.'

'Anywhere I want?'

'Of course! I mean, ideally with me in the car too.'

Silence.

Please don't be angry. Please don't be—

'Hope.' Jamie's entire face lights up. 'This is *incredible*. What a sweet gesture. And *of course* I want you to come too.'

I let all my breath out at once. 'You really like it?'

'Absolutely!' Jamie beams and puts a hand on either side of my face. 'You're just something else, you know that, Hope Valentine?'

382

It's everything I can do not to punch the air. That line is back to its original, positive emphasis.

I did it!

Now I've just got to wait until the coconut water is cracked open, the grapes are out and then I'll subtly pop the question—

'Would you look at that?' Jamie cries, clicking a button so the roof starts to open. 'Isn't that the coolest thing in the world? Whoa, listen to that engine! A six-point-five-litre V12, eight-hundred horsepower, zero to sixty miles per hour in two point nine seconds!'

I beam as the sunlight pours over our faces.

'Awesome!' I smile. 'Although, quick question. How do they get eight hundred horses into a car?'

Jamie laughs loudly and it's so surprising I suddenly realise it's the first time I've heard him do it since I got to America. A wave of bliss washes over me.

'Hey.' Jamie turns to me. 'Give me a kiss.'

Holding my breath, I lean slowly towards him, staring at the countless shades of blue in his eyes, the white-gold hairs across his forehead, the freckles across his nose and the delicate Cupid's bow. As our lips touch, Jamie's golden hand goes round the back of my head and his tongue briefly touches mine. My stomach abruptly clenches.

I kiss him back, eyes tightly shut.

Huh, Mercy says in my ear. *Wonder what he's staring at this time? Probably the handbrake.*

Get out of my head, Mer! You are not invited.

Whatever, my sister snarks. *As if I'd* want *to come on a date with you and your terrifying Ken doll. Get a grip, muppet.*

Then she vanishes again.

'Right.' Jamie grins as we pull away out of the driveway. 'Let's get this show on the road.'

47

HOPE and JAMIE drive through HOLLYWOOD in an open-top sports car. Spiky palm trees and tropical flowers line the highway, soft wind tugs at their hair, sunshine pours across their skin, the engine of the yellow Lamborghini purrs.

HOPE leans back in her seat, staring at the cloudless sky: an unreal, dazzling blue. Then she rolls her head to the left and watches the sea glitter as the car races along the winding road. Hazy mountains slowly materialise as if they're the painted backdrop of a movie.

HOPE VALENTINE is SO VERY HAPPY.

This is it.

I have *found* my movie trailer.

It's me and Jamie, sunglasses on, wind in our hair, sunshine on our skin, speeding smoothly down the Pacific Coast Highway towards San Diego. The scenery is sublime, the weather is perfect and frankly my co-star has never looked more gorgeous.

The camera focuses on our glowing faces. We glance at each other and smile – no need to speak – and the shot pulls back to focus on the open road, stretching out in front of us. The road that subtly implies that we have no obstacles any more, that we're facing our destiny together, that luck is on our side, the only way is forward, the—

Oooh, I should add a soundtrack!

Beaming, I grab my phone, click on 'God Only Knows (What I'd Be Without You)' by the Beach Boys and send it to the car stereo. I've grown very fond of these ancient hippy guys over the past week. Then I start warbling along under my breath.

'Can you not?' Jamie clicks it off again. 'Such a cliché.'

'Is it?' I pull my bare feet up on to the seat and

wrap my arms round my legs. 'Sorry, I . . . didn't realise. So . . .' Swallowing, I smile brightly. 'Did you have a nice week, Jamie? What have you been up to? Anything fun?'

'Not much.' A small shrug. 'Some surfing, hung out with Abs quite a bit, went to that barbecue, did some work for that charity I told you about. You know, the guy whose life I saved? I had this great idea about how we could diversify our resources and totally—'

'Abi?' I clear my throat. 'You saw a lot of Abi this week?'

'. . . Yup.'

He didn't have time to text you back, but he had time to see Abi 'quite a bit', Mer whispers in my ear. *Hilarious.*

'Do you . . . spend a lot of time with Abi?'

Jamie's jaw clenches so hard I'm worried his teeth are about to break. 'She's a very good friend. So, yes.'

'And she surfs too? As well as that gymnastic thing tha—'

'I told you it's called *Acroyoga*.' Jamie clicks the indicator and moves lanes. 'You know, jealousy is a very unattractive quality, Hope.' His voice is flat. 'Do I think Abi is gorgeous? Yes. Is she hilarious and smart? Yes. Would I maybe date her in the future? Yes. Am I dating her right now? No. I am currently dating you, Hope. And I *do not like* where this conversation is heading.'

My eyes open wide.

Wait – *what* did he just say?

Did Jamie just say he's *dating me*?

Has he just *officially confirmed* that We Are A Couple?

Oh my gosh, this is so unexpected. I'm completely unprepared. I don't even have the coconut water ready! There should be glasses to clink, a pink and yellow sunset, a long, tender kiss—

Not right now, though. I don't want to make him crash.

'And you should know,' Jamie continues, 'that this was a problem I had with Ella, and with Kaylee, and with Andrea . . .'

He's dating me! WE'RE DATING! We're *already* a couple! Wow, have we been a couple this whole time?

I can't believe I didn't *realise*. It was obviously so

clear it didn't need saying. It transcended words! It was an unspoken agreement between hearts and souls and—

'. . . and with Layla, and with Amelia . . .'

Should I confirm it anyway? Just for the sheer joy of hearing the words?

'. . . and with Zoe and I *do not like it.*'

Maybe I should ask him to stop the car so we can hold hands.

I blink. 'Umm, who are—'

'My ex-girlfriends.' Jamie abruptly changes lanes again. 'Ella was a model, Kaylee was a DJ, Andrea was a yoga instructor, Layla was heir to a billionaire's fortune, Amelia was an artist and Zoe . . . Well, Zoe is the first girl I was ever really in love with. And I didn't tolerate this kind of *crazy* behaviour from any of them, either.'

Mercy snorts loudly. Then she points and I can suddenly see a line of girls' heads stuck on a wall like hunting trophies with little bronze plaques underneath.

The Model

The DJ

The Yoga Instructor

The Billionairess

The Artist

The First Big Love

Thought he didn't date? my big sister laughs, giving me a thumbs up. *And ooh, look! You've made it up there too, Poodle!*

The Movie Star's Daughter

I scowl at her.

'I'm not c-crazy,' I say uncertainly, but the hard muscle in his jaw has set again. I look out at the

390

sea, then Mercy kicks me hard in the shin and forces me to turn back towards the driving seat again. *Ow.*

'Jamie . . . did I say something wrong? Are you . . . angry with me?'

'No.'

'Are you sure?'

'Yes.'

'Because . . .' His jaw is still stiff and pulsing slightly. 'I didn't mean to upset you, I was just . . . curious.'

Silence.

'It's only that . . . sometimes . . .'

Silence. Mercy kicks me again.

'It feels like it's a little bit different between us to how it was in London.'

Silence.

'So I suppose I was asking so I could understand why there's—'

'It's not different. It's exactly the same.'

'Is it?'

'Yes.'

'Are you . . . sure?'

'Yes.' He scowls. 'Although if we're being *completely* honest, Hope, *you're* pretty different to how you were when I met you. I wasn't going to say anything, but you've brought it up so there you go.'

I stare at him. 'Am I?'

'Yeah.' Jamie shakes his head and narrows his eyes. 'It's always the same pattern – I just don't get it. I meet a girl and she's amazing. Chilled, sunny, happy, funny. We have a brilliant time together. I'm totally into it. And then she just . . . *changes*.'

He flashes turquoise eyes at me.

'I've been tricked, because she's not who she pretended to be. And I'm disappointed *again*. Don't take it personally.'

I think I'm going to vomit.

'Jamie.' My voice is wobbling. 'I don't understand what I've done wrong, but I'm trying really hard. If you explain what it is, I can do something about it. I can be a better girlfriend and—'

'Whoa.' Jamie holds his hand up. 'Hope, you are *not* my girlfriend.'

And just like that the film stops, the cameras switch off and the curtains close.

'B-but you said—'

'I have *never* said we were in a relationship.'

'But—' I curl instinctively into my legs. 'OK, not a *relationship* as such, not yet, but it's . . .'

Mercy prods my arm gently this time.

'You said in London that, if I was in California, you'd date me in a hot second. You said I'd be your girlfriend so fast my head would spin. So I thought, now I'm here . . . and if I visit regularly, that maybe—'

'I didn't say that.'

I stare at him.

Am I actually going crazy?

'I am almost certain you did say that, Jamie. You said I was basically your perfect girl.'

Jamie's face has turned to stone again.

'Well, even if I did – which I didn't – *basically* is not the same as *literally*, is it?'

A wave of intense pain pulses over me.

We're here too, baby, Effie suddenly whispers, slipping her hand into mine.

The cavalry has arrived! Max announces from behind her. *Oh, did you have to pick a two-seater, Poodle? Where are we going to sit? On the bonnet?*

Quickly, I turn the other way while I attempt to control my face. I try to steady my breathing as the

393

Californian mountains rise and fall and the sea sparkles and the sunshine pours down and the palm trees whizz by and a bird soars over the—

Ow, stop kicking me, Mercy.

'Jamie, you said you were in love with me.'

'I said I was *falling* in love,' he says in a hard voice, shaking his head. 'Fall-*ing*. *ING*. It's a *process*. I didn't say I was *there* yet. Or anywhere near it. Please don't twist my words.'

There's another pulse of pain.

Surprised, I put my hand up and touch my face. It's wet. I haven't cried in years.

We've got you, Effie whispers. *All of us.*

'What's going on?' Jamie glances to the side in confusion, his lips very thin. 'What are you doing? Are you . . . crying? What do you want me to do about it, Hope? Do you want me to *lie* to you, to make you feel better? I am not your emotional Band-Aid.'

A clean sob bursts out of me. And it doesn't break Jamie to see me cry – not even one little bit, not even a fraction, not even at all.

The car stops.

I guess at some point he must have turned the

car round and driven back to Beverly Hills without me even noticing. Mercy has leapt across the boot before the engine's off.

I am going to kick this stupid douche-baguette right in the—

Not yet, Effie says, holding her back. *Po's got this.*

I'm not totally certain that I have.

'Look,' Jamie says as we sit in silence outside the house. He grabs my hand and suddenly smiles. 'We have a nice time together, don't we?'

I nod. 'Of course.'

'And who *knows* what will happen in the future? When we're older, when you live here, when I've established my career trajectory, when we're both more settled, maybe we can have a proper relationship then.'

My eyes widen. 'Really?'

'*Sure.*' Jamie's smile grows and he lifts my chin with his finger, blue eyes burning into mine. 'You're amazing, Hope. And I am going to miss you *so* much when you're gone. I'm just not emotionally available right now, you know? But let's see each other one more time before you go back to England, OK?'

I swallow. 'Absolutely.'

Jamie leans over. I freeze and he kisses me. Then we climb out of the yellow Lamborghini. With a hug, Jamie gets back into his own car and I wave goodbye cheerfully until he's disappeared out of sight.

I start stumbling up the driveway.

Hold it hold it hold it hold it hold it hold it hold it hold it—

'Hope!' Roz says as the front door swings open. 'My goodness, what's happened?'

Somebody starts to cry.

48

It's not *me*, I know that.

There's no way this wild wailing is coming from my mouth.

I've practised crying in front of a mirror, and *my* tears are beautiful. They're small, neat crystals; they trickle one at a time down my left cheek, shiny and devastating for my audience.

My eyes are eloquent and sparkling. Maybe my chin wobbles sweetly – the tragedy! – and a quiet but dignified sob catches in my throat as I turn with self-control towards a window just in time.

Mine is definitely not this ugly, raw wail of pain: an explosion of tears and saliva and snot rushing down my face and rolling into my ears. It's soaking into Roz's shoulder and trickling down my neck and dripping into my mouth and dribbling back out again until everything's loud and soggy and swollen.

This isn't me. It's not who I am. It's not what I do. Nobody ever wants to see *this*.

'That's good,' Roz says, stroking my head as I shake and splutter. I cough and make weird *uhhh uhhh uhhh* noises as I struggle to breathe. 'Good girl. Get it all out.'

I don't seem to be able to stop.

Years of water must have been stored up in my feet, because I cry and cry until my face aches. My nose is blocked and my eyes swell and my lips puff. And every time I think I'm done another wave of pain surprises me and I start all over again. It's like there's so much sadness inside me I can't hold it in any more and it's spilling everywhere.

At some point, Roz must have guided me patiently into the living room. When I finally come to, forty minutes later, I'm curled up in an armchair, covered in a soft blanket, hiccuping. At some point, I think I might have had my hair stroked because it's all fluffy and vertical at the front.

'Cookies?' Roz asks calmly as I brush it down again. 'I made double-chocolate chip and peanut butter with strawberry jam. This might be California, but nobody actually wants to live forever.'

Trying to steady my breathing, I wipe my eyes and nod.

Roz places a mug of hot tea on the tiny table in front of me, clinks a plate of massive cookies next to it and sits neatly opposite.

There's a very long silence and a lot more hiccups.

'Boy?' she says finally.

Embarrassed, I nod again and wipe my face. 'H-his name is Jamie. Y-you were r-right – the – the t-tall blond one y-you saw w-when you dropped me off. I m-met h-him in London b-before I c-c-came out here.'

'Ah, I see.'

'I th-th-th—' I take a deep breath. 'I-I think m-maybe I've wrecked everything, Roz. I think m-maybe it's o-over.' I start crying again.

'Well.' Roz sips her tea calmly. 'I'm sure that's not true. Don't be too hard on yourself, Hope. We all make mistakes sometimes.'

'N-not mistakes like this.' Chest heaving, I stick an entire cookie in my mouth and chew with claggy, breathless grunts. 'I d-don't know what I'm doing, Roz. I thought I'd b-be the perfect girlfriend, but this is all n-new to me. I didn't realise it would be so *hard to get right*.'

Another wave of pain pierces through me.

'And—' My mouth is doing that ugly crying-shape again. 'N-now I'm losing my dream guy and i-it's all my fault, Roz. I d-disappointed him. I've *changed*. I've become clingy and jealous and selfish and crazy.' Another tiny wail pops out. *'And I don't know how to make it better.'*

'He *is* a very handsome boy.' Roz takes a cookie from the plate. 'I could see that, even from the car.'

'Yes.' My face lights up. 'But he's s-so much m-more than that. Jamie's *good*. He does so much charity work, and loves whales, and swings from things, and he knows so much clever stuff. H-he's just . . .' I swallow. 'He's a-amazing and I've screwed it all u-u-up.'

I start crying into the blanket. Slowly, I calm down again. And Roz nods and asks soft questions until I've haltingly outlined every detail of how Jamie and I met: what happened in London, how I followed him out here and how I got it so wrong.

Roz is chewing thoughtfully.

'I do feel sorry for him,' she says eventually, shaking her head. 'The poor, poor guy.'

I nod, welling up once more. 'I *know*.'

'I mean, making him go on a date he wasn't even interested in. After all those dates in London, with you dragging him round the city, forcing him to do whatever you wanted, day after day, thinking only of yourself—'

'Oh no.' I wipe my nose on my wrist. 'No, those dates were Jamie's idea. I've lived in London all my life. I've already been on the London Eye, like, six times.'

'Ah.' Roz lifts her eyebrows. 'But you probably complained and rolled your eyes at it. I bet you gave the poor guy a real hard time . . .'

'Not at all.' A vigorous shake of my head. 'He was so excited to be in London I pretended I hadn't done any of it before. And it was so much fun because he was so happy.'

A sudden wave of homesickness and my eyes fill again.

I miss London.

'OK,' Roz says quietly. 'I understand. But after he told you right at the start that he was leaving in a week's time and laid the whole situation out so clearly—'

'I genuinely don't remember that. Swear on my life.'

'A very easy conversation to forget, I'd imagine. Except then, of course, Jamie asks you to keep things light and casual so nobody gets the wrong idea and there you go with all your gifts and compliments and emotional declarations . . .'

'But they weren't me,' I explain earnestly. 'At least, not to start with. That's what makes it so confusing. Jamie was the one pushing it faster and faster, and I was just trying to . . . keep up. You know, go at the same speed as him. Except I obviously misunderstood, because now he seems to think I'm . . . *insane*. And maybe I am. I'm certainly starting to *feel* insane.'

'Well, you did follow him across the Atlantic.' Roz nibbles on another cookie and leans back in her chair, watching me calmly through lowered eyelids. 'And after he'd ended things so cleanly with no mixed messages in London.'

'*Exactly*,' I say, shoving my third cookie into my mouth. 'That's my point *exactly*.'

There's a silence while I chew.

'Except,' I add, 'he did also say that he wanted me out here and that he missed me. And he said that he was falling in love with me and it was only circumstances stopping us from being a couple. So I just – you know. Changed the circumstances.'

'And you tried to surprise him by turning up unannounced.' Roz shakes her head. 'When he actually had other plans, much like you did in London. Put yourself in his shoes, Hope. How would *you* have felt if it was the other way round?'

I blink. 'Really happy. That's why I did it.'

'But then you start asking questions about the other girl he's talking about constantly, even though he's *told* you that he loves you—'

'Fall-*ing*,' I correct quickly. 'It's, like, a . . . grey scale of love, and he was actually at the . . . other end of it. You know. Quite far from love itself. It was another misunderstanding on my part.'

'Ah. Well, that *does* clear things up. I mean, what's love if not a moderately sloped gradient you can slip back down at any given moment? More tea?'

Humming, Roz boils the kettle as I stare at the wall.

'Do you know the worst thing?' she says, handing me another cup of tea and sitting down again. 'It sounds like you weren't really this way before you met Jamie. So I guess you must have saved all of the unhinged behaviour just for him, much like all those other crazy girls he's been with. I mean, what were the chances?' Roz pauses for a few seconds. 'Like, seriously. That boy has *such* bad luck.'

'He says he's drawn to broken people.'

'My goodness, what a hero.' Roz smiles. 'But it's not too late, Hope! I still think there's a solution. I really do. When are you seeing him next?'

I sit forward, heart lifting. 'In a few days? Maybe?'

'Well.' She claps her hands together. 'I've got quite a few boring errands to run tomorrow, so why don't you keep me company? Your dad's busy in the studio, fixing that continuation problem. And you'd be a huge help. Plus, it'll give us plenty of time to work out our next step.'

A bolt of hope shoots across my chest. 'Really? You honestly think there's still a chance for us?'

'Absolutely.' Roz smiles. 'We'll figure out what to do together.'

49

I take the longest bath of my entire life.

Roz lights dozens of vanilla-fragranced candles and puts them round the edge of the sunken marble tub, then pours in so much bubble bath that it looks like the top of a lemon-meringue pie. I soak for two whole hours, and once I'm out – wrapped in fluffy warm towels – I'm so sleepy and wrinkled I'm like a little yawning raisin.

'Right,' Roz says as I crawl into bed and shuffle under the covers. She pulls the duvet up to my chin. 'Sleep for as long as possible, please. Twelve or thirteen hours, fourteen if you want to be a champ.'

Then she starts tucking the duvet under the mattress, all the way round the bed like a pie.

I stare at her sleepily. *What is she doing?*

'Roz,' I say, eyes drifting. 'Thanks for your help,

but I'm nearly sixteen years old. I don't need tucking i—'

It's midday when I wake up.

Roz is already waiting in the dining room. On the table is an enormous brunch: a jug of orange juice, a vat of coffee, croissants, eggs, bacon, jam, peanut butter, maple syrup.

'Sit,' she commands as I stare at it. 'Eat. I want it all gone, please. If the Californian government find out it's not kale and grapes, they'll take us both straight to federal prison.'

I have literally never been this hungry. What have I been eating over the last few weeks? Have I been eating? Did I just completely forget food and drink existed? At what point did I start surviving purely off air and sunshine without even noticing?

Unbearably starving, I grab a piece of bacon and stuff it straight into my mouth.

'Sit down,' Roz laughs. 'And chew – you're not an alligator.' Then she sticks a neon-yellow Post-it on the table next to me. 'Your dad left this for you before he went to work. He's had to leave early again and he's sorry, but he should be done by the weekend. So just hold on a few more days.'

I look at the note:

Remember that time Dad was blown away by how kind his youngest daughter is, and how much he loves her xxx

My eyes well up again.

What is wrong with me? Where is all this salt water coming from?

'Cool,' I nod, carefully folding the note up and putting it in my pocket. 'Sure, whatever.'

With a tiny smile, I polish off everything on the table. Then I start looking round for more food.

'*Soooo*—' *Oooh, brioche!* 'I was just thinking, Roz. The thing with Jamie is he doesn't like casual people, but he doesn't like intense people, either. So maybe I should back off, give him some space, not text for a while, come across as more aloof—'

'Hmmm, that might work.' Roz nods as we wander into the sunshine towards her dusty grey car. 'Let's ponder over it as we run these errands, shall we?

I'm afraid our first stop is The Grove mall so I can source a gift for my friend's daughter. Something fashionable. It's out of my comfort zone – as you can see from my awesome khaki shorts – so I'm going to need your help.'

'Mall?' My stomach starts to fizz violently. 'We're going . . . *shopping*?'

I haven't been shopping in—

Have I *ever* been shopping?

I went once or twice with Mum when I was little, but the paparazzi followed us so she changed her mind and brought me home again. I don't have my own credit card yet (such a shame) so online is out too. My version of *shopping* is breaking into my sisters' rooms, seeing what fits best and sneaking it out again.

'Umm,' I swallow, heart hammering. *Be cool be cool be cool.* I lean effortlessly on the car door. 'Oh yeah, I don't mind shopping, I guess, maybe, for a bit. I mean, no pain, no game, right?'

Shopppppppiinnnnnnngggggggg.

'No pain no game indeed,' Roz smiles, turning on the engine.

★

The Grove is nothing like anything I've ever seen. It's outdoors, with pretty fountains and statues and cute little tables with parasols lining the sunny streets. Every building is a unique, beautiful design – a tower or a castle or a glass box – and each is also a shop.

It's exactly how I imagine Disney World is, except way better because instead of massive mice there are shoes and clothes and earrings and make-up and handbags you can take home with you. Maybe *this* is the happiest place on earth.

'Oooh!' I say three hours later. 'What about this?'

Roz and I have been wandering slowly, carefully exploring every shop we find – Barneys, Nordstrom, Banana Republic, Sephora – and we've managed to find her friend's daughter a really nice cheekbone highlighter. We also found me one too, plus a denim jumpsuit, a pair of Nike trainers, a new coat, my very own MAC palette, suede flats and a whole new moisturising system.

Platinum is just not the right metal for my skin type.

'I love it!' Roz nods approvingly at the dress I'm holding up. It's short and red and blue and green and purple and blue, which sounds gross, but I promise you it is a thing of beauty and wonder. 'I'm not sure if it'll fit my friend's daughter, though. Could you try it on for me so I can see?'

I beam widely. It's *so* lucky I'm exactly the same size and height as whatever-her-name-is.

'Sure.' I shrug, hopping into a changing room. 'On it.'

Then I come out and stand in front of the mirror and my chest pings with happiness. The dress isn't neon Lycra sports gear. It's not loaned designer and it's not black. It isn't too big, or too small, or too long. It's not Mercy, Faith or Mum: it's bright and happy.

It's . . . *me*.

'We'll take it, please.' Roz smiles at the assistant. 'I'm not completely sure if this is my friend's daughter's style, Hope, so you might have to keep this one until I've checked with her mom.'

Yes yes yes—

'Oh,' I say coolly, putting a hand on my hip. *Be the Orange, Hope.* 'Yeah. I mean, if I absolutely have to.'

Shopppinnngggggg.

Arms now laden with shopping bags, Roz and I keep wandering. 'We used to do this all the time when I was your age,' she tells me as we each chew on a red liquorice stick. 'Me and my buddies. We'd hang out here after school, try on lipsticks, eat cheesecake and maybe go see a terrible movie. What about you?'

'Oh,' I say, nodding. 'Yeah. Me too! I mean, my school is in the library at home so . . . But I do totally try on lipsticks and eat cheesecake and watch movies, though.'

'With your sisters?'

'Absolutely.' I nod fervently. 'Almost always. Sometimes.' I shuffle a bag on my arm. 'Now and then. I mean, when they're around. Although . . . Effie's got a boyfriend and Mercy's a bit of a party animal. And Max isn't really interested in that stuff because he's nearly twenty. So . . . it's usually just me.'

A short silence.

'At least you've got that lovely huge mansion in Richmond.' Roz smiles gently. 'All to yourself. I've seen photos. It's *incredible*: all those big rooms and beautiful grounds. There must be so much to do!'

'Absolutely!' I smile, perking up. '*So* much to do. It's *so* fun, and *so* pretty, and – and—' I pause for a few moments. 'I mean, it is quiet a lot of the time. And empty. Sometimes I can go literally days and days and days without seeing or speaking to another human being.'

Another silence.

'But that's completely fine,' I add quickly. 'There's only three months left to go so I've had time to prepare properly.'

Roz's eyebrows lift. 'Three months until what?'

'Until I turn sixteen and my *real* life starts.' I breathe out with a familiar flash of excitement. 'I'm not sure how it'll happen exactly, but when it does it's going to be *brilliant*.'

'That must be very reassuring.' Roz smiles and clicks open her car boot to start loading the bags with my – I mean her friend's daughter's – things in them. 'When I was a teenager, I didn't have a clue what I wanted to do with my future.' She grimaces. 'My parents were both dentists and I have a phobia of teeth and blood and . . . dentists, sadly.'

I giggle.

'I guess I've always known,' I explain

sympathetically. 'I'm going to be a great Hollywood acting legend, just like my mum, my grandma and my great-grandma. I'm a Valentine, you see, so it's kind of figured out for us.'

'Very handy.' Roz grins. 'Wow, all that time I spent trying to work out who I was and what I loved. Worrying about what I wanted my life to look like. You know, Hope, this is so embarrassing . . . but I actually used to go down to the fortune-teller machines on Santa Monica Pier and get my fate printed out on chits of paper. To see if they could give me a pointer as to what direction to take. Some comfort. I don't know . . . support? Ridiculous, huh?'

'Yeah,' I laugh. 'I mean, how are *machines* going to know? I tend to use horoscopes. That kind of knowledge is usually reserved for the zodiac and the universe and the internet.'

Roz gazes steadily at me over the top of the car roof.

'And yet somehow you've managed to escape all of that teenage angst,' she says in a soft voice. 'All that chaos. All that worry. All that mess. All those decisions and choices.'

'Yes.' I nod. 'I am very, very lucky.'

My eyes are abruptly full of tears again and I have zero idea why.

'Sorry.' I turn away quickly and brush my face. 'I'm not normally like this, I promise. I'm normally a really upbeat person. It's, like, my thing.'

We climb into the car.

With a shake of my head, I clear my throat, rearrange my features and start going through the shopping bag in my hand. *Oooh, my new eyeshadow palette.* I think when I get home I'm going to start with a neutral base, then put that light blue one on the lid, then a dark navy cut-in and a cat's eye of this liquid liner so that—

'You know,' Roz says as she taps the steering wheel thoughtfully. 'Sometimes I think happiness is overrated.'

Blinking, I look up. 'Huh?'

'Well, maybe happiness is somewhat like a road. And maybe we get so focused on the stretch directly ahead of us, we forget that sadness and pain and anger and fear are the signposts, telling us which direction to go. They're not much fun to look at. Sometimes it feels like they're spoiling the view. But we need them there to stop us driving the wrong way.'

I stare at Roz for a few seconds, trying to work out what she's saying.

'Where does the road go?'

Roz laughs and turns the car engine on.

'God only knows.' She pushes her glasses up her nose. 'That's probably what makes it oh so difficult to navigate.'

50

Roz runs the best errands in the *world*.

With a boot full of shopping, she insists we stop off at a swanky restaurant in the centre of Hollywood because she needs to 'check out the menu for a friend's birthday party next week'. I choose steak and fries and also lobster ravioli: they're declared very suitable.

Then – because *another* friend likes ice cream, but is apparently super fussy about where she gets it from – we drive all the way to Malibu to test three scoops of Italian gelato. I have strawberry, coconut and cantaloupe, which I originally thought was one of those little deer that lives in the desert, but turns out to be a kind of melon.

After that, we have to survey a luxury spa.

Yet *another* of Roz's friends needs to make sure that the facilities are up to scratch: pool, sauna, steam room, fluffy white towels, bubbly Jacuzzi situated in a beautiful rooftop garden in the centre of the city, etc.

It takes me nearly a full day to realise what's going on.

It's only as we're sitting with our feet dangling in the rooftop Jacuzzi that evening, sipping fizzy orange juices and watching the sun go down over Los Angeles, that it finally hits me. Roz doesn't have *friends*. We're running errands for *celebrity movie-star clients*, but she can't tell me which ones without breaking confidentiality.

Which – because I am also a very discreet professionalist – I will respect and would never, ever even dream of asking her who they are—

'Reese Witherspoon?' I lean forward. 'Do you work for Reese? I promise you, Roz, I am the *sold* of discretion. I will never tell the newspapers for as long as I live.'

The deer ice cream was so for her, wasn't it?

'I'm not able to say, Hope.' Roz smiles modestly and sips her orange juice. 'Or I'd never be employed in this town again. Hollywood's a funny place, isn't it? I've lived in LA my entire life, but I'm still not sure I entirely understand the appeal of the movie industry.'

I stare at my father's movie secretary in amazement.

Just when I was thinking how cool Roz is for somebody my parents' age who wears shorts with multiple pockets in them, she comes out with an unfathomable comment like that.

'You don't like *films*?'

'I don't mind the movies.' She shrugs, watching me carefully. 'I've seen a few of your dad's, obviously – they're excellent. But the unholy fuss people make? The adulation? The *frenzy*? I'm not sure I totally get it.'

I don't know how to – I can't even – what do I say that will—

How do I even *begin* to explain?

Putting my drink down, I stare at Los Angeles – dusty cityscape glowing beneath us – and then at the sky for a few minutes. I've finally caught my first Californian sunset: pale lilac blue, shot with golden slices of yellow, pink, peach and red.

'Movies are life,' I say finally. 'Except better. They're the beautiful bits, the happy bits, the good bits, the kind bits. And you get to *choose* them. Even if it's just for a couple of hours, you get to pick the life you want. You can take out all the parts you don't like, pause them, rewind them, fast-forward them. Play the bits you love over and over again. Stop them when you need to. Look away when it gets too hard.'

I pause and stare back at the sunset. Something at the bottom of my chest is starting to hurt.

'I understand,' Roz nods, sipping her drink. 'The ability to edit a life must be incredibly appealing.'

Then she looks straight at me. 'But I wonder what would happen if you didn't?'

I don't know if that's a real question or not.

It might be one of those rhetory-thingies Mr Gilbert taught me about, that sounds like a question but actually isn't. But it sticks in my head for the rest of that night and all of the next day anyway.

Mainly because I don't know the answer.

I've always turned my life into a film: always scripted, tweaked and paused it whenever I needed to. I've always known how I want it to go.

And I've always switched it off when I didn't like what was happening and rerun it when I did. Always lingered on the happy bits and closed my eyes through the parts that weren't.

I'm not entirely sure what would happen if I turned it off. If the screen in my head went dark and the cameras powered down completely.

I'm not sure what I'd see.

The next day, Dad is at the studio again so I have the house to myself once more. And – instead of keeping myself busy with Sophia and Olivia and Madison or Computer – I impulsively grab Mercy's black halter-neck bikini and head outside to the swimming pool.

My phone beeps just as I get to the edge.

I hesitate for a few seconds. Then I point my hands over my head and dive in. The water is surprisingly cold, but, as I swim up and down the sparkling turquoise pool, I start to feel warm and calm and strong. As if I'm being cleaned from the outside in, in the same way crying cleaned me from the inside out.

And I begin to wonder . . . what *would* happen if I tried to see things as they actually are, and not as I want them to be? What would happen if I took the filter off and looked at the world as it is instead of as *I* am?

What if the sky was more real with clouds in it and the facade came tumbling down?

Would it even be a life worth watching?

Forty minutes later – when my legs and arms are aching and my lungs are exhausted – I pull myself, dripping, out of the pool. Then I push Olivia off one of the sunloungers (she is properly doing my head in), perch on the end and grab my phone.

There are three messages.

Hey! So it turns out I'm free tomorrow after all, fancy a hike? Meet at 4? Looking forward to it! Jx

Hello?

God you're so sensitive fine be like that

My stomach twists sharply.

You want us to come with you? Effie whispers in my ear. *I know you're not really talking to us right now, but we could probably do with the exercise.*

Yeah, Max agrees, stretching. *You're not answering any of our real-life messages and it's getting quite cramped inside your head, Poodle.*

I'm bored, Mercy sighs. *There's nothing to do in here – your brain sucks.*

I think about it for a few seconds. On one hand, it would be nice to have my siblings with me for advice and support and completely unnecessary insults. On the other, they wouldn't actually be there . . . because in reality they're thousands of miles away and – much like Sophia, Madison, Olivia and my oil-painting pal, Elaine – these versions are literally the products of my overactive imagination.

I want to see what it's like when I turn that off.

'Thanks, guys,' I say, patting my sopping curls with a towel. 'But I think I've got this.'

Quickly, I type back:

Hey! Sorry, I was swimming! That sounds great! Send me the address and I'll meet you there! Hope xx

Roz walks on to the terrace with a paper bag in hand.

'Lunch!' she calls, holding it up. 'Your father should be back in time for dinner. He's given orders for pepperoni pizza and ice cream with his favourite youngest daughter.'

I smile: pretty sure that's me.

'Hey, Roz?' I glance at my phone again. 'We never really got round to talking about Jamie. You know, what I should do to make it better?'

'Oh, that.' Roz nudges her glasses. 'Well, I'm not sure you really need my advice, Hope. Keep your eyes open and look for the signs.' She smiles. 'And not just the ones you find in a newspaper.'

51

'. . . and this girl who looks like a rat, seriously she's all teeth and nose, she's been brought into the charity, but only because her parents are friends with the boss. It is just so unfair when I've been putting all the hard work in. I'm way more talented, plus, don't forget, I saved the boss's life! You'd think he'd be a bit more grateful, but *noooo* . . . I think it's more—'

'Hey there!' An older couple in I HEART LOS ANGELES T-shirts amble past us. 'There's the greatest view up at the top! *What* a day for the walk! Enjoy, you two!'

'Thanks so much!' Jamie calls, waving cheerfully. As soon as they've gone, he says: 'Check out the gross furry overspill on that guy's shorts. Though in fairness they probably don't come in his size, hahaha.'

We've been walking for over half an hour now.

The steep, dusty path winds through the mountains that curve behind Los Angeles. With every step, the scenery gets prettier – the landscape melting into a blue haze – but Jamie hasn't noticed any of it.

'You know,' he adds, striding ten metres ahead of me, 'I did tell you we were coming on a hike, Hope. What possessed you to dress like that? I don't know who you're trying to impress all the time.'

I look down at my bright, colourful new dress and silver pumps.

Me. I'm trying to impress *me*.

'Peanut-butter jam cookie?' I take one out of my bag. 'They're home-made.'

'Are you kidding?' Jamie grabs the cookie out of my hand and throws it into the bushes. 'You shouldn't be eating trash like that, either. They've done loads of studies: sugar totally damages brain cells, impairs body function and accelerates the ageing process. I *personally* stay away from it.'

I pull another one out of my bag and take a big bite.

'Fine,' Jamie sighs. 'Ignore me. I'm only looking out for your *health and well-being*, Hope.'

Then he starts powering off up the hill, arms pumping, toned, muscled legs shining in the sun, SAVE THE TURTLES T-shirt rippling, golden hair sparkling. I'm trailing behind him like a panting puppy on a lead. I tilt my head to the side slightly. Is there a tiny chance that he highlights his hair?

'Jamie?' I'm getting seriously out of breath. 'Please . . . could you . . . slow down? For a second? My legs aren't as . . . long as yours, it's really hot and quite steep—'

He pauses with an elaborate eye-roll.

'You Brits don't do much exercise, do you? Don't take it personally, but as a nation you're pretty lazy. This is just a casual walk for me. You should see how quickly I can climb Half Dome in Yosemite. I can do it in, like, six hours. Without refreshment breaks.'

An unexpected bubble of laughter pops out of my mouth.

'What?' His mouth has gone thin again. 'What are you laughing at? Are you laughing at me? I'd like to see *you* climb a mountain with only a rope and the strength of your upper arms.'

Jamie starts pounding up the hill again.

'And you may recall,' he adds over his shoulder, 'we have to walk faster because you were late. Because of you, we are *running out of sunshine*.'

Six minutes. There was a lot of LA traffic and I was *six minutes* late.

Puffing, I run to catch up. 'So I was thinking—'

'Me too.' Jamie nods. 'It's fascinating how influential your family is. You've handed down that privilege to each other through generations of nepotism and— Are you listening?'

With a concerted effort, I jog to his side again. I was actually noticing for the first time how tight his little blue shorts are. Do they *have* to be that tight? Does his T-shirt *have* to always have a good cause on it? How many turtles do T-shirts save?

'I'm listening!'

'But acting. How hard can it really be? You could do *so* much good with that fame and power. So, I was thinking I should have a go at it. I mean, I'm here in Los Angeles and I *was* asked to be a model. Twice actually. Obviously, I said no, because I have got so much more to offer than just standing in front of a camera.'

I blink at his back three times.

'So maybe acting could be my *springboard*, you know? I'm thinking a film, for starters. A way to get the really important causes heard. Then I could – oh, you're kidding me.'

I'm currently bent over at the waist, chest heaving, my hands on my hips.

'G . . . g . . . give . . . me . . . a . . .'

'*Fine.*' Jamie waits on the path ahead, impatiently tapping his foot. 'But once it starts getting dark we'll have to head back down again, whether we reach the top or not, because there are *mountain lions.*'

Another giggle pops up so I swallow hard.

'And – umm.' What was he talking about again? 'So . . . does . . . being famous appeal to you?'

Jamie's eyes are blue glass marbles; it is *amazing* how fast that happens.

'And what exactly is that supposed to mean?'

'Being famous.' I take a couple of deep breaths and wipe sweat from my forehead. 'You know, having literally every single thing that happens to you or your family spread around the media for the entertainment of strangers. Because—'

'You think that's what I want? That I want fame?'

Jamie looks furious. 'This isn't about *being famous*, Hope. It's about *helping others*, making *art*, being *part of a team*—'

'OK.' I hold up a hand. 'Honestly, it's a question I've only just started asking myself.'

'A question for you maybe.' His jaw is tense. 'We all know how much attention you need. You and your whole family. But I can't even believe that it would cross your mind for me. We've known each other nearly a month now, Hope, but you clearly don't know me at all.'

We stare at each other in silence.

It feels like I have butterflies in my stomach again, and they're fluttering, trembling, flickering around my—

No.

NO.

Turn the happy filter off, *Hope.*

This isn't fluttering. It's not flickering. They're not even butterflies. They're tiny monsters. Thudding and clanging, banging and clawing, biting and scratching with sharp teeth and nails.

Jamie's right. I *don't* know him.

Not really.

Not in any way that matters.

All I know for sure is that he's American and handsome and six-packed and a Gemini. And – very much like the famous twins of the zodiac – he appears to have two faces. One is lovely and bright and charming, and the other is a hard stone wall that scares the living daylights out of me.

And I have no idea which Jamie I'm going to get at any given moment.

All I've been seeing is the boy I wanted. In exactly the same way that I always pick the horoscope I like best and how I crossed out the parts of the compatibility test that suggested it might not work out between us.

Except now I know they're not happy, excited butterflies in my stomach any more, and I don't want to keep pretending they are.

'You're right,' I say finally, breathing out.

Jamie's face softens, the mask flipping again.

'I know,' he smiles warmly. 'Don't take it so hard. Right, I can't continue at this slow pace. I need to stretch my legs. See you at the top.'

And off he goes.

It's so quiet.

All around me, California sprawls lazily across hazy, jagged hills into the sea. Groups, couples and solo hikers are chatting, arguing, laughing, sweating, jogging, shouting and jumping to make cute aerial shots. Scattered across the view I can see tiny churches with miniature graveyards, rolling golf courses, farm fields with electricity pylons marching across them, tidy vineyards, roads snarled with endless traffic and towering high-rises.

And, for the first time possibly ever, I don't edit anything.

I don't move the camera away from the crumpled energy-bar packet on the ground or fire the girl picking her nose to my left. I don't fix the gross, smelly sweat under my armpits in post-production, or Photoshop my hair to look shinier. I don't delete the spiralling electrical cables running from an enormous, ugly tower over my head; I don't make the grass greener, or pretend it's a glorious sunset when it isn't.

I don't ignore the pain in my chest or the sting in my eyes.

And I don't shut out the signposts telling me which way to go.

For once, I force myself to see it all. The good and the bad, the ugly and the beautiful, the bright and the dark, the bits I like and the bits I don't.

Then I take a huge breath and keep walking. I round the bend towards an immense six-metre steel pylon that completely ruins the view. And I finally see giant white letters perched on scaffolding in the prickly bushes:

ᗡOOWY⅃⅃OH

A helicopter buzzes overhead.

'*There* you are,' a voice says from several metres above me. 'Check out this view!'

I look up. Jamie's on all fours, one arm stretched

out in front, the opposite leg stretched out behind. As I carefully climb over the last few rocks, I gaze at his golden hair, his scattered freckles, his sapphire eyes. How insanely leading-man good-looking he is.

'What are you doing?'

'Yoga,' he says, lowering smoothly on to his stomach and stretching upwards. 'I like to do yoga when I'm in inspirational places. It really helps me to *de-stress*, you know? Hang on.'

I wait while Jamie stands up, then bends over to touch his toes. Then he reaches to the sky. Bends to a strong plank, then into a downward dog. Smoothly, he bounces into a squat, arms above his head.

Then into a tree position.

Some kind of bird.

And a muscle in my mouth starts to twitch.

'There,' Jamie says eventually, bounding up and clapping. 'All done.' He reaches out, takes my hand and pulls me towards him. 'Isn't this the most awesome view, Hope? Aren't you glad I thought to bring you here?'

Then he puts a practised hand under my chin and leans towards me, blue eyes focused on mine.

With a *click*, I feel it.

HOPE and JAMIE stand on top of the Hollywood Hills, behind the world-famous HOLLYWOOD sign. As the sun sets in front of them, the sky is on fire.

JAMIE
(*passionately*)
Kiss me.

I put a hand on his chest.

I'm biting my bottom lip as hard as I can, but it's no good. I just keep picturing his bottom poking in the air on top of a mountain – little blue shorts shining in the sun, sports socks, turtle T-shirt tucked in – and my nose-twitching is out of control.

Oh my days, *the monkey bars.*

Jamie, swinging backwards and forwards with that smug, self-important look on his face. His sulky expression under that bright red MEGA HOLLYWOOD TOURS cap: furious and selfish, like a petulant six-year-old. How many times he referred *to himself* as a hero, while also pushing a young kid off the unicycle in Covent Garden so he could show everyone how to do it properly.

My shoulders start shaking.

All the pompous monologues, the nasty criticism of everything that isn't him, the total lack of empathy or compassion, the lies, the alarming inconsistencies, the sugar-coated insults, the self-styled chivalry and hypocrisy and vanity, the – *ahahahahaha* – the *push-ups*.

How much of a *nice guy* he is, how many *lives* he seems to save constantly, all the good causes he supports so he can tell everyone he supports good causes at literally three-second intervals.

A loud snort bursts out of my nose.

Oh oh oh oh – that stupid park video I've been watching over and over again. Jamie wasn't gazing adoringly up at me, was he?

He was gazing adoringly at *himself on the screen*.

'What?' Jamie says as I abruptly cover my face with my hands. 'For the love of – what's wrong with you this time? No way, are you *crying again?*'

I squeeze my lips together, but it's too late.

My nostrils flare out of control and I'm giggling hysterically. Jamie takes a step backwards.

He didn't get back on the train to ask me out. He got back on because he forgot his coat.

He never told me he was leaving because it didn't matter if it hurt me. He had zero intention of ever seeing me again.

All through those first dates in London, he was play-acting the hero I was so desperately looking for, not caring if it broke my heart.

Jamie is who he has always been. The signs were there from the beginning, I was just reading the wrong ones.

Hahahahaha – the push-ups the push-ups the push-ups.

'Oh gosh,' I whimper with wet eyes, looking up and trying to catch my breath. 'Oh my goodness. I-I—'

Nope. Just started giggling again.

'You're insane,' Jamie tells me with aggressive certainty. 'IN. SANE. *Why* do I always pick the nutjobs? What is it about me that seems to only attract crazy girls?'

I laugh a little harder. *Push-up, grunt, clap!*

'Oh, Jamie,' I chuckle, finally wiping my eyes. 'You don't date crazy girls. *You turn the girls you date crazy.*'

He stares at me blankly.

Because it suddenly hits me: maybe my ancient

friend Elaine didn't defy the curse to shatter the mirror and see her knight. Maybe she just wanted into the real world and Lancelot was the only way to get there. Maybe – at the very end – she didn't give a rat's bottom whether he thought she had a lovely face or not.

And maybe, when that boat turned the bend in the river, the Lady of Shalott opened her eyes, sat up, flicked off the flowers and jumped out.

To start her brand-new life without him.

'I don't understand what's going on,' Jamie says slowly, face hardening dramatically. 'Are you having some kind of . . . nervous breakdown?'

The mask has flipped again. It's quite amazing, really: two entirely different faces and I don't think I really like either of them.

'What's going on,' I beam happily, 'is you're a douche-baguette, this romance is over and I'm going home.'

He stares. 'Are you dumping me?'

'Oh my goodness, *no*.' I shake my head, patting him on those rock-hard abs. 'Of *course* not, Jamie. I can't dump you, because we were never going out. Remember?'

Grinning, I turn and start walking at my own sweet pace back down the hill. The air is fresh, the flowers are blooming and everything's so beautiful, so bright, so full of hope.

'You're unstable!' Jamie shouts after me. 'Girls, man! You're all as bad as each other!'

Still laughing, I give him a thumbs up over my shoulder without looking back.

It is a doggy-dog world indeed.

53

And that's it, film's over.

Thanks for coming; you've been a wonderful audience. If you could make your way out quietly while the credits roll, take your rubbish with you and don't forget to leave a five-star review on the—

'. . . TALKING ABOUT! SHE HAS EVERY-THING! EVERYTHING A YOUNG GIRL COULD POSSIBLY—'

Frowning, I let myself into Dad's borrowed house.

Then I quietly put Mercy's cookie-crumb-filled handbag on the floor. Dad appears to be yelling at someone in the living room and I'm guessing it's not the pizza-delivery boy. Silently, I slip my silver pumps off.

Don't leave just yet; it looks like there's a little more story left to tell.

'Michael,' Roz says calmly from the other side of the wall. 'You're being ridiculous and you know it.'

'I do *not* know it!' Dad continues yelling. 'There's a swimming pool! There's a mini-spa! There's a wall-sized television and a – a bathtub that sinks into the—' He slows to a stop. 'OK, yeah, I am being ridiculous. What were you saying again?'

'That none of those things matter, right? Money, designer clothes, fancy houses, swimming pools. Hope is fifteen years old. What she needs is support and love and security, especially after everything that's—'

'*You think I don't know that? You think I don't—*' Another pause. 'OK, I'm yelling again. Look, Roz, I know all this. Hope *has* love and support, but you have to understand that what with the divorce and the film demands and the budget and the—'

'What I *understand*, Mike, is that your youngest daughter has no friends. At all. Apart from a talking house, a woman in a painting from the nineteenth century and three imaginary mean girls who I can only assume she picked out of an American high-school movie.'

Blinking, I take a tiny step closer.

Olivia? Madison? Sophia? You're not mean girls, are you? I just thought you were super sassy and cool.

'What are you talking about?' Dad snaps defensively. 'Of *course* my youngest daughter has friends. There's her sisters and brother – that's three. And—'

'Friends who aren't related to her by blood,' Roz sighs. 'Ones she's chosen. For herself.'

'Well, then, she has *loads*. There's . . .' A pause. 'Well, there's . . .' A pause. 'How about . . .' Another longer pause. 'Well, there must be . . .'

I'm staring at the door frame.

Oh my days. I don't have any friends.

'Maggie's son!' Dad sounds way too triumphant. 'What's his name? Barney! Bob! Short, shiny, hasn't learnt how to shave yet. He's *always* in the house. Can't get rid of the boy. Pretty sure he's crushing on one of the girls, but we can't work out which one.'

Umm, Ben moved to Scotland *eighteen months ago*.

'Mike,' Roz says quietly. 'Why isn't Hope at school? Why is she rattling around that mansion on her own? Why isn't she with people her own age, learning things, working out what she's good at, what she wants?'

I lean forward curiously.

Was there an option for me not to be home-tutored? Could I actually have a . . . Sophia? A Madison and an Olivia? Desks with other people sitting at them? Could I wander down corridors, holding books to my chest? Could there be lockers with stickers on them and a bell that rings every hour and choreographed dances in the hallways?

Could I have all of that?

'It's only with everything . . .' Dad's gone very quiet. 'Oh, Roz, we just wanted to protect them. We wanted them to be safe. Happy. As normal as possible for as long as possible.'

'You can't do that by locking them away from the world, Mike. Hope's a bright girl, but she doesn't know it because she's never had a chance to learn it.'

My father sighs. 'She doesn't even know the difference between pacific and specific. I've told her over and over again, but it never seems to sink in. I don't understand it.'

I scowl. *All right, Dad, it's two letters. Jeez.*

'She's adorable,' Roz laughs. 'But she's incredibly lonely, Mike. She's an inherently optimistic, lonely teenage girl who is desperate for love of any kind. And that has made her vulnerable to textbook love-bombing, devaluation and triangulation from a narcissistic boy who—'

Uh-oh.

'BOY? BOY! WHAT BOY? SHE'S FIFTEEN YEARS OLD! WHAT ARE YOU TALKING ABOUT A BOY FOR?'

My father is so broken he may need rewiring after this.

'Oh, Michael. You *must* have known there was a boy. Didn't you see Hope's face when she arrived at the airport? She was all lit up with excitement and wearing bright red lipstick after an eleven-hour flight.'

Silence.

'I thought that was for me.'

'Of course you did.' Roz sounds vaguely amused. 'I don't want to overstep my boundaries, Michael, but in my professional opinion you and Juliet need to pull it together right now. Your children should not be bearing the brunt of this mess.'

I take another tiny step forward.

You and Juliet need to pull it together right now?

OK, I'm not entirely sure what Roz's professionalist boundaries are exactly – she doesn't seem to have any – but I am *fully* behind this brilliant logic. Finally, an adult is actually making sense.

'You're right,' Dad sighs tiredly after another long silence. 'About everything. Juliet and I need to sort things out immediately. Shooting's wrapped so I can edit the rest from London. I'll alert the studio, make the necessary arrangements and fly back at the end of the week.'

My mouth drops open.

Umm, did I hear that correctly? Did Dad just say he's *coming home?* Because, if he did, that means . . . that means—

I DID IT!

I fixed *everything*, exactly like the typical Cancerian I am! Oh, I'm *such* a water sign, taking my little crab shell with me everywhere I go: putting my home back together, creating an environment of protection and harmony, making everyone feel welcome and—

'And Roz,' Dad continues quietly, 'I'd very much

like you to come with me. If you want. If you can. Whenever suits you. There are some really great private practices in London.'

I stop bouncing on my tiptoes. Huh?

Practising what?

'Sure thing,' Roz laughs warmly. 'I mean, there's always room for one more clinical psychologist.'

54

Umm – *hold cameras.*

'Hello, what on earth are you talking about, please?'

Roz and Dad both jump.

'Hope!' Dad looks horrified. 'How long have you been—'

'Oh, ages. I'm trained in the art of being quiet backstage, so I heard literally everything you said.' I turn back to Roz. 'You're a *psychologist*? Not a movie secretary or a personal assistant? You don't run errands for celebrities? Or file papers and fetch coffees for movie stars? You're a *shrink*?'

Suddenly, everything makes sense. All those conversations with Roz prompting me to tell her everything: the nudges, the questions, the 'mmms' and 'ahs' and 'I sees'. I thought I was just being very wise, but it turns out I've been firmly guided on this whole emotional journey by a licensed professionalist.

Also . . . there *was* that time Dad straight up told me she wasn't my personal assistant.

Ooh, they're *good*.

'Yes, Hope.' Roz smiles at me. 'I am. Though we're not big fans of the word "shrink" because it makes us sound really tiny and old. But basically, yup.'

Holy horoscopes, we weren't going on *errands*.

All those ice creams and saunas and Jacuzzis and restaurant meals were excuses for Roz to spend time assessing the fascinating contents of my extremely complex brain.

I had the lobster *and* the steak. I am such a high-class client.

'So Dad paid you to follow me around for two whole weeks? To get right inside my head and figure me out? Wow, that is just *so* Hollywood. I can't believe I've got my very own full-time personal *therapist*. Thanks, guys.'

Roz has been so very helpful. I should probably tip. How much, do you think? A hundred dollars? Two hundred? Except most of the cash I've been spending has been coming from her, so I guess I'll need to get it and then hand it back somehow—

'Hope.' Roz's eyes have widened. 'I'm not *your* therapist.'

I stare at her.

'You're . . . Dad's therapist?' I frown. 'Well, obviously he needs to address his work-life balance, but I do think that this whole situation is maybe a little bit inappropriate. You need to start drawing some lines somewhere.'

Dad and Roz look at each other.

'Hope,' my father says slowly. 'Roz isn't my therapist, either. She's my girlfriend.'

I blink.

'Umm.' Still blinking.

'No.'

'Yes, sweetheart.'

'No.'

Blink blink blink.

'Dad, you *literally* just said you're working things out with Mum. And, even if you *did* have a secret girlfriend, she'd be some blonde, twenty-year-old wannabe with a perky nose and tiny feet and a too-small bikini and an eye on a lead role she can't handle.'

Dad laughs loudly. 'Wow. I just saw Mercy flash in front of my eyes.'

I fold my arms.

'Sweetheart,' he says, walking slowly towards me. 'I told you all this in the very, *very* long email I sent you before you left Richmond because I didn't want you to get a big shock on arrival. And I also said that, if you weren't ready to talk about it quite yet, I wouldn't bring it up until you did. Didn't you read it?'

Oh, as *if* I've ever read emails from my parents. I might be bored stiff at home, but I'm not in a *coma*.

'Michael.' Roz's whole face has gone pink. 'How could we have let this happen? How? This is *awful*. I'm a psychologist, for pity's sake. We should have sat Hope down, talked about it, made sure she understood. I assumed that —'

'Back to Mum,' I interrupt. 'Dad, it's been *four months* since you left. *What is wrong with you?*'

'It hasn't, baby.' Dad looks so sad. 'You know it hasn't.'

I shake my head. 'No, I don't,' I say firmly. 'Nope, you love each other – it's the real thing. None of this is true, just a figment of your—'

See it all, Hope.

My beautiful, charismatic parents are suddenly in front of me: laughing together, kissing, gifting scarves and lipsticks and ties, hosting glamorous parties, cooking gigantic family breakfasts, stopping for gelato, turning up late, accepting awards and thanking each other.

Except now I can see that those memories are years and years and years old. Tiny scraps of film left over from when I was a little girl, run so many times in my head they're all grainy and faded.

Dad has been gone a really long time.

Every time I go into Mum's room to steal – I mean borrow – it's only full of her things: clothes and jewellery and photos and perfume.

For goodness' sake, I call it *Mum's room.*

The reality I've refused to face is that my parents have slept on opposite sides of our enormous house for years; arranging film schedules that overlapped so they were always in different countries; making elaborate statements to the media about how close they still were and how much they still loved each other and then sitting in the car on the way home in total, rigid silence.

I close my eyes briefly. Because all I can see now are the huge fights: the shouting, the crying, the screaming and the silences. Days and days where us kids would hide together in our bedrooms because the air was so solid with unhappiness we couldn't breathe in it.

Why on earth would I want either of my parents to keep going through that?

That's not epic or romantic. It's just *awful*.

'But.' I open my eyes again. 'Mum—'

'Your mom is gonna be OK,' Dad says firmly. 'She needs some rest and support from people who know what they're doing, but she will be fine. Me giving her some space by filming out here was her idea, and, sweetheart, she knows all about Roz. When I said we'll work things out, I meant as your parents but not as a couple.'

A wave of pain hits my stomach, but this time I don't push it away.

I think that, on some level I'm still not quite ready to face, I knew Mum's sadness had nothing to do with my father.

Instead, I look at Roz.

With her unfashionable hair and her glasses and

her khaki shorts, her brilliance and calmness and generosity, her wisdom and – oh my gosh, she spent two weeks being my unpaid taxi and food-delivery service! And I bet there's no friend's daughter, is there? She totally took me shopping to cheer me up – what a compassionate *trickster*.

Roz bites her lip.

'You need to buy her new glasses,' I say abruptly, turning to my father. 'Roz is a wonderful lady and she needs glasses she doesn't have to push up her nose every five seconds.'

'I'm a highly paid professional who can buy my own specs,' Roz smiles, visibly relieved. 'And they actually fit. It's just a thirty-year tic left over from school. We've all got our flaws.'

'Not a flaw,' Dad grins. 'A detail.'

And I see that he's looking at Roz as if she's light.

I feel my heart starting to lift and glow, because aren't we *all* a little bit broken in one way or another? And isn't that what romance really is?

Seeing and loving the pieces of each other anyway.

A wave of affection rushes through me.

'*You guys*,' I say, dragging them together for a massive cuddle and accidentally smashing their heads together. 'So have you looked at your compatibility chart yet? Dad, you're Sagittarius, and Roz you're clearly a Libra. So that's a *pacifically* good combo, but Dad, try not to be so impatient and, Roz, you can be indecisive so don't get pushed around. But overall you're very balanced and harmonious, guys. Congrats.'

'I *am* a Libra,' Roz says in surprise as Dad laughs loudly. 'How on earth did you know that?'

'Special intuition,' I grin. 'Water sign. So, the *real* question is when are we going back to England? And please can we fly First Class so I can bring all the extra clothes and shoes . . . ? And, while we're at it, is there any way that I can maybe get a puppy?'

Because in this brand-new world anything is possible.

I have hope, I have hope, I have hope.

55

HOPE walks slowly down the long driveway towards a red-brick mansion on the outskirts of Richmond. Around her stretch green, familiar fields.

A black limo follows behind her very slowly because there are seven suitcases in the boot.

As she approaches the house, she feels a rush of happiness and HOPE starts smiling, then laughing, walking faster and faster until she's running.

The front door swings open.

SHE IS HOME.

                    FAITH
     Po! You're back! Oh my God, we've
           missed you so much!

                    MERCY
        We literally didn't notice
        she wasn't here for three
                    days.

                    MAX
     Pipe down, Mermaid. It hasn't been
     the same without her and you know
                     it.

I push the door open.

'Noah?' Effie's head pokes out over the bannister
– eyes slightly swollen, with toothpaste on her
beautiful chin – followed by an enormous flannel
shirt and a pair of grey tracksuit bottoms. 'Noah,
is that– '

Her gorgeous face lights up.

'*Po!* Oh, Po, you're home, you're home, you're
home!' My sister thunders down the stairs and
flings her arms round me, covering my face with

fluttery little kisses. 'We missed you *so* much! Are you OK? We're *so* sorry, honestly – please forgive us! We love you! Now come in and tell us *everything*.'

Mercy appears directly behind her.

'I mean,' my big sister says drily, folding her arms in front of her, 'we *literally* didn't notice she wasn't here for three days, but sure, whatever.'

But she's trying not to smile and I grin at her: *nailed it.*

'Pipe down, Mercury!' Max shouts, hopping to the bottom of the stairs and wrapping me and Eff in an enormous, long-armed hug. 'It hasn't been the same here without the Poodle-Pie and you know it.'

Then Max reaches out an arm and hooks Mercy in too.

'Ugh,' Mer sighs into my right shoulder. 'This is *soooo* codependent. You're all so annoying. This is too tight. I can't breathe. You're messing up my hair. Why can't any of you hug properly?'

I kiss her lovely, crotchety face.

'Leave the suitcases,' Max says, dramatically dragging me through the hallway to the living room by my hands. 'We need juicy details, Po. Hold

nothing back. We want gossip. Drama. *Embellishments.*
Tell us about your big solo adventure because there's
nothing on telly and we're bored *stiff.*'

'Solo adventure with *my* wardrobe,' Mercy
grumbles.

'Shhh,' Effie says, pinching her lightly. 'We've got
an epic story to hear.'

Delighted, I stand in the middle of the room.
Finally, an enraptured audience focused directly on
me.

I am obviously much wiser and more mature than
I was at the start of this journey so I shall deflect
this spotlight with dignity and—

Oh, screw it.

'People,' I say, holding a hand up and swishing
myself thoughtfully towards the window. 'Life is
complex. It's a pyramid of tiny moments, some that
change us forever, like a fork in the road that defines
the *essence* of our—' I turn. 'Max, it's six pm. Why
aren't you on stage?'

'Huh? Oh.' My brother stares at the ceiling.
'Apparently, even ephemeral spirits with no earthly
dimensions have to show up for work occasionally
or they'll replace you with somebody who does.'

'Oh, *Max*. I'm sorry.'

'I'm not.' He sounds genuinely cheerful. 'I had an audition yesterday for the First Commoner in *Julius Caesar*. Watch this.' Max flings his arms out. 'Why, sir, a carpenter! Why, *sir*, a *carpenter*! *Why*, sir! A *carpenter*? Four words, *so* many possibilities. Fingers crossed I get it or Nanny Vee is going to be as livid with me as she is with Mer.'

I turn to Mercy. 'What have you done now?'

'*Pffft*.' My sister folds her arms even more tightly and glowers from the sofa. 'You have *one* little argument at *one* little party and make *one* little gesture with your hands . . . The next thing you know you're the girl who pushes TV presenters into toilets.'

Even I'm shocked. 'Who was it?'

'Never you mind,' Mer says airily. 'Let's just say her head ended up where her career was going anyway.'

Blinking, I turn to Faith. 'What about you? Any big dramas while I've been gone? Nicked a car? Robbed a bank? Because, no offence, you're all kind of stealing my big scene.'

'Nope.' Eff smiles, picking at a thread on the sofa

arm. '*Nada* going on here. You know me. Same old, same old.'

'Well,' Max coughs, 'Effpot, that's not *completely*—'

Faith kicks him.

'Right.' I straighten my so-Los-Angeles denim jumpsuit. 'If you're quite *done* with your flagrant limelight hogging, I shall continue. Where was I?'

Gracefully holding a hand up again, I search for my next line. (I rehearsed this speech all the way from Los Angeles to London – Dad's flying out in a few days – and it was word-perfect, scripted brilliantly and very, very moving.) My siblings are *such* interrupting attention-seekers.

'I think you were defining your essence,' Faith prompts with a small smile. 'There was definitely a pyramid of some kind.'

'And a fork!' Max shouts. 'There was a fork somewhere!'

'In her head?' Mer suggests.

OK, if they don't start taking me seriously *right now*, when this is a blockbuster movie, I'm not even going to let them appear on the holding-image poster.

'So . . .' I continue, 'some moments alter our direction and give our lives a new purpose. Picture this.' I hold my hands up in a rectangle. 'A young girl, on the very *pinnacle* of adulthood . . .'

'Precipice. She means precipice.'

'What's going on with her hands? Can we all just notice that Hope's hands are in charades "film" shape?'

'That's not film, that's *television*. Film is an old projector. See?' Max holds both fists up and rotates one. 'Film.' He makes a rectangle. 'Television.'

'SOMETHING HAS ACTUALLY HAPPENED TO ME FOR THE FIRST TIME IN MY LIFE! WILL YOU PLEASE SHUT YOUR GOBBY MOUTHS FOR ONE SINGLE MINUTE AND LISTEN!'

Huh.

I should definitely consider yelling more often. I seem to be getting good at it.

'And in that *moment*,' I continue sternly, giving them a warning glance, 'the one we were talking about, the one with the pyramids, and the essences, and the whatever that was—'

Oh, I can't be bothered.

460

'GUYS, I AM GOING TO BE A FILM DIRECTOR!'

Faith, Mercy and Max stare at me.

I know, right? I cannot believe it took me nearly sixteen years and over five hundred Director's Cut films to figure this ending out. Being a movie star is cool – nice food, big parties – but a *director*?

They get to *decide how the story is told*.

And that is The Dream, my friends.

So, yes, it's a huge loss to the acting industry, but at least now there's room for other, less towering talents.

'I'm going to be a film director like Dad,' I repeat triumphantly. 'Once I've trained and done lots of internships and worked my way up. Did you know that only *eleven per cent* of film directors are women? I have decided that *I* shall be Director Number Twelve.'

'Po, I don't think that eleven per cent is the same as—'

'I'M NOT DONE YET, MAXWELL.' I clap my hands and start jumping up and down. 'And I'm going to *school*! Dad says we'll find a good one nearby. I'm going to be in a class with other real people in it! Obviously, I'm going to be super popular, but also kind and generous and I'll throw lots of parties and *everyone* will be invited. It's going to be *awesommmmmme*.'

Delighted, I spin in a circle.

'Well,' Mercy observes flatly. 'If anyone is a perfect candidate for going into full-time intensive education, it's you.'

I beam at her. 'Thanks!'

'I'm also very glad that Mr Gilbert can finally retire.' Max nods. 'That poor old man has been waiting for us to fly the nest for at least thirty years. He must be all Valentined out. You know, I'm pretty sure he taught Grandma.'

Faith has leapt to her feet, eyes shining.

'Hope, we can use my debit card. You're going to need a pencil case, a backpack, some kind of little white socks – do they wear little white socks? – heaps of pens and—'

Eff and I squeak and jump up and down together.

'Umm.' Max holds up a finger. 'I confess to being a little bit confused, Poodle. Wasn't this supposed to be a love story? I'm pretty sure this was marketed as a romance. Hearts and flowers, swirly writing and bad transatlantic accents?'

'Yeah,' Mer agrees. 'What happened to the boy?'

'Oh.' I grin at them. 'That didn't work out. Sometimes it doesn't. Also, I just want to let you smarty-pants know-it-alls know that I have access to the internet too. The *Bechdel test* isn't even from Italy! It's the test that examines whether or not there is a single scene in a work of fiction in which two female characters successfully have a conversation about something other than a man. So there.'

'Which you just failed,' Mercy points out. 'Again.'

My eyes widen. 'I was talking to *Max*,' I say quickly, crossing my arms. 'He is a *boy* and therefore that conversation doesn't count.'

All three of my siblings laugh.

And I laugh too, a bright, happy glow spreading through me. It stretches along my arms and my toes and my fingers and my cheeks and my— *Now* why are they all looking at each other?

'*What?*' I burst out in frustration. '*What is it? Will you please stop it with your fake invisible coded language? I CAN ALWAYS ALWAYS SEE YOU.*'

'Well . . .' Mercy says.

'Here's the thing . . .' Effie says.

463

'There's just one update we didn't give you,' Max says, looking over my shoulder.

Slowly, I turn round.

'Hello, darling,' Mum says. 'I'm home.'

THE END

56

Except it's not the end, is it?

Because that's not how it works. We don't get to choose when the credits roll and the auditorium lights come up. Our scenes just keep happening – passing from person to person – until eventually they become other people's stories to tell.

Which sounds pretty good to me.

Mum goes straight to bed.

It's going to take a while before she's fully back with us. Max, Faith and Mercy lean over the bannisters together. 'Coming, Mousebear? We're going to watch a film.'

I smile. 'Be there in a second.'

Once my siblings have disappeared into Faith's room, I open the door to the library. There's a faint layer of dust over everything and *The Lady of Shalott* is still where I threw it, lying open on the desk.

I carefully close the book and slide it back on to the shelf. Then I walk over to the small brown oily painting and stand as close to it as I can. 'Hey,' I say, touching the frame with one finger.

Elaine keeps her eyes closed, blonde hair fanned out.

'I just wanted to say you're going to be OK. Any second now you're going to open your eyes and hop out of this boat. You're going to live your own life your way. And I promise you the real world will be even more beautiful than you thought it was.'

Her eyes are still shut, so I lean forward.

'Your face was *always* lovely,' I whisper. 'You don't need anyone else to give you your happy ending.'

For a split second, Elaine gives me a tiny smile.

Joking: she's a painting.

Standing on my tiptoes, I give her a brisk little kiss. There's a loud crack and a line appears in the glass.

Whoops.

Then I turn to the chairs where Sophia, Olivia

and Madison are slouching. 'Thanks for everything, guys. I couldn't have done it without you. It's been pretty epic, huh?'

They wave, smile, then – without a sound – they disappear like bubbles.

Pop pop pop.

'HOPE!' Max yells from upstairs. 'WE'VE PAUSED THE TRAILERS. ARE YOU COMING OR NOT?'

'CHILL OUT!' I yell back. 'I'M COMING!'

Smiling, I take one last look round the library. Maybe I'll visit now and then, when I need a heavy encyclopedia to rest my camcorder on or something. Then I shut the door behind me softly and start walking up the long winding stairs.

Because life is not a romance.

It's not a thriller or a comedy; it's not a tragedy or a horror or a crime story. It's not a war film or an action movie, or a historical drama.

Life is every genre, all mixed up together: the scary bits and the funny bits and the sweet bits and the sad bits and the angry bits and the bits that hurt and the bits you want to rush through and the bits you want to hold on to forever.

And every single frame of the film is worth watching.

They're all part of the story.

'Poop-head?'

I must have automatically lingered at the window on the landing out of sheer habit. 'Yes, Mercy?'

'What the hell are you doing now?'

'Oh.' I glance up. Her dark curls are poking round the side of Faith's bedroom door. 'I dunno really. I guess I was thinking about what a doggy-dog world it is, you know?'

'For the love of—' Mer sighs. 'Please don't go around saying that at your new school, Hope. It's "dog-eat-dog". The expression is *it's a dog-eat-dog world*.'

I laugh brightly. 'Umm, no. Since when do dogs eat other dogs? At best it's a *dog-lick-dog* world, or a *dog-sniff-dog-butt* world. Also, why on earth would dogs eating dogs be a good thing?'

'It's not. That's why people use it to say life sucks. Idiot.'

Mercy disappears again and I stare at the door. *Huh.*

I knew I'd have to go back a school year to catch

up, but maybe we should try two just for good measure.

Still much prefer my version, though.

Giggling slightly – *doggy-dog* – I start climbing the stairs again. Oh yes, maybe I could write and direct a film for Drama Club at my new school; it'll be called *It's a Doggy-dog World* and it'll be all about this girl who meets this guy and goes to America and—

Wait a minute.

Spinning, I turn back to the window.

A boy with light brown hair has appeared in the driveway, wearing jeans and a blue-and-white stripy jumper. He keeps walking towards the house, stopping, looking up at it, scratching his head, turning, walking back a few steps, then staring at the house again.

I frown. What is he *doing*?

Although he's absolutely gorgeous, so he can keep doing it if he likes. I've got time.

Perching on the windowsill so I have a better view, I watch the hot stranger walk another ten steps towards our front door, then stop and turn away again, bite his lip, spin back and try again. It's hugely entertaining. He takes another six steps – spinning in little circles – and is just about close enough for me to see he's muttering away to himself, lifting a finger and rubbing it anxiously over his top—

BEN?

Oh my gosh, that's *Moustachio Ben*? Ben of the Scrabble Tiles? Ben of the Chess Club and Caterpillars? My old buddy, Crispy Benjamin?

Nice *work*, puberty: that is some *solid* glow-up.

Also a quick shout-out to razors.

'FAITH!' I scream happily from the windowsill. 'FAITH! COME OUT, THERE'S SOMEONE HERE TO SEE YOU!'

Delighted, I make myself comfortable.

From two floors up, I watch Ben scratch his head again, stare at the door, mutter a bit more, flush and straighten his jumper awkwardly. I'm sending down little supportive vibes, encouraging him with my mind.

Come on, Benjamin. You've waited over a decade – time to step up the romantic gesture. You can do it.

Pick up a kitten or something.

There's the soft click of a bedroom door opening behind me.

FAITH VALENTINE appears at the top of the stairs. She is glowing and pink-cheeked, wearing an electric-orange hoodie with neon-blue leggings and – oh good Lord – one red sock and one green.

                    FAITH
          What's going on? Who is it?

Grinning, I hold my hands up in a rectangle so my beautiful sister is framed perfectly. And—
   Lights. Cameras.
   Action.

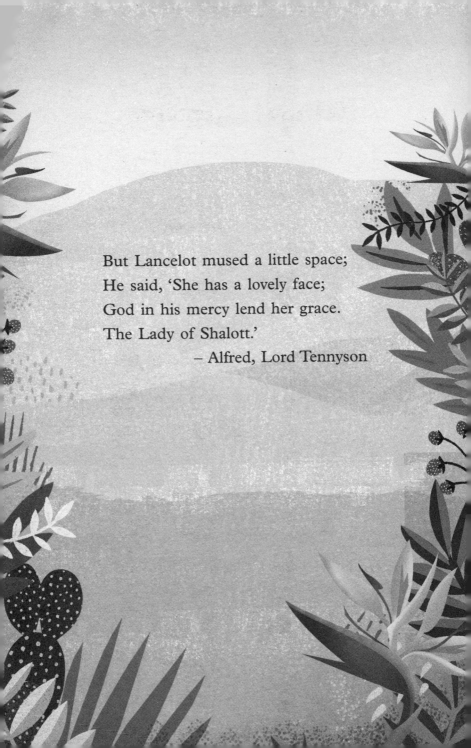

But Lancelot mused a little space;
He said, 'She has a lovely face;
God in his mercy lend her grace.
The Lady of Shalott.'
— Alfred, Lord Tennyson

Acknowledgements

My name may be on the cover, but an army of amazing people created this book.

Huge thanks to Lizzie Clifford, my wise and all-seeing editor: you have helped to guide me on so many stories, and I'd be lost without you. Thanks to Kate Shaw, my agent of a decade, for supporting me so tirelessly and with so much passion.

To everyone at HarperCollins: Rachel Denwood and Ann-Janine Murtagh; Samantha Stewart, Michelle Misra, Yasmin Morrissey, Jess Dean, Lowri Ribbons, Jane Tait and Mary O'Riordan; Elorine Grant and David McDougall; Elisa

Offord, Beth Maher, Alex Cowan; Geraldine Stroud, Jo-Anna Parkinson, Louise Sheridan; Robert Smith and Jessie Ford. Your hard work, talent and creativity brought this story alive, and I am so grateful.

As always, my infinitely awesome family deserve a shout-out. Mum and Dad, I owe you: thank you for never reminding me of just how much. Tara and Autumn, Grandad, Louise, Charlie, Adrian, Veronique, Caroline, Dan, Vincent, Simon, Lesley, Romaine, Dixie, Lorraine, Ellen, Freya, Robin, Judith and Grandma – thanks for always cheering me on, even if it's where I can't see you.

And finally, to my readers: old and new. I hope you love the Valentine family as much as I do.

Thanks for coming on this adventure with me too.